주홍글자

II

🎧 강독 MP3 파일 다운로드 방법 안내

1. 방송대출판문화원 홈페이지에 접속한다.
   http://press.knou.ac.kr
2. 첫 화면 오른쪽 상단의 "고객만족센터"를 클릭한 뒤 "자료실"로 이동한다.
3. 자료실에서 "주홍글자 Ⅰ, Ⅱ 강독 MP3 파일"을 다운로드하고, 압축 비밀번호를 입력해서 압축을 푼다.

※ 압축 비밀번호 찾아내는 방법
   첫째 자리: 〈주홍글자 Ⅰ〉 26쪽 첫째 줄의 첫 알파벳
   둘째 자리: 〈주홍글자 Ⅰ〉 98쪽 첫째 줄의 마지막 알파벳
   셋째 자리: 〈주홍글자 Ⅰ〉 157쪽 첫째 줄의 첫 알파벳
   넷째 자리: p

신현욱 교수의 명작 강독 시리즈-2

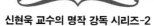

주홍글자

II

너새니얼 호손 지음
신현욱 주해

THE
SCARLET
LETTER

에피스테메
EPISTEME

신현욱 교수의 명작 강독 시리즈 - 2

주홍글자 II

초판 1쇄 펴낸날 | 2015년 9월 15일

지은이 | 너새니얼 호손
주 해 | 신현욱
펴낸이 | 이동국
펴낸곳 | 한국방송통신대학교출판문화원
　　　　110-500 서울시 종로구 이화장길 54
　　　　전화 02-3668-4764
　　　　팩스 02-741-4570
　　　　홈페이지 http://press.knou.ac.kr
　　　　출판등록 1982년 6월 7일 제1-491호

출판문화원장 | 권수열
편집 | 신경진·양영희
마케팅 | 이상혁
편집 디자인 | (주)성지이디피
표지 디자인 | BOOKDESIGN SM

ISBN　978-89-20-01668-4　94840
　　　　978-89-20-01673-8　(세트)

값은 뒤표지에 있습니다.

　이 도서의 국립중앙도서관 출판예정도서목록(CIP)은 서지정보유통지원시스템 홈페이지
(http://seoji.nl.go.kr)와 국가자료공동목록시스템(http://www.nl.go.kr/kolisnet)에서 이
용하실 수 있습니다. (CIP제어번호: CIP2015023093)

차례

The Scarlet Letter 11장

The Interior of a Heart

After the incident [last described], the intercourse between the clergyman and the physician,[1] {though externally the same}, was really of another character {than it had previously been}. The intellect of Roger Chillingworth had now a sufficiently plain path before it.[2] It[3] was not, indeed, precisely that[4] {which he had laid out for himself to tread}. {Calm, gentle, passionless, as[5] he appeared}, there was yet, {we fear}, a quiet depth of malice,[6] [hitherto latent, but active now], in this unfortunate old man, {which led him to[7] imagine a more intimate revenge than any mortal had ever wreaked upon[8] an enemy}. To make himself the one trusted friend, {to whom should be confided all the fear, the remorse, the agony, the ineffectual repentance, the backward rush of sinful thoughts, [expelled in vain]}![9] All that guilty sorrow, [hidden from the

---

1 the clergyman and the physician: clergyman은 딤즈데일(Dimmesdale), physician은 칠링워스(Chillingworth)

2 The intellect ... path before it: '로저 칠링워스(Roger Chillingworth)의 머릿속에는 이제 자신이 나아갈 길이 분명히 정해졌다'는 의미. 칠링워스의 지성(능)을 의인화하여, 이제 그 지성이 자기 앞에 매우 분명한 길을 두게 되었다고 묘사하고 있다.

3 It: =a sufficiently plain path

4 that: =the path

5 as: =though

6 quiet depth of malice: 조용한 깊은 원한

7 lead ... to: ~하도록 이끌다, 유도하다(=induce ... to.)

8 wreaked upon[=wreak (revenge) upon ...]: ~에게 (원한을) 품다

9 To make himself ... in vain!: 부정사로 표현된 감탄문. ＊그 뒤의 두 문장 역시 to be revealed, to be ravished가 중심에 자리한 부정사 감탄문으로 '~한다니!', '~하는 거야!' 정도의 의미로 파악할 수 있다.

world, {whose great heart[10] would have pitied and forgiven}], to be revealed to him, [the Pitiless—to him, the Unforgiving]! All that dark treasure to be lavished[11] on the very man, {to whom nothing else could so adequately pay the debt of vengeance}!

The clergyman's shy and sensitive reserve had balked[12] this scheme. Roger Chillingworth, however, was inclined to be [hardly, if at all, less[13] satisfied] with the aspect of affairs, {which Providence— [using the avenger and his victim for its own purposes, and, perchance, pardoning, where it seemed most to punish[14]]—had substituted for his black devices[15]}. A revelation, {he could almost say}, had been granted to him. It mattered little for his object, {whether celestial or from what other region}.[16] [By its aid], in all the subsequent relations

---

10 whose great heart: 'whose'의 선행사는 'the world'

11 to be lavished: 부정사가 주가 되어 '(~에게) 아낌없이 주어지도록 하는 거야', 혹은 '아낌없이 주어진다니…… 생각만 해도 흥분되는군' 정도의 의미를 띤 감탄문

12 balk: 방해하다(=hinder)

13 hardly ... less: 부정의 뜻을 가진 두 단어가 만나서 "(그래도) 거의"라는 긍정의 의미를 갖게 된다. *전혀 덜 만족스러운 것은 아니었다라고는 할 수 없어도, 거의 그런 것은 아니었다는 의미

14 using … punish: 복수자도 희생자도 모두 자신의 목적을 위해 사용하면서 벌해야만 할 때에 용서하기도 하는 [하늘의 섭리]

15 the aspect of affairs ... which Providence had substituted for his black devices: 신의 섭리가 그의 사악한 계략 대신에 제공해 준 사태의 양상. *substitute A for B: A로 B를 대신하다

betwixt him and Mr. Dimmesdale, not merely the external presence, but the very inmost soul of the latter,[17] seemed to be brought out before his eyes, {so that he could see and comprehend its every movement}. He became, thenceforth, not a spectator only, but a chief actor in the poor minister's interior world. He could play upon[18] him {as he chose}. Would he arouse him with a throb of agony? The victim was for ever on the rack; it needed only to know the spring {that controlled the engine}: and the physician[19] knew it well. Would he startle him with sudden fear? [As at the waving of a magician's wand[20]], uprose a grisly phantom,—uprose a thousand phantoms— in many shapes, of death, or more awful shame, all flocking round about the clergyman, and pointing with their fingers at his breast!

All this was accomplished with a subtlety so perfect,[21] that the minister, {though he had constantly a dim perception of some evil influence watching over him}, could never gain a

---

16 whether ... region: =whether (the revelation) was celestial, or from what other region (it had come). *'천상이 아닌 어떤 다른 곳(what other region)'은 지옥을 암시

17 the latter: 후자. 여기서는 딤즈데일

18 play upon: =play on. ~에 영향을 끼치다, ~을 이용하다

19 the physician: 칠링워스

20 As at the waving of a magician's wand: 마법사가 지팡이를 휘둘렀을 때처럼

21 so perfect: 그렇게나 완벽한. *subtlety를 수식

knowledge of its actual nature. True, he looked [doubtfully, fearfully—even, at times, with horror and the bitterness of hatred]—at the deformed figure of the old physician. [His gestures, his gait, his grizzled beard, his slightest and most indifferent acts, the very fashion of his garments], were odious in the clergyman's sight;[22] a token [implicitly to be relied on[23]] of a deeper antipathy in the breast of the latter {than he was willing to acknowledge to himself}. For, {as it was impossible to assign a reason for such distrust and abhorrence}, so Mr. Dimmesdale, [conscious[24] {that the poison of one morbid spot was infecting his heart's entire substance}], attributed all his presentiments to no other cause.[25] He took himself to task for his bad sympathies in reference to[26] Roger Chillingworth, disregarded the lesson {that he should have drawn from them}, and did his best to root them out.[27] [Unable to accomplish this], he nevertheless, [as a matter of principle], continued his habits of social familiarity with the old man, and thus gave him constant opportunities for perfecting the purpose {to which—

---

22 in the clergyman's sight: 목사의 눈에는, 목사가 보기에는

23 implicitly to be relied on: 은연중에 신뢰할 수 있는. *'a token'을 수식

24 conscious: = (who was) conscious. ~을 알고 있는

25 attributed ... to no other cause: 자신의 모든 예감을 어떤 다른 원인 탓으로 돌리지 않았다. *attribute A to B: A를 B의 탓으로 돌리다

26 in reference to: ~에 관해, ~에 대해

27 root ... out: 근절하다, 없애다

[poor forlorn creature that he was,[28] and more wretched than his victim]—the avenger had devoted himself}.

{While thus suffering under bodily disease, and gnawed and tortured by some black trouble of the soul, and given over to[29] the machinations of his deadliest enemy}, the Reverend Mr. Dimmesdale had achieved a brilliant popularity in his sacred office. He won it indeed, in great part, by his sorrows. [His intellectual gifts, his moral perceptions, his power of experiencing and communicating emotion], were kept in a state of preternatural[30] activity by the prick and anguish of his daily life. His fame, {though still on its upward slope}, already overshadowed the soberer reputations of his fellow-clergymen, {eminent as several of them were[31]}. There are scholars among them, {who had spent more years in acquiring abstruse lore, [connected with the divine profession], than Mr. Dimmesdale had lived}; and {who might well,[32] therefore, be more profoundly versed in such solid and valuable attainments than their youthful brother[33]}. There were men, too, [of a

---

28 poor forlorn creature that he was: =though he was poor, forlorn creature. 'he'는 칠링워스

29 given over to(=give over): 넘겨주다, 맡기다

30 preternatural: 이상한, 기이한, 초자연적인. *preter-: '과(過), 초(超)' 등의 뜻의 결합사

31 eminent as several of them were: =though several of them were eminent

32 might well: ~하는 것이 당연하다(고 여겨지다)

33 their youthful brother: 그들의 젊은 동료, 즉 딤즈데일

sturdier texture of mind than his], and [endowed with a far greater share of shrewd, hard, iron or granite understanding]; which[34], [duly mingled with a fair proportion of doctrinal ingredient], constitutes a highly respectable, efficacious, and unamiable variety of the clerical species. There were others again, true saintly fathers, {whose faculties had been elaborated by weary toil among their books, and by patient thought, and etherealised, moreover, by spiritual communications with the better world, [into which their purity of life had almost introduced these holy personages, with their garments of mortality[35] still clinging to them]}. All {that they lacked} was, the gift {that descended upon the chosen disciples at Pentecost,[36] in tongues of flame; [symbolising, {it would seem}, not the power of speech in foreign and unknown languages, but that[37] of addressing the whole human brotherhood in the heart's native language]}. These fathers, [otherwise so apostolic], lacked Heaven's last and rarest attestation of their office,[38] the Tongue of Flame. They would have vainly

---

34 which: 앞에 묘사된 그런 종류의 정신(mind)과 그런 종류의 오성 (understanding)을 가리킨다.

35 garments of mortality: 유한의 피복, 육신

36 Pentecost: 성령 강림절, 오순절(五旬節). 부활절 후의 제7일요일

37 that: =the power

38 Heaven's last and rarest attestation of their office: 그들의 임무 에 대한 하느님의 마지막이자 진귀한 증명. 뒤의 'the Tongue of Flame'과 동격. *예수의 부활 이후 성령이 불꽃 모양의 혀로 제자 들에게 내렸다고 함. 보통의 언어와는 달리 인간 공통의 깊은 가슴

sought — {had they ever dreamed of seeking[39]} — to express the highest truths through the humblest medium of familiar words and images. Their voices came down, afar and indistinctly, from the upper heights {where they habitually dwelt}[40].

Not improbably,[41] it was to this latter class of men {that Mr. Dimmesdale, by many of his traits of character, naturally belonged[42]}. [To the high mountain peaks of faith and sanctity] he would have climbed, {had not the tendency been

---

에 호소하는 힘을 의미함.

39 They would have ... of seeking: =If they had ever dreamed of seeking, they would have vainly thought .... 가장 지고한 진리를 표현하려 노력하겠다고 추구하지도 않았겠지만 설령 그것을 추구했더라도 소용없었을 것이라는 의미

40 Their voices ... dwelt: 이 문장에서 'their', 'they'가 가리키는 것이 분명치는 않으나, 앞에 열거한 여러 종류의 성직자 중 마지막 부류, 즉 타고난 능력이 끊임없는 수고와 인내로 더 정교해지고(elaborated) 천상과의 영혼적 교류를 통해 더 영묘해진(etherealised) 진정 성스러운 교부들을 가리키는 것으로 보인다. 이들은 삶의 순수함으로 인해 아직 육신을 벗지 않은 상태인데도 이미 천국에 든 듯하지만 일상의 익숙한 언어와 이미지들이라는 가장 소박한 매체를 통해 지고의 진리들을 전달하는 능력은 결여된 부류이다. 따라서 높으신 곳에 거(居)하는 이들의 목소리는 지상에서 들으면 정확히 무슨 의미인지 똑똑하게 분별되지 않고 일반 청중의 심금을 파고들지 못한다는 내용을 설명한 대목으로 볼 수 있다.

41 not improbably: =probably

42 it was ... belonged: 'it was ... that ...' 강조 구문. *이 대목과 다음 대목은 딤즈데일 목사가 앞에 열거한 부류들 중에 나중 부류에 속하지만 그와 동시에 그들과 전혀 다른 그만의 특장점이 있음을 설명하고 있다.

thwarted[43] by the burden, [whatever it might be], of crime or anguish, [beneath which it was his doom to totter]}. It kept him down on a level with the lowest; him, the man of ethereal attributes, {whose voice[44] the angels might else[45] have listened to and answered}! But this very burden it was {that[46] gave him sympathies so intimate with the sinful brotherhood of mankind; so that his heart vibrated in unison with theirs, and received their pain into itself and sent its own throb of pain through a thousand other hearts, in gushes of sad, persuasive eloquence}. Oftenest persuasive, but sometimes terrible! The people knew not the power {that moved them thus}. They deemed the young clergyman a miracle of holiness. They fancied him the mouth-piece[47] of Heaven's messages of wisdom, and rebuke, and love. In their eyes, the very ground {on which he trod} was sanctified. The virgins of his church grew pale around him, victims[48] of a passion [so imbued with religious sentiment, that they imagined it[49] to be all religion,

---

43 had not the tendency been thwarted: 〈가정법〉 그러한 경향이 저
    해되지 않았더라면

44 whose voice: 뒤의 'listened to'와 'answered'의 목적어

45 else: =otherwise

46 this very burden it was that: =it was this very burden that .... 'it
    was ... that ...'의 강조 구문

47 mouth-piece: 대변자

48 victims: 앞의 'virgins'와 동격

49 it: =a passion. *바로 다음의 'it' 역시 '열정'을 가리킨다. 처녀들
    이 목사를 향해 열정을 품고 있지만 여기에 종교적인 색채가 입혀진
    까닭에 자신들의 열정이 온통 종교적인 것이라고 상상한다는 의미

and brought it openly, in their white bosoms,[50] as their most acceptable sacrifice before the altar]. The aged members of his flock,[51] [beholding Mr. Dimmesdale's frame so feeble, {while they were themselves so rugged in their infirmity}], believed {that he would go heavenward before them}, and enjoined it upon their children {that their old bones should be buried close to their young pastor's holy grave}. And all this time, perchance, {when poor Mr. Dimmesdale was thinking of his grave}, he questioned with himself {whether the grass would ever grow on it, because an accursed thing must there be buried}![52]

It[53] is inconceivable, the agony {with which this public veneration tortured him}. It[54] was his genuine impulse [to adore the truth, and to reckon all things shadow-like, and utterly devoid of[55] weight or value, {that had not its divine

---

50 brought it openly ... bosoms: 그 열정을 당당하게 그들의 가슴에 품고 (교회로) 나왔다

51 flock: = congregation. 신도들, 회중

52 whether the grass ... be buried: 저주받은 이의 무덤에는 풀이 자라지 않는다는 속설이 있다.

53 It: = the agony

54 It: to adore ... 부분을 가리킨다. that 이하는 목적어인 'all things' 를 꾸며 주는 관계절로서 '생명 속의 생명[생명의 가장 소중한 것, 원동력]으로서 신성한 본질을 갖고 있지 않은 모든 것들'이라는 뜻이며, 'all things' 바로 다음의 'shadow-like, and utterly devoid of weight or value(그림자와 같은 것이며, 무게나 가치가 전혀 없다)' 는 목적보어이다.

55 devoid of: ~이 전혀 없는, 결여된

essence as the life within their life}. Then what was he? —
a substance? — or the dimmest of all shadows? He longed to
speak out from his own pulpit at the full height of his voice,
and tell the people {what he was[56]}. "I, {whom you behold
in these black garments of the priesthood} — I, {who ascend
the sacred desk, and turn my pale face heavenward, taking
upon myself to hold communion in your behalf with the Most
High Omniscience[57]} — I, {in whose daily life you discern the
sanctity of Enoch[58]} — I, {whose footsteps, as you suppose,
leave a gleam along my earthly track, whereby the Pilgrims
that shall come after me may be guided to the regions of the
blest[59]} — I, {who have laid the hand of baptism upon your
children} — I, {who have breathed the parting prayer over
your dying friends, to whom the Amen sounded faintly from a
world which they had quitted} — I, your pastor, {whom you so
reverence and trust}, am utterly a pollution and a lie!"[60]

More than once, Mr. Dimmesdale had gone into the
pulpit, [with a purpose never to come down its steps {until

---

56 what he was: 그가 어떤 사람인지, 그의 정체

57 the Most High Omniscience: 전지(全知)의 신

58 sanctity of Enoch: 에녹과 같은 신성함, 고결함. 여기의 에녹은 야
렛(Jared)의 아들로 아담의 자손들에게 내려진 피할 수 없는 죽음
을 면하고 신과 함께 나란히 걸은 인물을 가리킨다.

59 regions of the blest: 천국

60 인용부호 안에 들어 있는 이 긴 문장의 동사는 끝부분에 있는 'am'
이며 앞은 여러 차례 'I'와 'I'를 꾸며 주는 관계절로 이루어져 있다.

he should have spoken words like the above}]. More than once he had cleared his throat, and drawn in the long, deep, and tremulous breath, {which, when sent forth again, would come burdened with[61] the black secret of his soul}. More than once — nay, more than a hundred times — he had actually spoken! Spoken! But how? He had told his hearers {that he was altogether vile, a viler companion of the vilest,[62] the worst of sinners, an abomination, a thing of unimaginable iniquity}, and {that the only wonder was [that they did not see his wretched body shrivelled up before their eyes by the burning wrath of the Almighty]}! Could there be plainer speech than this?[63] Would not the people start up in their seats, by a simultaneous impulse, and tear him down[64] out of the pulpit {which he defiled}? Not so, indeed! They heard it all, and did but reverence him the more. They little guessed {what deadly purport lurked in those self-condemning[65] words}.

"The godly[66] youth!" said they among themselves. "The

---

61 when sent forth again, would come burdened with: (그 숨을) 다시 내뿜었을 때에는 ~와 함께 나왔을지도 모른다. * 'would'에 는 가정의 의미가 들어 있다.

62 viler companion of the vilest: 타락한 이들 가운데서도 가장 타락한 사람

63 Could there be plainer speech than this?: 〈수사의문문〉 "이보다 더 분명한 말이 있을까?"

64 tear ... down: 떼어 놓다, 끌어내리다

65 self-condemning: 자책하는

saint on earth! Alas! {if he discern such sinfulness in his own white[67] soul}, what horrid spectacle would he behold in thine or mine!"[68] The minister well knew — [subtle, but remorseful hypocrite that he was!] — the light[69] {in which his vague confession would be viewed}. He had striven to put a cheat upon[70] himself by making the avowal of a guilty conscience, but had gained only one other sin, and a self-acknowledged shame, without the momentary relief of being self-deceived. He had spoken the very truth, and transformed it into the veriest falsehood. And yet, by the constitution of his nature, he loved the truth, and loathed the lie, {as few men ever did}. Therefore, above all things else, he loathed his miserable self!

His inward trouble drove him to practices more in accordance with the old, corrupted faith of Rome[71] than with the better light of the church[72] {in which he had been born and bred}. [In Mr. Dimmesdale's secret closet, under lock and key], there was a bloody scourge.[73] Oftentimes, this Protestant and

---

66 godly: = pious

67 white: 결백한, 순수한

68 thine or mine: = thy(your) soul or my soul

69 light: 양상(= aspect)

70 put a cheat upon: 속이다

71 old, corrupted faith of Rome: 낡고 타락한 Roman Catholicism

72 better light of the church: Protestantism을 지칭함.

73 scourge: 채찍, 매. *딤즈데일이 자신의 정신적 고통을 속죄하기 위하여 스스로에게 육체적 형벌을 가한다.

Puritan divine[74] had plied it on his own shoulders, [laughing bitterly at himself the while, and smiting so much the more pitilessly because of that bitter laugh]. It was his custom, too, {as it has been that of many other pious Puritans}, to fast[75]—not however, like them, in order to purify the body, and render it the fitter medium of celestial illumination—but rigorously, and until his knees trembled beneath him, as an act of penance. He kept vigils,[76] likewise, night after night, sometimes [in utter darkness], sometimes [with a glimmering lamp], and sometimes, [viewing his own face in a looking-glass, by the most powerful light {which he could throw upon it}]. He thus typified the constant introspection {wherewith[77] he tortured, but could not purify himself}. In these lengthened vigils, his brain often reeled,[78] and visions seemed to flit before him; perhaps seen doubtfully, and by a faint light of their own, in the remote dimness of the chamber, or more vividly and close beside him, within the looking-glass.[79] Now it was a

---

74 divine: 성직자, 목사
75 fast: 금식하다
76 vigil: (밤샘) 간호; (철야) 기도
77 wherewith: =with which
78 reel: 어질어질하다, 현기증이 나다
79 In these ... the looking-glass: 환영들이 나타나는 양태를 설명하고 있다. 환영들이 있는지 없는지 불확실하게 보이는가 하면, 환영 자체의 빛인 듯 어슴푸레 보이기도 하고 때로는 생생하게 마치 곁에 서 있는 듯 보인다고 함으로써 딤즈데일의 혼란스러운 정신 상태를 묘사한다.

herd of diabolic shapes, {that grinned and mocked at the pale minister, and beckoned him away with them}; now a group of shining angels, {who flew upward heavily, as sorrow-laden, but grew more ethereal as they rose}. Now came the dead friends of his youth, and his white-bearded father, [with a saint-like frown], and his mother [turning her face away {as she passed by}]. Ghost of a mother—thinnest fantasy of a mother—methinks she might yet have thrown a pitying glance towards her son! And now, [through the chamber {which these spectral thoughts had made so ghastly}], glided Hester Prynne [leading along little Pearl, in her scarlet garb], and [pointing her forefinger, first at the scarlet letter on her bosom, and then at the clergyman's own breast].

None of these visions ever quite deluded him. At any moment, by an effort of his will, he could discern substances[80] through their misty lack of substance, and convince himself {that they were not solid[81] in their nature, like yonder table of carved oak, or that big, square, leather-bound and brazen-clasped volume of divinity}. But, [for all that[82]], they were, in one sense, the truest and most substantial things {which the poor minister now dealt with}. It is the unspeakable misery of

---

80 discern substances: 실체인지 아닌지 분간하다
81 solid: =substantial
82 for all that: =in spite of that

a life [so false as his], {that it steals the pith and substance[83] [out of whatever realities there are around us], and [which[84] were meant by Heaven to be the spirit's joy and nutriment]}. To the untrue man, the whole universe is false — it is impalpable — it shrinks to nothing within his grasp.[85] And he himself {in so far as he shows himself in a false light}, becomes a shadow, or, indeed, ceases to exist. The only truth {that continued to give Mr. Dimmesdale a real existence on this earth} was the anguish in his inmost soul, and the undissembled expression of it in his aspect.[86] {Had he once found power to smile, and wear a face of gaiety}, there would have been no such man![87]

On one of those ugly nights, {which we have faintly hinted

---

83 pith and substance: 가장 중요한 부분, 정수

84 which: which의 선행사를 무엇으로 보느냐에 따라 이 대목을 다음과 같이 해석할 수 있다. ① 'realities'로 보면, '우리 주위에 있으면서 하늘에 의해 영혼의 기쁨과 자양분이 되도록 의도된 현실'이 된다. ② which 앞의 and를 무시한 채 선행사를 'the pith and substance'로 보면, '우리 주위에 있는 모든 현실로부터 하늘이 영혼의 기쁨과 자양분이 되도록 의도한 가장 중요한 정수를 훔쳐가 버린다'는 의미가 된다. 문장구조와는 별도로 현실을 어떻게 보느냐에 따라 두 가지 해석 모두 의미가 통한다.

85 shrinks to nothing within his grasp: 그의 손 안에서 줄어들어 사라지고 만다

86 undissembled expression of it in his aspect: 그의 얼굴에 드러난 고통의 거짓 없는 표현

87 Had he once ... such man!: 그가 한 번이라도 미소를 짓고 즐거운 얼굴을 할 힘이 없었지만, 만일 그랬다고 하더라도, 미소와 즐거운 얼굴이 사람들에게 주는 일반적인 효과와는 달리 오히려 너무도 해괴한 느낌을 주는 볼썽사나운 얼굴이 되었을 것이라는 의미이다.

at, but forborne[88] to picture forth}, the minister started from his chair. A new thought had struck[89] him. There might be a moment's peace in it. [Attiring himself with as much care {as if it had been for public worship},[90] and precisely in the same manner], he stole softly down the staircase, undid the door, and issued forth.

---

88 forborne: forbear(삼가다, 참다)의 과거분사
89 strike: 갑자기 떠오르다
90 public worship: 교회의 예배

The Scarlet Letter 12장

The Minister's Vigil[1]

[Walking in the shadow of a dream, as it were, and perhaps actually under the influence of a species of somnambulism[2]], Mr. Dimmesdale reached the spot, {where, now so long since, Hester Prynne had lived through her first hour of public ignominy}. The same platform or scaffold, [black and weather-stained[3] with the storm or sunshine of seven long years, and foot-worn[4], too, with the tread of many culprits[5] {who had since ascended it}], remained standing beneath the balcony of the meeting-house. The minister went up the steps.

It was an obscure night of early May. An unvaried pall[6] of cloud muffled[7] the whole expanse of sky from zenith to horizon. {If the same multitude [which had stood as eyewitnesses[8] while Hester Prynne sustained her punishment] could now have been summoned forth}, they would have discerned no face above the platform, nor hardly the outline of a human shape, in the dark gray of the midnight. But the town was all asleep. There was no peril of discovery. The minister might stand there, {if it so pleased him}, {until morning should

---

1 vigil: 밤샘 기도
2 somnambulism: 몽유병
3 weather-stained: 날씨로 더럽혀진
4 foot-worn: 밟아서 닳은
5 culprit: 범죄자, 죄인
6 pall: 장막
7 muffle: 덮다
8 eyewitnesses: 목격자

redden in the east}, [without other risk than {that the dank[9] and chill night-air would creep into his frame, and stiffen his joints with rheumatism, and clog[10] his throat with catarrh[11] and cough; thereby defrauding[12] the expectant audience of to-morrow's prayer and sermon[13]}]. No eye could see him, [save that ever-wakeful one {which had seen him in his closet[14], wielding the bloody scourge[15]}]. Why, then, had he come hither? Was it but the mockery[16] of penitence[17]? A mockery, indeed, but {in which his soul trifled with[18] itself}! A mockery {at which angels blushed and wept, while fiends rejoiced, with jeering laughter[19]}! He had been driven hither by the impulse of that Remorse[20] {which dogged him everywhere}, and {whose own sister and closely linked companion was that Cowardice[21] [which invariably drew him back, with her tremulous gripe[22],

---

9 dank: 축축한, 습기 찬
10 clog: 막히게 하다
11 catarrh: 카타르(점막의 염증)
12 defraud: 속이다, (권리, 재산 따위를) ~에게서 빼앗다
13 defraud the expectant audience of to-morrow's prayer and sermon: 다음날의 기도와 설교를 고대하던 청중들의 기대를 저버리다. *defraud A of B: A에게서 B를 사취하다, 빼앗다
14 closet: 밀실
15 scourge: 회초리, 채찍
16 mockery: 흉내, 모방, 조롱
17 penitence: 회개
18 trifle with: 희롱하다, 경시하다, 하찮게 보다
19 with jeering laughter: 조롱하는 웃음으로
20 Remorse: 양심의 가책
21 Cowardice: 비겁함

just when the other impulse had hurried him to the verge of a disclosure]}. Poor, miserable man! what right had infirmity[23] like his to burden itself with crime? Crime is for the iron-nerved[24], {who have their choice either to endure it, or, [if it press too hard], to exert their fierce and savage strength for a good purpose, and fling it off at once}! This feeble and most sensitive of spirits could do neither, yet continually did one thing or another, {which intertwined, in the same inextricable[25] knot, the agony of heaven-defying guilt[26] and vain repentance}.

And thus, {while standing on the scaffold, in this vain show of expiation[27]}, Mr. Dimmesdale was overcome with a great horror of mind, {as if the universe were gazing at a scarlet token on his naked breast, right over his heart}. On that spot, in very truth, there was, and there had long been, the gnawing and poisonous tooth of bodily pain. [Without any effort of his will, or power to restrain himself], he shrieked aloud; an outcry {that went pealing[28] through the night, and was beaten back from one house to another, and reverberated from[29] the hills in

---

22 with her tremulous gripe: 비겁함의 떨리는 손으로 움켜쥐고.
   * her = Cowardice
23 infirmity: 허약, 병약
24 the iron-nerved: 대담한 사람
25 inextricable: 풀 수 없는, 풀리지 않는
26 heaven-defying guilt: 하늘을 거역한 죄
27 expiation: 속죄
28 peal: 울리다

the background; as if a company of devils, [detecting so much misery and terror in it], had made a plaything of the sound, and were bandying it to and fro[30]}.

"It is done!" muttered the minister, covering his face with his hands. "The whole town will awake, and hurry forth, and find me here!"

But it was not so. The shriek had perhaps sounded with a far greater power, to his own startled ears, than it actually possessed. The town did not awake; or, if it did, the drowsy slumberers mistook the cry either for something frightful[31] in a dream, or for the noise of witches; {whose voices, at that period, were often heard to pass over the settlements or lonely cottages, as they rode with Satan through the air}. The clergyman, therefore, [hearing no symptoms of disturbance], uncovered his eyes and looked about him. At one of the chamber-windows of Governor Bellingham's mansion, {which stood at some distance, on the line of another street}, he beheld the appearance of the old magistrate himself, [with a lamp in his hand, a white night-cap on his head, and a long white gown enveloping his figure]. He looked like a

---

29 reverberate from: ~로부터 울려 퍼지다

30 and were bandying it to and fro: 그 소리를 이리저리 치고받는 것 같았다. *it=the sound

31 frightful: 무서운, 무시무시한

ghost, [evoked unseasonably[32] from the grave]. The cry had evidently startled him. At another window of the same house, moreover, appeared old Mistress Hibbins, the Governor's sister, also with a lamp, {which, even thus far off, revealed the expression of her sour[33] and discontented face}. She thrust forth her head from the lattice, and looked anxiously upward. Beyond the shadow of a doubt, this venerable witch-lady had heard Mr. Dimmesdale's outcry, and interpreted it, [with its multitudinous[34] echoes and reverberations], as the clamor[35] of the fiends and night-hags[36], {with whom she was well known to make excursions into the forest[37]}.

Detecting the gleam of Governor Bellingham's lamp, the old lady quickly extinguished her own, and vanished. Possibly, she went up among the clouds. The minister saw nothing further of her motions. The magistrate, after a wary[38] observation of the darkness — {into which, nevertheless, he could see but little farther than he might into a mill-stone[39]} — retired from the

---

32 unseasonably: 때 아니게, 때에 맞지 않게
33 sour: 심술궂은, 시큰둥한
34 multitudinous: 다수의, 무수한
35 clamor: 시끄러운 소리, 아우성
36 night-hag: 마녀, [모욕적] 할망구
37 make excursions into the forest: 숲 속으로 여행을 가다
38 wary: 경계하는, 조심하는
39 mill-stone: 맷돌, 〈성서〉 무거운 짐. *여기에서 'see into a mill-stone'의 의미가 분명하지 않으나 '맷돌을 꿰뚫어본다'는 말이 '도

window.

The minister grew comparatively calm. His eyes, however, were soon greeted by a little, glimmering light, {which, at first a long way off, was approaching up the street}. It threw a gleam of recognition on here a post, and there a garden-fence, and here a latticed window-pane[40], and there a pump, [with its full trough of water], and here, again, an arched door of oak, [with an iron knocker[41]], and a rough log for the door-step. The Reverend Mr. Dimmesdale noted all these minute particulars, even while firmly convinced {that the doom of his existence was stealing onward, in the footsteps which he now heard}; and {that the gleam of the lantern would fall upon him, in a few moments more, and reveal his long-hidden secret}. {As the light drew nearer}, he beheld, within its illuminated circle, his brother clergyman, — [or, to speak more accurately, his professional father, as well as highly valued friend], — the Reverend Mr. Wilson; who, {as Mr. Dimmesdale now conjectured}, had been praying at the bedside of some dying man. And so he had. The good old minister came freshly

---

저히 불가능한 것도 통찰한다'는 의미로 쓰인다는 점을 염두에 두고 보면, 이 대목에서는 '암흑'(darkness)과 '맷돌'을 병치시켜 그만큼 조금 앞의 거리도 보이지 않는 어두운 상황임을 나타내는 것으로 볼 수 있다.

40 a latticed window-pane: 격자로 된 창의 유리
41 knocker: 문 두드리는 고리쇠

from the death-chamber of Governor Winthrop[42], {who had passed from earth to heaven within that very hour}. And now, [surrounded, like the saint-like personages of olden times, with a radiant halo[43], {that glorified him amid this gloomy night of sin,—[as if the departed Governor had left him an inheritance of his glory], or [as if he had caught upon himself the distant shine of the celestial[44] city, while looking thitherward to see the triumphant pilgrim pass within its gates]}],—now, in short, good Father Wilson was moving homeward, aiding his footsteps with a lighted lantern! The glimmer of this luminary[45] suggested the above conceits to Mr. Dimmesdale, {who smiled,—nay, almost laughed at them,—and then wondered if he were going mad}.

{As the Reverend Mr. Wilson passed beside the scaffold, [closely muffling[46] his Geneva cloak about him with one arm, and holding the lantern before his breast with the other]}, the minister could hardly restrain himself from speaking.

---

42 the death-chamber of Governor Winthrop: 윈스롭 총독의 임종의 방. * 비록 호손이 이 시점을 '5월 초'로 설정하고 있으나 존 윈스롭 총독이 실제로 죽은 날은 1649년 3월 26일이다. 윈스롭은 1630년 에 매사추세츠 베이 식민지를 세운 이래 죽을 때까지 거의 계속해 서 총독이나 부총독으로 일했다.

43 with a radiant halo: 밝은 후광에 싸인 채

44 celestial: 천상의, 거룩한

45 luminary: 등불

46 closely muffling: 바짝 감싸면서. * muffle: 감싸다

"A good evening to you, venerable[47] Father Wilson! Come up hither, I pray you, and pass a pleasant hour with me!"

Good Heavens! Had Mr. Dimmesdale actually spoken? For one instant, he believed that these words had passed his lips. But they were uttered only within his imagination. The venerable Father Wilson continued to step slowly onward, [looking carefully at the muddy pathway before his feet, and never once turning his head towards the guilty platform]. {When the light of the glimmering lantern had faded quite away}, the minister discovered, [by the faintness which came over him], that the last few moments had been a crisis of terrible anxiety; {although his mind had made an involuntary[48] effort to relieve[49] itself by a kind of lurid playfulness[50]}.

Shortly afterwards, the like grisly[51] sense of the humorous again stole in among the solemn phantoms of his thought. He felt his limbs growing stiff with the unaccustomed chilliness of the night, and doubted {whether he should be able to descend the steps of the scaffold}. Morning would break, and find him there. The neighbourhood would begin to rouse

---

47 venerable: 존경할 만한
48 involuntary: 무의식중의
49 relieve: 덜다, 완화하다
50 lurid playfulness: 으스스한 장난, 무서운 장난
51 grisly: 소름끼치게 하는

itself. The earliest riser, [coming forth in the dim twilight], would perceive a vaguely defined figure[52] [aloft on the place of shame]; and, [half crazed betwixt alarm and curiosity], would go, [knocking from door to door, summoning all the people to behold the ghost—as he needs must think it—of some defunct transgressor[53]]. A dusky tumult would flap its wings from one house to another. Then—[the morning light still waxing stronger]—old patriarchs would rise up in great haste, [each in his flannel gown], and matronly dames, [without pausing to put off their night-gear[54]]. The whole tribe of decorous personages[55], {who had never heretofore been seen with a single hair of their heads awry[56]}, would start into public view, with the disorder of a nightmare in their aspects. Old Governor Bellingham would come grimly forth, [with his King James's ruff[57] fastened askew[58]]; and Mistress Hibbins, [with some twigs of the forest clinging to her skirts, and looking sourer than ever, as having hardly got a wink of sleep after her night ride]; and good Father Wilson, too, [after spending half the night at a death-bed[59], and liking ill to be

---

52 a vaguely defined figure: 윤곽이 희미한 모습
53 defunct transgressor: 죽은 죄인
54 night-gear: =night clothes
55 personage: 저명인사, 명사
56 awry: 빗나간, 엉망인
57 ruff: 주름 칼라
58 askew: 삐딱하게
59 death-bed: 죽음의 자리, 임종의

disturbed, thus early, out of his dreams about the glorified saints]. Hither, likewise, would come the elders and deacons of Mr. Dimmesdale's church, and the young virgins {who so idolized their minister, and had made a shrine for him in their white bosoms; which, now, by the by, in their hurry and confusion, they would scantly have given themselves time to cover with their kerchiefs}. All people, in a word, would come stumbling over their thresholds, and turning up their amazed and horror-stricken visages around the scaffold. Whom would they discern there, with the red eastern light upon his brow? Whom, but the Reverend Arthur Dimmesdale, [half frozen to death, overwhelmed with shame, and standing where Hester Prynne had stood]!

[Carried away by the grotesque horror of this picture], the minister, unawares, and to his own infinite alarm, burst into a great peal of laughter. It was immediately responded to by a light, airy, childish laugh, {in which, with a thrill of the heart, — but he knew not whether of exquisite[60] pain, or pleasure as acute, — he recognized the tones of little Pearl}.

"Pearl! Little Pearl!" cried he, after a moment's pause; then, suppressing his voice[61], — "Hester! Hester Prynne! Are you

---

60 exquisite: 격렬한(=acute)
61 suppressing his voice: 목소리를 가라앉히며

there?"

"Yes; it is Hester Prynne!" she replied, in a tone of surprise; and the minister heard her footsteps approaching from the sidewalk, {along which she had been passing}.—"It is I, and my little Pearl."

"Whence come you, Hester?" asked the minister. "What sent you hither?"

"I have been watching at a death-bed," answered Hester Prynne;—"at Governor Winthrop's death-bed, and have taken his measure for a robe[62], and am now going homeward to my dwelling."

"Come up hither, Hester, thou and little Pearl," said the Reverend Mr. Dimmesdale. "Ye have both been here before, but I was not with you. Come up hither once again, and we will stand all three together!"

She silently ascended the steps, and stood on the platform, holding little Pearl by the hand. The minister felt for the child's other hand, and took it. {The moment that he did so}, there

---

62 robe: (신분의 상징이나 특별한 의식을 위한) 예복. 여기서는 수의 를 의미한다.

came {what seemed a tumultuous rush of new life[63], [other life than his own], pouring like a torrent into his heart[64], and hurrying through all his veins[65], as if the mother and the child were communicating their vital warmth to his half-torpid system[66]}. The three formed an electric chain.

"Minister!" whispered little Pearl.

"What wouldst thou say, child?" asked Mr. Dimmesdale.

"Wilt thou stand here with mother and me, to-morrow noontide?" inquired Pearl.

"Nay; not so, my little Pearl!" answered the minister; for, [with the new energy of the moment], all the dread of public exposure[67], {that had so long been the anguish of his life}, had returned upon him; and he was already trembling at the conjunction[68] {in which—with a strange joy, nevertheless—

---

63 there came what seemed a tumultuous rush of new life: 세차게 요동치며 솟구치는 새 생명 같은 것이 생겼다

64 pouring like a torrent into his heart: 급류같이 그의 가슴속으로 쏟아져 들어오는

65 hurrying through all his veins: 아주 빨리 혈관으로 고루 퍼지는

66 half-torpid system: 반쯤은 무기력해진 신체. *torpid: 무기력한, 활기 없는

67 exposure: 드러남

68 conjunction: (특별한 결과를 초래하는 사건·상황 등의) 결합, 연

he now found himself}. "Not so, my child. I shall, indeed, stand with thy mother and thee one other day, but not to-morrow!"

MP3 ★
12장 (2)
시작 Pearl laughed, and attempted to pull away her hand. But the minister held it fast.

"A moment longer, my child!" said he.

"But wilt thou promise," asked Pearl, "to take my hand, and mother's hand, to-morrow noontide?"

"Not then, Pearl," said the minister, "but another time!"

"And what other time?" persisted the child.

"At the great judgment day!" whispered the minister,—and, strangely enough, the sense {that he was a professional teacher of the truth} impelled him to answer the child so. "Then, and there, before the judgment-seat, thy mother, and thou, and I, must stand together. But the daylight of this world shall not see our meeting!"

Pearl laughed again.

결, 동시발생

38

But, {before Mr. Dimmesdale had done speaking}, a light gleamed far and wide over all the muffled sky. It was doubtless caused by one of those meteors[69], {which the night-watcher may so often observe burning out to waste, in the vacant regions of the atmosphere}. So powerful was its radiance, that it thoroughly illuminated the dense medium of cloud betwixt the sky and earth. The great vault[70] brightened, like the dome[71] of an immense lamp. It showed the familiar scene of the street, with the distinctness of mid-day, but also with the awfulness {that is always imparted to familiar objects by an unaccustomed light}. The wooden houses, [with their jutting[72] stories and quaint[73] gable-peaks[74]]; the doorsteps and thresholds, [with the early grass springing up about them]; the garden-plots[75], [black with freshly turned earth]; the wheel-track, [little worn[76], and, even in the market-place, margined with green on either side];— all were visible, but with a singularity of aspect {that seemed to give another moral interpretation to the things of this world than they had ever borne before}. And there stood the minister, [with his hand over his heart]; and Hester Prynne,

---

69 meteor: 유성
70 vault: 둥근 천장, 하늘
71 dome: 반구형 모양의 것
72 jutting: 튀어나온
73 quaint: 기묘한, 기괴한
74 gable-peaks: 박공 꼭대기
75 plot: 작은 구획의 땅
76 little worn: 거의 닳지 않은, 거의 지워지지 않은

[with the embroidered letter glimmering on her bosom]; and little Pearl, [herself a symbol, and the connecting link between those two]. They stood in the noon of that strange and solemn splendor[77], {as if it were the light [that is to reveal all secrets], and the daybreak[78] [that shall unite all who belong to one another]}.

There was witchcraft in little Pearl's eyes; and her face, {as she glanced upward at the minister}, wore that naughty[79] smile {which made its expression frequently so elvish[80]}. She withdrew her hand from Mr. Dimmesdale's, and pointed across the street. But he clasped both his hands over his breast, and cast his eyes towards the zenith[81].

Nothing was more common, in those days, than to interpret all meteoric appearances, and other natural phenomena, {that occurred with less regularity than the rise and set of sun and moon}, as so many revelations from a supernatural[82] source. Thus, a blazing spear, a sword of flame, a bow, or a sheaf[83]

---

77 splendor: 광휘, 광채
78 daybreak: 새벽
79 naughty: 장난기 서린
80 elvish(=elfish): 꼬마 요정 같은
81 zenith: 천정(天頂)
82 supernatural: 초자연적인
83 sheaf: 다발

of arrows, [seen in the midnight sky], prefigured[84] Indian warfare. Pestilence[85] was known to have been foreboded[86] by a shower of crimson light. We doubt whether any marked event, for good or evil, ever befell New England, from its settlement down to Revolutionary times, {of which the inhabitants had not been previously warned by some spectacle of this nature}. Not seldom, it had been seen by multitudes. Oftener, however, its credibility[87] rested on the faith of some lonely eyewitness, {who beheld the wonder through the colored, magnifying, and distorting medium of his imagination[88], and shaped it more distinctly in his after-thought}. It was, indeed, a majestic idea, {that the destiny of nations should be revealed, in these awful hieroglyphics[89], on the cope of heaven}. A scroll[90] [so wide] might not be deemed too expansive for Providence to write a people's doom upon. The belief was a favorite one with our forefathers, as betokening[91] {that their infant commonwealth was under a celestial guardianship of peculiar intimacy and strictness}. But what shall we say, {when an individual

---

84 prefigure: 예시하다, 예상하다

85 pestilence: 역병

86 forebode: 전조하다, 예시하다

87 credibility: 진실성, 신빙성

88 magnifying, and distorting medium of his imagination: 과장하기도 하고 왜곡하기도 하는 상상력이라는 매개체로 보는

89 hieroglyphics: 상형 문자로 쓰여진 것

90 scroll: 두루마리

91 betoken: 나타내다

discovers a revelation, [addressed to himself alone], on the same vast sheet of record}! In such a case, it could only be the symptom of a highly disordered mental state, {when a man, [rendered morbidly [92] self-contemplative by long, intense, and secret pain], had extended his egotism over the whole expanse of nature, [until the firmament [93] itself should appear no more than a fitting page for his soul's history and fate]}.

We impute it, therefore, solely to the disease in his own eye and heart, {that the minister, [looking upward to the zenith], beheld there the appearance of an immense letter,—the letter A,—marked out in lines of dull red light}. Not but the meteor may have shown itself at that point, burning duskily through a veil of cloud; but with no such shape {as his guilty imagination gave it}; or, at least, with so little definiteness [94], {that another's guilt might have seen another symbol in it}.

There was a singular circumstance {that characterized Mr. Dimmesdale's psychological state, at this moment}. All the time {that he gazed upward to the zenith}, he was, nevertheless, perfectly aware {that little Pearl was pointing her finger towards old Roger Chillingworth, [who stood at no great distance

---

92 morbidly: 병적으로
93 firmament: 창공, 하늘
94 definiteness: 한정됨

from the scaffold]}. The minister appeared to see him, with the same glance {that discerned the miraculous letter}. To his features, as to all other objects, the meteoric light imparted a new expression; or it might well be {that the physician was not careful then, [as at all other times], to hide the malevolence[95] [with which he looked upon his victim]}. Certainly, {if the meteor kindled up the sky, and disclosed the earth, with an awfulness [that admonished[96] Hester Prynne and the clergyman of the day of judgment]}, then might Roger Chillingworth have passed[97] [with them[98]] for the arch-fiend[99], [standing there, with a smile and scowl[100], to claim his own[101]]. So vivid was the expression, or so intense the minister's perception of it, that it seemed still to remain painted on the darkness, {after the meteor had vanished}, with an effect {as if the street and all things else were at once annihilated[102]}.

"Who is that man, Hester?" gasped Mr. Dimmesdale, overcome with terror. "I shiver at him! Dost thou know the

---

95 malevolence: 악의, 증오
96 admonish A of B: A에게 B를 알리다, 일깨우다, 경고하다
97 pass for: ~로 통하다
98 with them: 헤스터와 딤즈데일에게는
99 arch-fiend: 대악마
100 scowl: 얼굴을 찌푸리다, 찌푸린 얼굴
101 the arch-fiend ... his own: 자신의 몫을 주장하려고 미소와 찌푸림을 동시에 띠고 거기에 서 있는 대악마
102 annihilate: 전멸시키다, 소멸시키다

man? I hate him, Hester!"

She remembered her oath, and was silent.

"I tell thee, my soul shivers at him," muttered the minister again. "Who is he? Who is he? Canst thou do nothing for me? I have a nameless horror of the man."

"Minister," said little Pearl, "I can tell thee {who he is}!"

"Quickly, then, child!" said the minister, bending his ear close to her lips. "Quickly!—and as low as thou canst whisper."

Pearl mumbled something into his ear, {that sounded, indeed, like human language, but was only such gibberish[103] as children may be heard amusing themselves with, by the hour together[104]}. At all events, {if it involved any secret information in regard to old Roger Chillingworth}, it was in a tongue [unknown to the erudite[105] clergyman], and did but increase the bewilderment[106] of his mind. The elvish child then laughed aloud.

"Dost thou mock me now?" said the minister.

---

103 gibberish: 횡설수설
104 by the hour together: 한 번에[쉬지 않고] 몇 시간씩
105 erudite: 박학한
106 bewilderment: 당황함

"Thou wast not bold!—thou wast not true!" answered the child. "Thou wouldst not promise to take my hand, and mother's hand, to-morrow noontide!"

"Worthy Sir," said the physician, {who had now advanced to the foot of the platform}. "Pious Master Dimmesdale! can this be you? Well, well, indeed! We men of study, {whose heads are in our books}, have need to be straitly[107] looked after! We dream in our waking moments, and walk in our sleep. Come, good Sir, and my dear friend, I pray you, let me lead you home!"

"How knewest thou that I was here?" asked the minister, fearfully.

"Verily[108], and in good faith," answered Roger Chillingworth, "I knew nothing of the matter. I had spent the better part of the night at the bedside of the worshipful Governor Winthrop, doing {what my poor skill might to give him ease}. He [going home to a better world], I, likewise, was on my way homeward, {when this strange light shone out}. Come with me, I beseech you, Reverend Sir; else you will be poorly able to do Sabbath duty to-morrow. Aha! see now, how they trouble the brain,— these books!—these books! You should study less, good Sir,

---

107 straitly: 엄하게, 꼼꼼하게
108 verily: 참으로, 진정

and take a little pastime[109]; or these night-whimseys[110] will grow upon you!"

"I will go home with you," said Mr. Dimmesdale.

With a chill despondency[111], like one [awaking, all nerveless, from an ugly dream], he yielded himself to the physician, and was led away.

[The next day, however, being the Sabbath], he preached a discourse {which was held to be the richest and most powerful, and the most replete[112] with heavenly influences, [that had ever proceeded from his lips]}. Souls, it is said, more souls than one, were brought to the truth by the efficacy[113] of that sermon, and vowed within themselves to cherish[114] a holy gratitude towards Mr. Dimmesdale throughout the long hereafter[115]. But, {as he came down the pulpit-steps}, the gray-bearded sexton[116] met him, holding up a black glove, {which the minister recognized

---

109 pastime: 오락, 기분전환
110 night-whimseys(=night-whimsies): 밤의 변덕. *whimsey: 엉뚱한 생각이나 행동
111 despondency: 낙담, 의기소침
112 replete: 충만한
113 efficacy: 효능
114 cherish: (추억을) 고이 간직하다
115 hereafter: 앞으로, 장차
116 sexton: 교회관리인

as his own}.

"It was found," said the sexton, "this morning, on the scaffold, {where evil-doers are set up to public shame}. Satan dropped it there, {I take it}, intending a scurrilous jest[117] against your reverence. But, indeed, he was blind and foolish, {as he ever and always is}. A pure hand needs no glove to cover it!"

"Thank you, my good friend," said the minister gravely, but startled at heart; for, so confused was his remembrance, that he had almost brought himself to look at the events of the past night as visionary. "Yes, it seems to be my glove, indeed!"

"And, {since Satan saw fit to steal it}, your reverence must needs handle him without gloves, henceforward," remarked the old sexton, grimly smiling. "But did your reverence hear of the portent[118] {that was seen last night}? a great red letter in the sky, — the letter A, — {which we interpret to stand for[119] Angel}. For, {as our good Governor Winthrop was made an angel this past night}, it was doubtless held fit {that there should be some notice thereof}!"

"No," answered the minister; "I had not heard of it."

---

117 scurrilous jest: 상스러운[악마적인] 희롱
118 portent: 조짐, 전조, 경이적인 존재
119 stand for: 나타내다, 의미하다

Another View of Hester

In her late singular interview[1] with Mr. Dimmesdale, Hester Prynne was shocked at the condition {to which she found the clergyman reduced}. His nerve[2] seemed absolutely destroyed. His moral force was abased into more than childish weakness. It grovelled helpless[3] on the ground, {even while his intellectual faculties retained their pristine strength, or had perhaps acquired a morbid energy, [which disease only could have given them]}. {With her knowledge of a train of circumstances [hidden from all others]}, she could readily infer that, [besides the legitimate action[4] of his own conscience], a terrible machinery had been brought to bear, and was still operating, on Mr. Dimmesdale's well-being and repose. Knowing {what this poor fallen man had once been}, her whole soul was moved by the shuddering terror {with which he had appealed to her — the outcast woman — for support against his instinctively discovered enemy}. She decided, moreover, that he had a right to her utmost aid.[5] [Little accustomed, in her long seclusion from society, to measure her ideas of right and wrong by any standard external to herself], Hester saw — or seemed to see — that there lay a responsibility upon her in reference to[6] the clergyman, {which she owned

---

1 singular interview: 이상한 상황에서의 만남

2 nerve: = vigor, energy

3 grovelled helpless: 힘없이 쓰러져 있었다[기다시피 했다]

4 legitimate action: 당연한 작용

5 utmost aid: 최대한의 도움

to no other, nor to the whole world besides}. The links {that united her to the rest of humankind—links of flowers, or silk, or gold, or whatever the material}—had all been broken. Here was the iron link of mutual crime[7], {which neither he nor she could break}. Like all other ties, it brought along with it its obligations.

Hester Prynne did not now occupy precisely the same position {in which we beheld her during the earlier periods of her ignominy}. Years had come and gone. Pearl was now seven years old. Her mother, [with the scarlet letter on her breast, glittering in its fantastic embroidery[8]], had long been a familiar object to the townspeople. {As is apt to be the case[9] when a person stands out in any prominence before the community, and, at the same time, interferes neither with public nor individual interests and convenience}, a species of general regard had ultimately grown up in reference to Hester Prynne. It is to the credit of human nature that, [except where its selfishness is brought into play[10]], it loves more readily than it hates. Hatred, by a gradual and quiet process, will even be

---

6 in reference to: ~에 관하여
7 iron link of mutual crime: 함께 저지른 죄로 얽힌 끊기 어려운 고리
8 glittering in its fantastic embroidery: 색다르게 수놓여 번쩍거리는
9 As is apt to be the case: 흔히 그럴 수 있듯이
10 except where its selfishness is brought into play: 이기심이 개입하는 경우를 제외하고는

transformed to love, {unless the change be impeded[11] by a continually new irritation of the original feeling of hostility}. [In this matter of Hester Prynne] there was neither irritation nor irksomeness. She never battled with the public, but submitted uncomplainingly to its worst usage[12]; she made no claim upon it in requital for {what she suffered}; she did not weigh upon its sympathies. Then, also, the blameless purity of her life during all these years {in which she had been set apart to infamy} was reckoned[13] largely in her favour. {With nothing now to lose, in the sight of mankind, and with no hope, and seemingly no wish, of gaining anything},[14] it could only be a genuine regard for virtue that had brought back the poor wanderer to its paths.

It was perceived, too, that {while Hester never put forward[15] even the humblest title to share in the world's privileges[16]— further than to breathe the common air and earn daily bread for little Pearl and herself by the faithful labour of her hands—} she was quick to acknowledge her sisterhood with the race of man[17] {whenever benefits were to be conferred}.

---

11 impeded: =hindered, obstructed

12 to its worst usage: 세상 사람들의 가장 혹독한 대우에도

13 reckoned: =considered

14 With nothing now to lose ... anything: 뒤의 'the poor wanderer' 를 수식하는 형용사구

15 put forward: 제안하다, 주장하다

16 humblest title to share in the world's privileges: 세상의 특권을 나누겠다는 아주 소박한 권리

None so ready as she to give of her little substance to every demand of poverty, {even though the bitter-hearted pauper threw back a gibe[18] in requital of the food [brought regularly to his door], or the garments [wrought for him by the fingers that could have embroidered a monarch's robe]}. None so self-devoted as Hester when pestilence stalked[19] through the town. In all seasons of calamity,[20] indeed, whether general or of individuals, the outcast of society at once found her place. She came, not as a guest, but as a rightful inmate, into the household {that was darkened by trouble}, as if its[21] gloomy twilight were a medium {in which she was entitled to hold intercourse with her fellow-creatures}. There glimmered the embroidered letter, with comfort in its unearthly ray. Elsewhere the token of sin, it was the taper[22] of the sick chamber. It had even thrown its gleam, in the sufferer's hard extremity[23], across the verge of time. It had shown him[24] where to set his foot, {while the light of earth was fast becoming dim, and ere the light of futurity could reach him}. In such emergencies Hester's

---

17 the race of man: 인류, 세상 사람들

18 gibe: 헐뜯음, 비웃음

19 stalk: 활보하다(= stride, spread)

20 In all seasons of calamity: 재난이 있을 때는 언제나

21 its: = the household's

22 taper: 가는 양초. ＊양초의 의미와 약한 빛이라는 비유적인 의미
    두 가지로 쓰였다.

23 extremity: 임종

24 him: = the sufferer

nature showed itself warm and rich—a well-spring of human tenderness, [unfailing to every real demand, and inexhaustible by the largest]²⁵. Her breast, with its badge of shame, was but the softer pillow for the head that needed one²⁶. She was self-ordained a Sister of Mercy²⁷, or, we may rather say, the world's heavy hand had so ordained her, {when neither the world nor she looked forward to this result}. The letter was the symbol of her calling²⁸. Such helpfulness was found in her—so much power to do, and power to sympathise—that many people refused to interpret the scarlet A by its original signification²⁹. They said that it meant Able, so strong was Hester Prynne, with a woman's strength.

It was only the darkened house {that could contain her}. When sunshine came again, she was not there. Her shadow had faded across the threshold. The helpful inmate had departed, {without one backward glance to gather up the meed³⁰ of gratitude, [if any were in the hearts of those whom she had served so zealously]}. [Meeting them in the street], she never raised her head to receive their greeting. {If they were resolute

---

25 largest: =largest demand
26 one: =a pillow
27 a Sister of Mercy: 'the Sisters of Mercy'는 자비의 성모 동정(童貞) 수녀회
28 calling: 소명, 천직(天職)
29 its original signification: 주홍글자 A의 원래 의미인 adultery
30 meed: =reward

to accost her}, she laid her finger on the scarlet letter, and passed on. This might be pride, but was <u>so</u> like humility, <u>that</u> it produced all the softening influence of the latter quality[31] on the public mind. The public is despotic in its temper; it is capable of denying common justice {when too strenuously demanded as a right}; but quite as frequently it[32] awards more than justice, {when the appeal is made}, as despots love to have it made, entirely to its generosity. [Interpreting Hester Prynne's deportment[33] as an appeal of this nature], society was inclined to show its former victim a more benign countenance <u>than</u> she cared to be favoured with, or, perchance, <u>than</u> she deserved.

The rulers, and the wise and learned men of the community, were longer in acknowledging the influence of Hester's good qualities than the people. The prejudices {which they shared in common with the latter[34]} were fortified in themselves by an iron frame-work of reasoning[35], {that made it a far tougher labour to expel them}. Day by day, nevertheless, their sour and rigid wrinkles were relaxing into something {which, in the due course of years[36], might grow to be an expression of

---

31 latter quality: ＝humility

32 it: ＝the public

33 deportment: 행동, 품행

34 the latter: ＝the people

35 iron frame-work of reasoning: 무쇠처럼 단단한 논리라는 틀.
    ＊'of'는 동격관계

36 in the due course of years: 세월이 흐르면, 때가 되면

almost benevolence}. Thus it was with the men of rank[37], {on whom their eminent position imposed the guardianship of the public morals}. Individuals in private life, meanwhile, had quite forgiven Hester Prynne for her frailty[38]; nay, more, they had begun to look upon the scarlet letter as the token, not of that one sin {for which she had borne so long and dreary a penance}, but of her many good deeds since. "Do you see that woman with the embroidered badge?" they would say to strangers. "It is our Hester — the town's own Hester — who is so kind to the poor, so helpful to the sick, so comfortable to the afflicted![39]" Then, it is true, the propensity of human nature to tell the very worst of itself, {when embodied in the person of another}, would constrain[40] them to whisper the black scandal of bygone years. It was none the less a fact, however, that [in the eyes of the very men {who spoke thus}], the scarlet letter had the effect of the cross on a nun's bosom. It imparted to the wearer a kind of sacredness, {which enabled her to walk securely amid all peril}. {Had she fallen among thieves}, it[41] would have kept her safe. It[42] was reported, and believed by many, {that an Indian had drawn his arrow against the badge},

---

37 the men of rank: 신분이 높은 사람들
38 frailty: =fault
39 the afflicted: 고통 받는 사람들
40 constrain: =compel
41 it: =the scarlet letter
42 It: 뒤의 that 절을 받는 가주어

and {that the missile struck it, and fell harmless to the ground}.

The effect of the symbol — or rather, of the position [in respect to society] {that was indicated by it} — on the mind of Hester Prynne herself was powerful and peculiar. All the light and graceful foliage of her character had been withered up by this red-hot brand[43], and had long ago fallen away, leaving a bare and harsh outline, {which might have been repulsive [had she possessed friends or companions to be repelled by it]}. Even the attractiveness of her person[44] had undergone a similar change. It might be partly owing to the studied[45] austerity of her dress, and partly to the lack of demonstration[46] in her manners. It was a sad transformation, too, that her rich and luxuriant hair had either been cut off, or was so completely hidden by a cap, that not a shining lock of it ever once gushed into the sunshine. It was due in part to[47] all these causes, but still more to something else, that there seemed to be no longer anything in Hester's face for Love to dwell upon[48]; nothing in Hester's form, [though majestic and statue like], {that Passion would ever dream of clasping in its

---

43 red-hot brand: 붉은 낙인. *주홍글자를 의미한다.

44 person: =bodily figure

45 studied: =deliberate, intentional

46 lack of demonstration: 과시하지 않는 것

47 It was due in part to: 부분적으로는 ~ 때문이었다. *'It was due to ...' 구문 사이에 'in part'가 삽입된 것

48 for Love to dwell upon: 사랑이 깃들 만한 (여지)

embrace}; nothing in Hester's bosom [to make it ever again the pillow of Affection]. Some attribute had departed from her, {the permanence of which[49] had been essential to keep her a woman}. Such is frequently the fate, and such the stern development, of the feminine character and person, {when the woman has encountered, and lived through, an experience of peculiar severity[50]}. {If she be all tenderness[51]}, she will die. {If she survive}, the tenderness will either be crushed out of her, or — and the outward semblance is the same[52] — crushed <u>so</u> deeply into her heart <u>that</u> it can never show itself more. The latter[53] is perhaps the truest theory. She {who has once been a woman, and ceased to be so[54]}, might at any moment become a woman again, {if there were only the magic touch to effect the transformation}. We shall see whether Hester Prynne were ever afterwards so touched and so transfigured.

Much of the marble coldness[55] of Hester's impression was to be attributed to the circumstance {that her life had turned, in a

---

49 which: 선행사는 'some attribute'
50 an experience of peculiar severity: 유달리 가혹한 경험. 앞의 'encountered'와 'lived through'의 목적어
51 all tenderness: =very tender
52 outward semblance is the same: 겉보기는 같아도
53 latter: =the tenderness will be crushed so deeply into her heart ... more.
54 so: =a woman
55 marble coldness: 대리석 같은 차가움

great measure, from passion and feeling to thought}. [Standing alone in the world—alone, as to any dependence on society, and with little Pearl to be guided and protected—alone, and hopeless of retrieving her position, {even had she not scorned to consider it[56] desirable}] — she cast away the fragment a broken chain. The world's law was no law for her mind. It was an age {in which the human intellect, [newly emancipated[57]], had taken a more active and a wider range than for many centuries before}. Men of the sword[58] had overthrown nobles and kings. Men bolder than these had overthrown and rearranged—[not actually, but within the sphere of theory,[59] which was their most real abode]—the whole system of ancient prejudice, {wherewith was linked much of ancient principle}. Hester Prynne imbibed this spirit. She assumed a freedom of speculation[60], then common enough on the other side of the Atlantic[61], but {which our forefathers, [had they known it], would have held to be a deadlier crime than that stigmatised by the scarlet letter}. In her lonesome cottage, by the seashore, thoughts visited her, {such as dared to enter no

---

56 it: = retrieving her position

57 newly emancipated: 이제 막 해방된

58 Men of the sword: 군대, 군인

59 not actually, but within the sphere of theory: 실제로가 아니라, 이론적인 영역에서

60 freedom of speculation: 사색의 자유

61 the other side of the Atlantic: 대서양 건너 저편. *영국을 가리킨다.

other dwelling in New England[62]}; shadowy guests[63], {that would have been as perilous as demons to their entertainer, [could they have been seen so much as knocking at her door]}.

It is remarkable that persons {who speculate the most boldly} often conform with the most perfect quietude to the external regulations of society. The thought suffices them, without investing itself in the flesh and blood[64] of action. So it seemed to be with Hester.[65] Yet, {had little Pearl never come to her from the spiritual world}, it might have been far otherwise. Then[66] she might have come down to us in history, hand in hand with Ann Hutchinson[67], as the foundress of a religious sect. She might, in one of her phases, have been a prophetess. She might, and not improbably[68] would, have suffered death from the stern tribunals of the period, for attempting to

---

62 such as … in New England: 이 대목은 앞의 'thoughts'를 꾸미는 것으로 보아서 '뉴잉글랜드의 다른 집을 감히 들어가지 못하는 그런 생각들'로 해석

63 shadowy guests: 앞의 'thoughts'를 받아 헤스터의 사상을 비유적으로 표현한 것

64 flesh and blood: =substance and reality

65 So it seemed to be with Hester: 헤스터는 그렇게 여겼다

66 Then: =If little Pearl had never come to her from the spiritual world, then ….

67 Ann Hutchinson(1591~1643). 앤 허친슨은 자유주의 사상의 감화를 받아, 교회의 법칙에 따르지 않고도 각 개인 속에 깃든 Holy Spirit를 통한 직관에 의해 신의 은총을 얻을 수 있다고 믿었다.

68 not improbably: =with probability

undermine the foundations of the Puritan establishment. But, in the education of her child, the mother's enthusiasm of thought had something to wreak itself upon[69]. Providence, in the person of this little girl, had assigned to Hester's charge, the germ and blossom of womanhood, to be cherished and developed amid a host of[70] difficulties. Everything was against her. The world was hostile. The child's own nature had something wrong in it, {which[71] continually betokened [that she had been born amiss—the effluence of her mother's lawless passion]—and often impelled Hester to ask, in bitterness of heart, whether it were for ill or good that the poor little creature had been born at all}.

Indeed, the same dark question often rose into her mind with reference to[72] the whole race of womanhood. Was existence worth accepting even to the happiest among them? {As concerned[73] her own individual existence}, she had long ago decided in the negative, and dismissed the point as settled. A tendency to speculation, {though it may keep women quiet, as it does man[74]}, yet makes her sad. She discerns, it may be, such a hopeless task before her. [As a first step], the whole system

---

69 wreak ... upon: 분출하다, 터뜨리다, 쏟아붓다
70 a host of: 많은, 다수의
71 which: 선행사는 앞의 주절 전체
72 with reference to: ~에 관하여
73 as concerned: ~에 대해서는(=concerning)
74 as it does man: =as it keeps man quiet

of society is to be torn down and built up anew. Then the very nature of the opposite sex[75], or its long hereditary habit, {which has become like nature}, is to be essentially modified {before woman can be allowed to assume [what seems a fair and suitable position]}. Finally, [all other difficulties being obviated[76]], woman cannot take advantage of these preliminary reforms until she herself shall have undergone a still mightier change, {in which, perhaps, the ethereal essence, [wherein she has her truest life], will be found to have evaporated}. A woman never overcomes these problems by any exercise of thought. They are not to be solved[77], or only in one way. If her heart chance to come uppermost[78], they vanish. Thus Hester Prynne, {whose heart had lost its regular and healthy throb}, wandered without a clue in the dark labyrinth of mind; now turned aside by an insurmountable precipice; now[79] starting back from a deep chasm. There was wild and ghastly scenery all around her, and a home and comfort nowhere. At times a fearful doubt strove[80] to possess her soul, {whether it were not better to send Pearl at once to Heaven, and go herself to such futurity as Eternal Justice should provide}.

---

75 opposite sex: 남성

76 obviate: = remove

77 They are not to be solved: = They cannot be solved. *be 동사
와 to 부정사가 '가능'의 의미로 쓰였다.

78 uppermost: = foremost

79 now ... now: = at one time ... at another time

80 strive: = make efforts

The scarlet letter had not done its office.

Now, however, her interview with the Reverend Mr. Dimmesdale, on the night of his vigil, had given her a new theme of reflection, and held up[81] to her an object {that appeared worthy of any exertion and sacrifice for its attainment}. She had witnessed the intense misery {beneath which the minister struggled, or, to speak more accurately, had ceased to struggle}. She saw that he stood on the verge of lunacy[82], {if he had not already stepped across it}. It was impossible to doubt that, {whatever painful efficacy there might be in the secret sting of remorse[83]}, a deadlier venom had been infused into it by the hand {that proffered relief}. A secret enemy had been continually by his side, under the semblance of[84] a friend and helper, and had availed himself of the opportunities [thus afforded for tampering with the delicate springs of Mr. Dimmesdale's nature]. Hester could not but ask herself {whether there had not originally been a defect of truth, courage, and loyalty on her own part, in allowing the minister to be thrown into position [where so much evil was to be foreboded[85] and nothing auspicious to

---

81 hold up: =to present to notice
82 on the verge of lunacy: 미쳐 버릴 지경
83 secret sting of remorse: 남모르는 후회, 양심의 가책
84 under the semblance of: ~을 가장하여
85 forebode: =portend. ~의 전조(징조)가 되다

be hoped]}. Her only justification lay in the fact {that she had been able to discern no method of rescuing him from a blacker ruin than had overwhelmed herself except by acquiescing in[86] Roger Chillingworth's scheme of disguise}. [Under that impulse] she had made her choice, and had chosen, {as it now appeared}, the more wretched alternative of the two. She determined to redeem her error {so far as it might yet be possible}. [Strengthened by years of hard and solemn trial], she felt herself no longer so inadequate to cope with Roger Chillingworth as on that night, [abased by sin and half-maddened by the ignominy {that was still new}, {when they had talked together in the prison-chamber}]. She had climbed her way since then to a higher point. The old man, on the other hand, had brought himself nearer to her level, or, perhaps, below it, by the revenge {which he had stooped for}.

In fine, Hester Prynne resolved to meet her former husband, and do {what might be in her power for the rescue of the victim [on whom he had so evidently set his gripe]}. The occasion was not long to seek. One afternoon, [walking with Pearl in a retired part of the peninsula], she beheld the old physician with a basket on one arm and a staff in the other hand, stooping along the ground in quest of roots and herbs to concoct his medicine withal.

---

86 acquiesce in (a plan): (계획을) 묵인하다, 보아 넘기다

The Scarlet Letter 14장

Hester and the Physician

Hester bade little Pearl run down to the margin of the water, and play with the shells and tangled sea-weed, {until she should have talked awhile with yonder gatherer of herbs[1]}. So the child flew away like a bird[2], and, [making bare her small white feet], went pattering[3] along the moist margin of the sea. Here and there, she came to a full stop[4], and peeped curiously into a pool, [left by the retiring tide[5] as a mirror for Pearl to see her face in]. Forth peeped at her, out of the pool[6], with dark, glistening curls around her head, and an elf-smile[7] in her eyes, the image of a little maid[8], {whom Pearl, having no other playmate, invited to take her hand and run a race with her[9]}. But the visionary little maid[10], on her part, beckoned likewise, {as if to say, — "This is a better place! Come thou into the

---

1 gatherer of herbs: 약초를 채집하는 사람으로 칠링워스를 지칭

2 fly away like a bird: 새처럼 내달리다

3 go pattering: 물 위를 찰박거리며 가다

4 come to a full stop: 완전히 멈춰 서다

5 left by the retiring tide: 썰물이 남겨 놓은

6 out of the pool: 물웅덩이 밖으로

7 an elf-smile: 요정 같은 미소

8 the image of a little maid: 작은 소녀의 형상(웅덩이에 비친 펄의 모습). *이 문장의 주어로 술어를 도치 이전의 어순으로 바꾸면 'peeped forth at her ...'가 된다.

9 whom Pearl, having no other playmate, invited to take her hand and run a race with her: 놀아 줄 친구가 없는 펄은 이것[whom: 웅덩이에 비친 작은 소녀]에게 자기 손을 잡고 함께 달리기를 하자고 말했다

10 visionary little maid: 환영 같은 작은 소녀, 작은 소녀의 환영. *물에 비친 펄의 형상을 가리킨다.

pool!"} And Pearl, stepping in, mid-leg deep, beheld her own white feet at the bottom; {while, out of a still lower depth, came the gleam of a kind of fragmentary smile[11], floating to and fro[12] in the agitated water[13]}.

Meanwhile, her mother had accosted[14] the physician.

"I would speak a word with you," said she, — "a word {that concerns us much[15]}."

"Aha! And is it Mistress Hester {that has a word for old[16] Roger Chillingworth}?" answered he, raising himself from his stooping posture[17]. "With all my heart! Why, Mistress, I hear good tidings of you on all hands[18]! No longer ago than yester-eve[19], a magistrate, a wise and godly man, was discoursing of

---

11 fragmentary smile: 조각난 미소

12 floating to and fro: 이리저리 앞뒤로 떠다니는

13 fragmentary smile ... in the agitated water: 흔들리는 물에 비친 부서진 미소. *물에 비친 자기 모습을 보고 그 영상 위로 발을 디디자 물이 흔들리면서 거기에 비치던 영상도 함께 부서지는 것을 묘사하고 있다.

14 accost: 다가가 말을 걸다

15 a word that concerns us much: 우리 둘 모두에 관계가 매우 많은 한마디

16 old: 늙은. *이 형용사에는 칠링워스의 자의식이 투영되어 있다.

17 raising himself from his stooping posture: 굽혔던 자세에서 몸을 일으키며

18 on all hands: 사방팔방으로[에서], 모두가

your affairs, Mistress Hester, and whispered me {that there had been question concerning you in the council}. It was debated whether or no, with safety to the common weal[20], yonder scarlet letter might be taken off your bosom[21]. On my life, Hester, I made my entreaty[22] to the worshipful magistrate {that it might be done forthwith[23]}!"

"It lies not in the pleasure[24] of the magistrates to take off this badge," calmly replied Hester. "{Were I worthy to be quit[25] of it}, it would fall away of its own nature, or be transformed into something {that should speak a different purport}."[26]

---

19 No longer ago than yester-eve: 바로 어제 저녁에

20 with safety to the common weal: 공공의 안녕에 지장을 주지 않고

21 It was debated whether or no, with safety to the common weal, yonder scarlet letter might be taken off your bosom: 공공의 안녕에 지장을 주지 않고 저 주홍글자를 당신 가슴에서 떼어 내도 좋을지 어떨지에 대한 논쟁이 있었다

22 entreaty: 간청, 애원

23 that it might be done forthwith: 당장 그렇게 되어야 할 거라고 [간청했다는 말]

24 pleasure: 보통 '기쁨', '즐거움'의 의미이나 여기에서는 '의지', '희망'의 의미. *자신의 가슴에 단 상징 표식을 떼고 말고는 행정관 [지사]들의 의지에 달린 것이 아니라는 말

25 quit: 면하게 하다

26 Were I worthy to be quit of it, it would fall away of its own nature, or be transformed into something that should speak a different purport: 내가 그것[주홍글자의 상징]에서 면하게 될 자격이 있다면, 그것은 그 자체의 본성에 따라 자연히 떨어져 사라질 것이고 아니면 어떤 다른 의미를 말해 주는 것으로 변화될 것이다

"Nay, then, wear it, {if it suit you better}," rejoined he, "A woman must needs follow her own fancy, touching the adornment of her person[27]. The letter is gayly embroidered[28], and shows right bravely on your bosom!"

All this while[29], Hester had been looking steadily at the old man, and was shocked, as well as wonder-smitten[30], to discern {what a change had been wrought[31] upon him within the past seven years}. It was not so much[32] {that he had grown older}; for {though the traces of advancing life were visible}, he bore his age well, and seemed to retain a wiry[33] vigor and alertness[34]. But the former aspect of an intellectual and studious[35] man, calm and quiet, {which was what she best remembered in him}, had altogether vanished, and been succeeded by an eager, searching,

---

27 touching the adornment of her person: 자기 몸을 치장하는 것에 관해서는

28 gayly embroidered: 화려하게 수놓아진

29 All this while: 이러는 사이 내내

30 wonder-smitten: 기이함에 깜짝 놀란

31 wrought: work의 과거형을 나타내는 고어. (변화 등을) 초래하다 [일으키다]

32 not so much: 뒤의 문장과 연결지어 not so much A as B 꼴의 변형으로 보아 'A라기보다는 B다'로 해석해야 한다. 바로 뒤의 'that ...'은 '이유'로 보는 것이 자연스럽다.

33 wiry: 철사 같은, 마르고도 강인한

34 for though the traces ... alertness: 왜냐하면 비록 나이가 들어 가는 인생의 자취들이 보이기는 했으나 그는 늙어 가는 것을 잘 견뎌 내서 말랐지만 강단 있는 활력과 민첩성을 유지해 온 듯 보였다

35 studious: 학구적인

almost fierce, yet carefully guarded look[36]. It seemed to be his
wish and purpose to mask this expression with a smile; but
the latter[37] played him false, and flickered[38] over his visage so
derisively[39], that the spectator could see his blackness[40] all the
better for it[41]. Ever and anon[42], too, there came a glare[43] of red
light out of his eyes; {as if the old man's soul were on fire, and
kept on smouldering duskily[44] within his breast, [until, by some
casual puff of passion, it was blown into a momentary flame[45]]}.

---

36 an eager, searching, almost fierce, yet carefully guarded look: 열
    렬하고, 주도면밀하고, 거의 무시무시하다 싶지만 조심스럽게 억제
    된 표정

37 the latter: 후자. 바로 앞에 나온 'this expression'과 'smile' 중에서
    'smile'을 가리킴.

38 flicker: 명멸하다

39 played him false ... so derisively: 변모된 외양을 감추려는 듯한
    웃음을 묘사하는 대목으로 "[웃음이] 그에게 거짓되게 작용하여 그
    의 얼굴 위에 너무나 조롱하듯 어른거렸다"는 뜻. *play ... false:
    ~을 속이다, 기만하다, 배신하다. 'so derisively'의 'so'는 바로 뒤
    의 'that'과 연결되어 'so ... that ...'의 용법으로 쓰였다.

40 blackness: 검음, 음흉

41 all the better for it: 그것 때문에 더 잘 (~하게 되다)

42 ever and anon: 때때로(=now and then), 이따금

43 glare: 섬광, 쏘아보기

44 kept on smouldering duskily: 계속해서 거뭇하게 연기를 피워 올
    리고 있었다

45 by some casual puff of passion, it was blown into a momentary
    flame: 이따금 열정이 훅 일어나면 그 바람에 그것[그 노인의 영
    혼]은 찰나의 불꽃에 휩싸였다. *불 위에 얹어 놓은 갈탄이나 나
    무 등이 연기만 나다가 입김을 훅 불면 순간적으로 빨갛게 불꽃이
    일어나는 장면에 빗대어 칠링워스의 기이하게 빛나는 눈빛에 대해
    설명하고 있다. 불 위에 놓인 그의 영혼이 이따금씩 열정이라는 입

This[46] he repressed as speedily as possible, and strove to look {as if nothing of the kind had happened}.

In a word, old Roger Chillingworth was a striking evidence[47] of man's faculty of transforming himself into a devil, {if he will only, for a reasonable space of time[48], undertake a devil's office}. This unhappy person had effected such a transformation [by devoting himself, for seven years, to the constant analysis of a heart full of torture, and deriving his enjoyment thence[49], and adding[50] fuel to those fiery tortures {which he analyzed and gloated over[51]}].

The scarlet letter burned on Hester Prynne's bosom. Here was another ruin[52], {the responsibility of which came partly home to her[53]}.

김으로 인해 순간적으로 불이 붙어 뿜어내는 불꽃이 눈빛으로 드러난다고 묘사하고 있다.

46 This: repressed의 목적어
47 striking evidence: 뚜렷한 증거
48 for a reasonable space of time: 적절한 시간 동안
49 thence: 〈고어 또는 격식〉 거기에서; 그 뒤에
50 by devoting ..., and deriving ..., and adding ...: [by devoting, deriving, and adding의 형태] 고뇌에 찬 한 사람의 속내를 7년 동안 끊임없이 분석하는 데 자신을 바치고, 거기에서 기쁨을 얻으며, 자신이 분석하고 흡족하게 여긴 그 불타는 듯한 고통을 더 악화시킴으로써
51 gloat over: 고소하게 여기다, 흡족해하다
52 ruin: 몰락, 영락, (옛 모습이 없는) 영락한 사람, 낙오자

"What see you in my face," asked the physician, "{that you look at it so earnestly}?"

"Something {that would make me weep, if there were any tears bitter enough for it[54]}," answered she. "But let it pass! It is of yonder miserable man {that I would speak}."

"And what of him?" cried Roger Chillingworth eagerly, {as if he loved the topic, and were glad of an opportunity to discuss it with the only person [of whom he could make a confidant[55]]}. "Not to hide the truth, Mistress Hester, my thoughts happen just now to be busy with the gentleman. So speak freely; and I will make answer."

"When we last spake together," said Hester, "now seven years ago, it was your pleasure to extort a promise of secrecy[56], [as touching[57] the former relation betwixt yourself and me].

---

53 the responsibility of which came partly home to her: [그것의] 책임이 어느 정도[부분적으로] 그녀의 가슴에 뼈저리게 와 닿았다. *which[another ruin]는 관계대명사 계속적 용법이며, '또 하나의 영락'(another ruin)은 칠링워스의 변화된 모습을 가리킨다.

54 if there were any tears bitter enough for it: 그럴 만큼[울 만큼] 쓰라린 눈물이 남아 있다면

55 make a confidant of: 비밀을 털어놓을 수 있는 상담상대로 만들 수 있는 [유일한 사람]. *make A of B: B를[에서] A로 만들다; confidant: 비밀을 털어놓을 수 있을 믿을 만한 친구, 상담상대

56 it was your pleasure to extort a promise of secrecy: 비밀을 유지 하겠다는 약속을 억지로 받아 낸 것이 당신에겐 기쁜 일이었겠지요

{As the life and good fame of yonder man were in your hands}, there seemed no choice to me, save to be silent[58], in accordance with your behest[59]. Yet it was not without heavy misgivings[60] {that I thus bound myself[61]}; for, [having cast off[62] all duty towards other human beings], there remained a duty towards him[63]; and something whispered me {that I was betraying it[64], in pledging myself to keep your counsel[65]}. Since that day, no man is so near to him as you. You tread behind his every footstep. You are beside him, sleeping and waking. You search his thoughts. You burrow and rankle[66] in his heart! Your clutch[67] is on his life, and you cause him to die daily a living death[68]; and still he knows you not. In permitting this, I have

---

57 as touching: ~에 관해서

58 save to be silent: 침묵하는 것 외에는. *여기에서 'save'는 'except'의 의미로 쓰인다.

59 in accordance with your behest: 당신의 명령[강요]에 따라[부합되게]

60 not without heavy misgivings: 극심한 불안감이 없지 않은

61 bind myself: 나 자신을 [당신의 강요에 따라] 속박하다, 맹세하다

62 cast off: ~을 (던져/벗어) 버리다

63 for ... towards him: 다른 사람들에 대한 모든 의무를 벗어던졌을 지언정 그 사람에 대한 의무는 여전히 남아 있었으므로

64 it: 딤즈데일에 대한 의무

65 keep your counsel: 당신의 비밀을 남에게 알리지 않다.
    *counsel: 〈고어〉 은밀한 의도[목적], 비밀

66 burrow and rankle: 파고들어 괴롭히다

67 clutch: 꽉 움켜쥠, 마수, 손아귀, 지배

68 die daily a living death: 나날이 산 채로 죽어 가는 죽음을 겪다.
    *'living death'에는 '즐거움이 전혀 없는 비참한 생활', '비참한 생

surely acted a false part by the only man {to whom the power was left me to be true[69]}!"

"What choice had you?" asked Roger Chillingworth. "My finger, [pointed at this man], would have hurled him from his pulpit into a dungeon, —thence, peradventure[70], to the gallows[71]!"

"It had been better so[72]!" said Hester Prynne.

"What evil have I done the man?" asked Roger Chillingworth again. "I tell thee, Hester Prynne, the richest fee {that ever physician earned from monarch} could not have bought such care {as I have wasted on this miserable priest}! [But for my

---

활'의 의미가 있으나 여기에서는 'die ... death'의 표현을 살리는 것
이 자연스럽다.

69 by the only man to whom the power was left me to be true: 내
가 진실하게 대할 수 있을 힘이 남아 있는 상대인 그 유일한 사람
에 대하여. *'the power to be true to [the only man]'의 문맥으로
보아야 한다. 전치사 by는 toward의 의미이다. He did well by his
children. 그는 자기의 아이들에게 잘 했다. She does her duty by
her friends. 그녀는 친구들에 대해[위하여] 의무를 다한다.

70 peradventure: 〈고어〉 아마, 우연히, 혹시나, 뜻밖에도; 만약

71 gallows: 교수대

72 It had been better so: 그게[그렇게 되는 게] 더 나았을 거예요.
*'so'에 칠링워스의 말을 받은 가정의 의미가 실려 있으며 'it had
better have been so' 혹은 'it would[might] have been better so'
의 의미로 파악할 수 있다.

aid[73]], his life would have burned away[74] in torments, within the first two years after the perpetration[75] of his crime and thine. For, Hester, his spirit lacked the strength {that could have borne up[76], [as thine has[77]], beneath a burden like thy scarlet letter}. O, I could reveal a goodly[78] secret! But enough! What art can do, I have exhausted[79] on him. {That he now breathes, and creeps about on earth}, is owing all to me[80]!"

"Better he had died at once!" said Hester Prynne.

"Yea, woman, thou sayest truly!" cried old Roger Chillingworth, letting the lurid fire of his heart blaze out before her eyes[81]. "Better had he died at once[82]! Never did mortal suffer {what

---

73 But for my aid: 내 도움이 없었다면. *but for＝without＝if it had not been for

74 burn away: 타 없어지다, ～을 태워 없애다

75 perpetration: 범함, 저지름

76 bear up: (～에도) 꿋꿋함을 잃지 않다, 끝까지 견디다. *'up'에는 '완전히', '끝까지'의 의미가 있다.

77 as thine has: ＝as thy strength has borne up beneath the burden of the scarlet letter

78 goodly: 엄청난, 굉장한

79 exhaust: 소모하다, 다 쓰다. *'what art can do'(의술이 할 수 있는 모든 것)이 'exhaust'의 목적어로 도치되었다.

80 is owing all to me: 다 내 덕분이다

81 letting the lurid fire of his heart blaze out before her eyes: 자기 가슴에 타오르는 끔찍한 불꽃을 그녀 눈앞에 이글거리게 하면서 (번뜩이면서)

82 had he died at once: ＝if he had died at once. *if가 생략되면서

this man has suffered}. And all, all[83], in the sight of his worst enemy! He has been conscious of me.[84] He has felt an influence dwelling[85] always upon him like a curse. He knew, by some spiritual sense[86], — for the Creator never made another being so sensitive as this[87], — he knew {that no friendly hand was pulling at his heart-strings[88]}, and {that an eye was looking curiously into him, [which[89] sought only evil, and found it]}. But he knew not that the eye and hand[90] were mine! With the superstition [common to his brotherhood], he fancied himself given over to a fiend[91], to be tortured with frightful

---

    'had'가 주어 앞으로 도치됨.

83 all: 여기서는 문맥상 'above all'의 의미로 쓰여 '하필', '무엇보다도', '게다가'의 뜻

84 He has been conscious of me: 그[딤즈데일]는 나를 의식하고 있다

85 dwell upon[on]: 머무르다, 떠나지 않다, 심사숙고하다

86 by some spiritual sense: 영적인 감각으로

87 for the Creator never made another being so sensitive as this: 창조주가 이처럼 예민한 존재를 또 하나 만든 적이 없었으므로

88 no friendly hand was pulling at his heart-strings: 결코 친구답다고 할 수 없는 손이 자기 심장의 가닥들을 잡아 뜯고 있다. *heart-strings: 심금(心琴), 마음의 가닥들

89 which: =an eye

90 the eye and hand: 예문을 들어 'She was the writer and teacher to devote herself to her country's reunification' 같은 경우에 정관사를 하나만 쓴 'the writer and teacher'는 동일인으로 '작가이자 교사'임을 가리키나, 'the eye and hand'처럼 동일한 것으로 오해될 여지가 없을 경우에도 관사를 하나만 써 준다.

91 fancy himself given over to a fiend: 자기 자신이 마귀에게 송두리째 맡겨졌다고 생각하다

dreams, and desperate thoughts, the sting of remorse[92], and despair of pardon; as a foretaste[93] of {what awaits him beyond the grave}. But it was the constant shadow of my presence! — the closest propinquity[94] of the man {whom he had most vilely wronged[95]}! — and {who had grown to exist only by this perpetual poison of the direst revenge[96]}! Yea, indeed! — he did not err[97]! — there was a fiend at his elbow[98]! A mortal man, with once a human heart, has become a fiend for his especial torment!"

The unfortunate physician, [while uttering these words], lifted his hands with a look of horror, {as if he had beheld some frightful shape, [which he could not recognize], usurping the place of[99] his own image in a glass}. It was one of those

---

92 the sting of remorse: 양심의 가책

93 foretaste: 전조, 맛보기

94 propinquity: (장소, 시간상으로) 가까움[근접]

95 the man whom he had most vilely wronged: 그[딤즈데일]가 가장 사악하게 욕보인 사람[칠링워스]

96 who had grown to exist only by this perpetual poison of the direst revenge: 가장 무시무시한 복수의 영원히 계속되는 이 독에 의지해서만 존재하게 된 사람[칠링워스 자신]

97 err: 틀리다, 빗나가다. *딤즈데일이 어떤 손길과 눈길이 자신을 괴롭히고 감시하고 있다고 상상하는 것이 틀리지 않았다는 것을 말하는 대목

98 at one's elbow: 가까이에, 바로 곁에

99 usurp the place of: ~의 자리를 빼앗다, ~을 쫓아내고 대신 들어 앉다

moments — {which sometimes occur only at the interval of years} — {when a man's moral aspect is faithfully revealed to his mind's eye[100]}. Not improbably[101], he had never before viewed himself as he did now.

"Hast thou not tortured him enough?" said Hester, noticing the old man's look. "Has he not paid thee all?"

"No! — no! — He has but increased the debt!" answered the physician; and, as he proceeded, his manner lost its fiercer characteristics, and subsided[102] into gloom. "Dost thou remember me, Hester, {as I was nine years agone[103]}? Even then, I was in the autumn of my days, nor was it the early autumn. But all my life had been made up of earnest, studious, thoughtful, quiet years, bestowed faithfully for the increase of mine own knowledge[104], and faithfully, too, {though this latter object was but casual to the other[105]}, — faithfully for

---

100 a man's moral aspect is faithfully revealed to his mind's eye: 한 사람의 도덕적 양상이 그의 마음의 눈에 여실히 드러나다

101 not improbably: 어쩌면, 혹 (~인지도 모르다)

102 subside: 잦아들다

103 agone: 지나간, ~전에(=gone by)

104 bestowed faithfully for the increase of mine own knowledge: 내 자신의 지식 함양을 위해 충실히 바쳐진

105 though this latter object was but casual to the other: 비록 이 후 자의 목표[인류 복지의 향상]가 다른 것[자신의 지식 함양]에 비 해 우연한[건성인] 것이기는 했으나

the advancement of human welfare. No life had been more peaceful and innocent than mine; few lives so rich with benefits conferred[106]. Dost thou remember me? Was I not, {though you might deem me cold}, nevertheless a man {thoughtful for others}, craving little for himself, — kind, true, just, and of constant, if not warm affections? Was I not all this?"

"All this, and more," said Hester.

"And what am I now?" demanded he, looking into her face, and permitting the whole evil within him to be written on his features[107]. "I have already told thee what I am! A fiend! Who made me so?"

"It was myself!" cried Hester, shuddering. "It was I, not less than he[108]. Why hast thou not avenged thyself on[109] me?"

---

106 No life had been more peaceful and innocent than mine; few lives [had been] so rich with benefits conferred: 내 삶보다 더 평화롭고 순수한 것은 없었으며, 그렇게 은혜로 풍성한 삶도 드물었다. ＊과거분사 'conferred'가 바로 앞의 'benefits'를 꾸며 주어 '수여된 은혜'의 의미

107 permitting the whole evil within him to be written on his features: 자신에게 내재된 악성을 모두 얼굴 전면에 드러내 보이면서

108 not less than he: 그에 못지않게, 그와 다름없이

109 avenge oneself on: ~에게 복수하다. ＊'avenge + 목적어 + on ...'의 표현은 목적어에게가 아니라 목적어 때문에 'on' 뒤의 ~에게 복수를 한다는 뜻이다.

"I have left thee to the scarlet letter," replied Roger Chillingworth. "If that have not avenged me, I can do no more!"

He laid his finger on it, with a smile.

"It has avenged thee!" answered Hester Prynne.

"I judged no less[110]," said the physician. "And now, what wouldst thou with me touching this man?"

"I must reveal the secret," answered Hester, firmly. "He must discern thee in thy true character.[111] {What may be the result}, I know not. But this long debt of confidence, [due from me to him], {whose bane[112] and ruin I have been}, shall at length be paid. {So far as concerns[113] the overthrow or preservation of his fair fame and his earthly state, and perchance[114] his life}, he is in thy hands. Nor do I,— {whom the scarlet letter has disciplined to truth, [though it be the truth of red-hot iron, entering into the soul]},—nor do I perceive such advantage in his living any longer a life of ghastly[115] emptiness, {that I

---

110 no less: 역시, 적잖이
111 He must discern thee in thy true character: 딤즈데일이 칠링워
      스의 정체를 알아야만 한다는 말
112 bane: 독, 해악, 고통의 씨앗, 골칫거리
113 so far as concerns ...: ~에 관한 한
114 perchance: 〈고어〉 아마 어쩌면
115 ghastly: 섬뜩한, 지독한, 끔찍한

shall stoop to implore thy mercy[116]}. Do with him as thou wilt! There is no good for him, — no good for me, — no good for thee! There is no good for little Pearl! There is no path to guide us out of this dismal maze!"

"Woman, I could wellnigh[117] pity thee!" said Roger Chillingworth, unable to restrain a thrill of admiration too; for there was a quality [almost majestic] in the despair {which she expressed}. "Thou hadst great elements[118]. Peradventure, {hadst thou met earlier with a better love than mine}, this evil had not been. I pity thee, for the good {that has been wasted in thy nature}!"

"And I thee[119]," answered Hester Prynne, "for the hatred {that has transformed a wise and just man to a fiend}! Wilt thou yet purge[120] it out of thee, and be once more human? If not for his sake[121], then doubly for thine own![122] Forgive, and leave his

---

116 nor do I perceive ... that I shall stoop to implore thy mercy: 엎드려 당신의 자비를 간청해야 한다고 생각하지 않는다

117 wellnigh: 거의

118 element: 옛날 자연계의 기본적 구성요소로 생각되었던 4대 요소 [원소](earth, water, air, fire)의 하나

119 I thee: =I pity thee

120 purge: 몰아내다, 제거하다

121 If not for his sake: 그를 위해서가 아니라면, 그의 명예를 위해서 가 아니라면

122 If not for his sake, then doubly for thine own!: 그를 위해서가 아니라면, 그렇다면 두 배로 당신 자신을 위해서라도!

further retribution[123] to the Power {that claims it[124]}! I said, but now, that there could be no good event for him, or thee, or me, {who are here wandering together in this gloomy maze of evil, and stumbling, at every step, over the guilt [wherewith we have strewn our path]}. It is not so![125] There might be good for thee, and thee alone[126], {since thou hast been deeply wronged, and hast it at thy will [to pardon]}. Wilt thou give up that only privilege? Wilt thou reject that priceless benefit?"

"Peace, Hester, peace!" replied the old man, with gloomy sternness. "It is not granted me to pardon[127]. I have no such power {as thou tellest me of}. My old faith, long forgotten, comes back to me, and explains all {that we do}, and all {we suffer}. By thy first step awry[128], thou didst plant the germ of evil; but, since that moment, it has all been a dark necessity. Ye {that have wronged me} are not sinful, save in a kind of typical illusion; neither am I fiend-like, {who have snatched a fiend's office from his hands}. It is our fate. Let the black flower blossom as it may! Now go thy ways, and deal as thou wilt with yonder man."

---

123 retribution: 응징, 징벌
124 claim it: 그것[응징]을 내릴 자격이 있는
125 It is not so: 그렇지 않다, 좋은 일이 아니다
126 There ... thee alone: 그대, 그대에게만은 좋은 일일 수도 있다
127 It is not granted me to pardon: 나에게 용서를 구할 일이 아니다
128 By thy first step awry: 첫걸음부터 빗나갔기 때문에

He waved his hand, and betook himself[129] again to his employment of gathering herbs.

---

129 betook himself: = displaced oneself; went from one location to another. *betake: 가다, 호소하다, 의지하다, ~에 전념하다

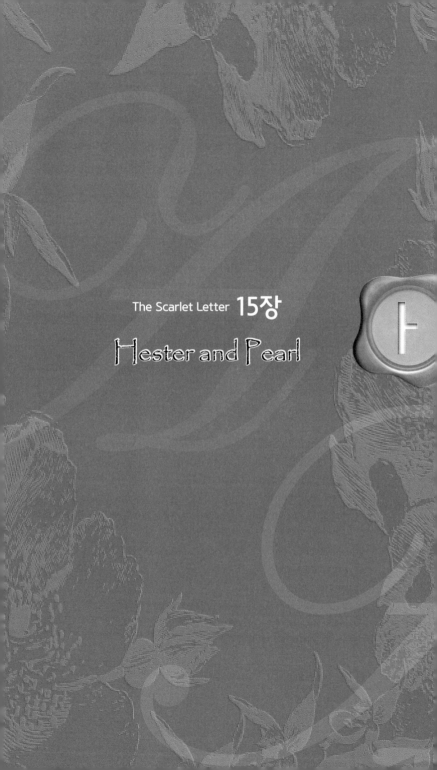

The Scarlet Letter 15장

Hester and Pearl

So Roger Chillingworth—a deformed old figure, with a face {that haunted men's memories longer than they liked}— took leave of Hester Prynne, and went stooping away along the earth. He gathered here and there an herb, or grubbed up[1] a root, and put it into the basket on his arm. His gray beard almost touched the ground, as he crept onward. Hester gazed after him a little while, looking with a half-fantastic curiosity[2] to see {whether the tender grass of early spring would not be blighted beneath him[3], and show the wavering track of his footsteps[4], sere and brown[5], across its cheerful verdure[6]}. She wondered what sort of herbs they were, {which the old man was so sedulous[7] to gather}. Would not the earth, [quickened[8] to an evil purpose by the sympathy of his eye], greet him with[9] poisonous shrubs, of species [hitherto unknown[10]], {that

---

1 grub ... up/out: (땅에서) ~을 파내다. * No work, no grub. 일하지 않는 자, 먹지도 말라; grub: 음식물

2 with a half-fantastic curiosity: 반쯤은 기이한 호기심으로

3 to see whether the tender grass of early spring would not be blighted beneath him: 이른 봄철의 부드러운 풀이 그의 발밑에서 말라죽어 버리지 않을까 지켜보기 위해

4 the wavering track of his footsteps: 오락가락한 발자국의 자취

5 sere and brown: 시들어 누렇게 된

6 verdure: 푸른 초목, 신록

7 sedulous: (자기 일에) 공을 들이는, 정성을 다하는

8 quicken: 빨라지다, 더 빠르게 하다, 더 활발해지다[활발하게 하다], 자극하다, 쑤석거리다

9 greet him with: 그를 ~으로 맞이하다

10 species hitherto unknown: 지금까지 알려지지 않은 종(種)

would start up under his fingers[11]}? Or might it suffice him[12], {that every wholesome growth should be converted into[13] something deleterious[14] and malignant[15] at his touch}? Did the sun, {which shone so brightly everywhere else}, really fall upon him? Or was there, {as it rather seemed}, a circle of ominous shadow[16] [moving along with his deformity[17]], {whichever way he turned himself}? And whither was he now going? Would he not suddenly sink into the earth, leaving a barren and blasted[18] spot, {where, in due course[19] of time, would be seen deadly[20] nightshade[21], dogwood[22], henbane[23], and whatever else of vegetable wickedness [the climate could produce], all

---

11 that would start up under his fingers: 그의 손길 밑에서 돋아났을

12 might it suffice him …?: 그의 욕구를 충족시켜 주지 않았을까?

13 be converted into: 전환되다, 바뀌다

14 deleterious: 해로운, 유해한

15 malignant: 악성의

16 ominous shadow: 불길한 그림자

17 moving along with his deformity: 그의 기형적인 몸을 따라 움직이는. *along with sb/sth: ~에 덧붙여, ~와 마찬가지로

18 blast: 시들게 하다, 망쳐 놓다

19 in due course: 적절한 때에, 때가 되면

20 deadly: 생명을 앗아가는[앗아갈], 치명적인

21 nightshade: 〈식물〉 가지속(屬)의 각종 식물(→ black nightshade, deadly nightshade). *deadly nightshade는 벨라도나(belladonna) 라고 불리는 유독식물을 가리킨다. 경련이나 위통 따위의 약제로 쓰이기도 한다.

22 dogwood: 층층나무. *여기에서는 poison dogwood(= poison sumac)로서 독성이 강한 옻나무를 가리키는 것으로 보인다.

23 henbane: 〈식물〉 사리풀[가짓과(科)의 유독 식물]

flourishing with hideous luxuriance[24]}?[25] Or would he spread bat's wings and flee away, looking so much the uglier, {the higher he rose towards heaven[26]}?

"Be it sin or no," said Hester Prynne bitterly, as she still gazed after him, "I hate the man!"

She upbraided herself for the sentiment[27], but could not overcome or lessen it. Attempting to do so, she thought of those long-past days, in a distant land, {when he used to emerge at eventide[28] from the seclusion of his study, and sit down in the fire-light of their home, and in the light of her nuptial[29]

---

24 all flourishing with hideous luxuriance: 모두 끔찍하도록 풍성하게 번성하는

25 Would he not ... luxuriance?: 그가 갑작스럽게 땅속으로 꺼져 버려 불모의 메말라 버린 자국만 남기지 않을까? 그러면 그 자리에서 어느 정도의 시간이 지나 때가 되면 치명적인 까마종이, 독옻나무, 독사리풀, 그 밖에 기후가 생산해 낼 수 있는 식물성의 사악함[유독성의 식물]을 지닌 것이라면 어떤 것이나 온통 끔찍스럽고 풍성하게 번성하는 것이 보이지 않을까?

26 looking so much the uglier, the higher he rose towards heaven: 그가 하늘을 향해 더 높이 날아오를수록 그만큼 더 추악하게 보이면서

27 upbraided herself for the sentiment: 그런 감정에 대해 자신을 질책했다. *upbraid a person with[for] a fault: 질책하다, 호되게 나무라다, 잘못에 대해서 ~을 비난하다

28 eventide: 저녁, 밤

29 nuptial: 결혼생활의, 결혼[혼인]의. *her nuptial smile: 아내의 미소, 결혼생활에서 그녀가 지은 미소

smile}. He needed to bask himself in that smile[30], he said, {in order that the chill of so many lonely hours among his books might be taken off the scholar's heart[31]}. Such scenes had once appeared not otherwise than happy[32], but now, [as viewed through the dismal medium of her subsequent life], they classed themselves among her ugliest remembrances[33]. She marvelled {how such scenes could have been}! She marvelled {how she could ever have been wrought[34] upon to marry him}! She deemed it her crime [most to be repented of[35]], {that she had ever endured, and reciprocated[36], the lukewarm[37] grasp of

---

30 bask himself in that smile: 그 미소의 볕을 쬐다. *바로 앞의 결혼 생활에서 헤스터가 지은 미소를 '빛·볕'(light)이라고 비유한 것을 이어받은 표현으로 볼 수 있다.

31 in order that ... off the scholar's heart: 책들 사이에서 외로운 시간을 너무나 많이 보낸 탓에 생긴 냉기가 학자의 심장에서 빠져나가도록 하기 위해

32 not otherwise than happy: 행복함과 다르지 않은

33 but now, as viewed through the dismal medium of her subsequent life, they classed themselves among her ugliest remembrances: 하지만 이제, 그 이후 자신의 삶의 암울한 매개체를 통해 보니 그것들[그 장면들]은 자신의 가장 추악한 기억들 사이에 속했다

34 wrought: work의 과거형을 나타내는 고어. (변화 등을) 초래하다 [일으키다]

35 She deemed it her crime most to be repented of: 그녀는 그것[뒤의 that 이하]을 자신이 가장 뉘우쳐야 할 죄로 여겼다

36 reciprocate: (어떤 사람에게서 받는 것과 비슷한 행동·감정으로) 화답[응답]하다

37 lukewarm: 미지근한, 미온적인

his hand, and had suffered[38] the smile of her lips and eyes to mingle and melt into his own}. And it seemed a fouler offence [committed by Roger Chillingworth], than any {which had since been done him}, {that, in the time [when her heart knew no better], he had persuaded her to fancy herself happy by his side}.[39]

"Yes, I hate him!" repeated Hester, more bitterly than before. "He betrayed me! He has done me worse wrong than I did him!"

Let men tremble to win the hand of woman[40], {unless they win [along with it] the utmost passion of her heart[41]}! Else it may be their miserable fortune, {as it was Roger Chillingworth's}, {when some mightier touch than their own may have awakened all her sensibilities}, [to be reproached even for the calm content, the marble image of happiness,

---

38 suffer 목적어 to ...: 목적어가 to ~하는 것을 견디다[허용하다]

39 it seemed ... to fancy herself happy by his side: 그녀의 마음이 분별력이 없었을 때 로저 칠링워스가 그녀를 꾀어 그의 곁에서 행복하다는 생각이 들도록 한 것은 이후에 그에게 가해진 어느 모욕보다도 더 불결한 그가 저지른 모욕으로 보였다

40 Let men tremble to win the hand of woman: 남성들이여 여인의 손을 얻으면 몹시 걱정할지어다. *tremble: 못 견딜 만큼 걱정하다

41 unless they win along with it the utmost passion of her heart: 그들이 그것[여인의 손]과 함께 그녀 마음의 최고의 열정을 얻지 못한다면. *along with it을 괄호로 묶어 놓고 보면 win the utmost ...의 꼴

{which they will have imposed upon her as the warm reality[42]}]. But Hester ought long ago to have done with[43] this injustice.[44] What did it betoken[45]? Had seven long years, under the torture of the scarlet letter, inflicted so much of misery, and wrought out no repentance?

The emotions of that brief space, {while she stood gazing after the crooked figure[46] of old Roger Chillingworth}, threw a dark light on Hester's state of mind, revealing much {that she might not otherwise[47] have acknowledged to herself}.

He being gone, she summoned back her child.

---

42 to be reproached even for the calm content, the marble image of happiness, which they will have imposed upon her as the warm reality: 차분한 만족감, 곧 그들이 그녀에게 따뜻한 현실이라고 속여 강요하게 될 대리석처럼 차가운 이미지의 행복조차 이유가 되어 비난받는 것. *문장 앞부분의 가주어 'it'이 가리키는 진주어에 해당하는 대목이다.

43 have done with: (불쾌한 것을) 끝내다, 절연하다, 관계를 끊다

44 But Hester ought long ago have done with this injustice: 하지만 헤스터는 이런 부당함과는 오래전에 관계를 끊었어야 했다. *미숙한 시절의 자신에게 칠링워스가 행한 부당함을 되새기며 헤스터가 7년의 세월이 지난 아직도 증오의 마음을 강렬하게 표출하는 것을 두고 작가가 끼어들어 훈계하듯 하는 장면이다. 이 앞뒤의 맥락을 보면, 적어도 헤스터의 7년간의 '참회'가 칠링워스에 대한 참회와는 거리가 한참 먼 것이 분명하다.

45 betoken: ~을 나타내다, ~의 전조이다

46 crooked figure: 기형적인 모습. *crooked: 구부정한, 기형의

47 otherwise: 다른 상황 아래에서는, 다른 경우라면

"Pearl! Little Pearl! Where are you?"

Pearl, {whose activity of spirit never flagged[48]}, had been at no loss for amusement[49] {while her mother talked with the old gatherer of herbs}. At first, as already told, she had flirted[50] fancifully with her own image in a pool of water, beckoning the phantom forth, and—as it declined to venture—seeking a passage for herself into its sphere of impalpable earth and unattainable sky.[51] Soon finding, however, {that either she or the image was unreal}, she turned elsewhere for better pastime. She made little boats out of birch-bark[52], and freighted[53] them with snail-shells, and sent out more ventures[54] on the mighty deep[55] than any merchant in New England; but the larger part of them foundered[56] near the shore. She seized a

---

48 flag: (돛 따위가) 축 늘어지다, (기력 따위가) 쇠퇴하다, 시들다

49 at no loss for amusement: 어찌 즐겁게 놀아야 할지 전혀 난처해 하지 않는

50 flirt: 희롱하다, 시시덕거리다

51 At first ... unattainable sky: 이미 말했듯이, 처음에 그녀는 상상에 가득 차서 물웅덩이에 비친 자기 자신의 이미지와 희롱거리며 놀면서 그 환영을 손짓으로 불러내는가 하면 그것[환영]이 감히 나오기를 거절하자 제 자신이 손으로 만져 알 수 없는 대지와 도달할 수 없는 하늘의 영역으로 들어가는 길을 찾으려 했다. * "손으로 만져 알 수 없는 대지와 도달할 수 없는 하늘의 영역"이라고 한 것은 그것들이 물에 비친 대지와 하늘이기 때문이다.

52 birch-bark: 자작나무 껍질

53 freight ... with ...: ~에 ~의 화물을 싣다

54 venture: 모험(성), 모험적 사업[투기]의 대상물(배·뱃짐·상품·도박에 건 돈 따위)

55 the mighty deep: 거대한 깊은 바다

live horseshoe[57] by the tail, and made prize of[58] several five-fingers[59], and laid out a jelly-fish[60] to melt in the warm sun. Then she took up the white foam, {that streaked the line of the advancing tide}, and threw it upon the breeze[61], scampering[62] after it with winged footsteps, to catch the great snow-flakes[63] {ere they fell}. Perceiving a flock of beach-birds, {that fed and fluttered along the shore}, the naughty child picked up her apron full of pebbles, and, [creeping from rock to rock after these small sea-fowl], displayed remarkable dexterity[64] in pelting[65] them. One little gray bird, with a white breast, {Pearl was almost sure}, had been hit by a pebble, and fluttered away with a broken wing. But then the elf-child[66] sighed, and gave up her sport; because it grieved her to have done harm to[67] a

---

56 founder: 침수하여 가라앉다, 실패하다

57 horseshoe: 참게(=horseshoe crab)

58 make prize of: ~을 포획[나포]하다

59 five-finger: 잎이 다섯 손가락 모양으로 갈라진 식물, 불가사리

60 laid out a jelly-fish: 해파리를 펼쳐 놓았다

61 took up the white foam, that streaked the line of the advancing tide, and threw it upon the breeze: 밀려오는 파도의 선을 따라 줄무늬를 만든 하얀 물거품을 걷어 내어 산들바람에 실어 던져 보냈다

62 scamper: 아동이나 작은 동물이 날쌔게 움직이다

63 the great snow-flakes: 커다란 눈송이. ＊펄 자신이 바람에 띄워 보낸 물거품을 가리킨다.

64 dexterity: (손이나 머리를 쓰는) 재주

65 pelt: (sb with sth) (무엇을 던지며) 공격하다

66 the elf-child: 요정 같은 아이

67 have done harm to: ~에게 해를 입혔다. ＊do harm to …: ~에게

little being {that was as wild as the sea-breeze[68], or as wild as Pearl herself}.

Her final employment was to gather sea-weed, of various kinds, and make herself a scarf, or mantle, and a head-dress[69], and thus assume the aspect of a little mermaid. She inherited her mother's gift for devising drapery[70] and costume. [As the last touch to her mermaid's garb[71]], Pearl took some eel-grass[72], and imitated, {as best she could}, [on her own bosom], the decoration {with which she was so familiar on her mother's[73]}. A letter,—the letter A,—but freshly green, instead of scarlet! The child bent her chin upon her breast, and contemplated this device[74] with strange interest; even as if the one only thing {for

---

해를 입히다

68 sea-breeze: 바닷바람, 해풍

69 head-dress: 머리쓰개, 머리장식

70 drapery: 휘장. 권의(卷衣)·현의(懸衣) 등의 남방계(南方系) 의복의 총칭. 원래는 주름을 잡아 늘어뜨린 휘장, 아래로 늘어진 주름, 의문(衣紋), 직물, 포목상 등을 이르는 말이다. 한 장의 천을 재봉하지 않고, 그대로 몸에 감거나 걸치거나 늘어뜨려서 착용한다. 고대 이집트·그리스·로마시대의 의복에서 그 전형을 볼 수 있으며, 지금도 인도의 사리나 미얀마의 승려복에서 볼 수 있다.

71 garb: (특이한 또는 특정 유형의 사람이 입는) 의복. *mermaid's garb: 인어처럼 꾸민 치장

72 eel-grass: 〈식물〉 거머리말[거머리말속(屬)의 바닷말], 나사말(= tape grass)

73 the decoration with which she was so familiar on her mother's: 자기 엄마의 가슴에서 본 그렇게나 친숙한 장식

74 device: 궁리, 계획, 고안물, (장식적) 도안, 의장, 문장(紋章)

which she had been sent into the world} was to make out its hidden import[75].

"I wonder if mother will ask me what it means!" thought Pearl.

Just then, she heard her mother's voice, and, [flitting along as lightly as one of the little sea-birds], appeared before Hester Prynne[76], dancing, laughing, and pointing her finger to the ornament upon her bosom.

★ MP3
15장 [2]
시작

"My little Pearl," said Hester, after a moment's silence, "the green letter, and on thy childish bosom, has no purport. But dost thou know, my child, what this letter means {which thy mother is doomed to wear}?"

"Yes, mother," said the child. "It is the great letter A. Thou hast taught it me in the horn-book[77]."

---

75 even as if the one only thing for which she had been sent into the world was to make out its hidden import: 심지어 마치 자신이 세상에 보내진 유일한 한 가지 이유가 그것의 감추어진 의미를 알아내는 것인 양

76 flitting along as lightly as one of the little sea-birds, appeared before Hester Prynne: 한 마리의 작은 바닷새처럼 가볍게 나풀거리며 날아와 헤스터 프린 앞에 나타났다

77 horn-book: 글씨판(옛날 아이들의 학습용구); 기본서, 입문서 (primer). *15세기 영국에서 유래한 이 글씨판은 마치 손잡이 거

Hester looked steadily into her little face; but, {though there was that singular expression [which she had so often remarked in her black eyes]}, she could not satisfy herself {whether Pearl really attached any meaning to the symbol}. She felt a morbid desire[78] to ascertain the point.

"Dost thou know, child, {wherefore[79] thy mother wears this letter}?"

"Truly do I!" answered Pearl, looking brightly into her mother's face. "It is for the same reason {that the minister keeps his hand over his heart}!"

"And what reason is that?" asked Hester, half smiling at the absurd incongruity of the child's observation[80]; but, on second thoughts[81], turning pale. "What has the letter to do with any heart, save mine[82]?"

올의 형태처럼 손잡이가 달린 나무판에 글자를 적은 종이나 양피지를 붙이고 그것을 보호하기 위해 그 위에 뿔 재질의 투명한 판을 씌워 만들었다.

78 morbid desire: 병적인 갈망
79 wherefore: 〈고어〉〈의문사〉왜(why), 무슨 이유로, 무엇 때문에
80 half smiling at the absurd incongruity of the child's observation: 터무니없이 부조리한 아이의 관찰에 반쯤 미소를 지으며
81 on second thoughts: 다시 한 번 생각하자
82 save mine: ＝save[＝except＝but] my heart

"Nay, mother, I have told all I know," said Pearl, more seriously than she was wont to speak[83]. "Ask yonder old man {whom thou hast been talking with}! It may be he can tell. But in good earnest now, mother dear, what does this scarlet letter mean? ─ and why dost thou wear it on thy bosom? ─ and why does the minister keep his hand over his heart?"

She took her mother's hand in both her own, and gazed into her eyes with an earnestness {that was seldom seen in her wild and capricious character}. The thought occurred to Hester, {that the child might really be seeking to approach her with childlike confidence, and [doing what she could], and [as intelligently as she knew how], to establish a meeting-point of sympathy[84]}. It showed Pearl in an unwonted[85] aspect. Heretofore[86], the mother, {while loving her child with the intensity of a sole affection}, had schooled herself to[87] hope for little other return than the waywardness of an April breeze[88]; which spends its time in airy sport, and has its gusts of inexplicable passion,

---

83 more seriously than she was wont to speak: 그녀가 평소 말하는 버릇보다 더 심각하게

84 to establish a meeting-point of sympathy: 공감대를 형성하려고. *앞의 'to approach'와 같이 seeking에 걸린다.

85 unwonted: 평소와 다른, 특이한, 뜻밖의

86 Heretofore: 지금까지는, 이전에는

87 schooled oneself to: 스스로 단련해 오다, 수양하다

88 to hope for little other return than the waywardness of an April breeze: 4월의 미풍이 지닌 변덕스러움 이외의 다른 보상은 거의

and is petulant[89] in its best of moods, and chills oftener than caresses you, {when you take it to your bosom[90]}; {in requital of[91] which misdemeanours[92], it will sometimes, [of its own vague purpose], kiss your cheek with a kind of doubtful tenderness, and play gently with your hair, and then be gone about its other idle business, leaving a dreamy pleasure at your heart}. And this, moreover, was a mother's estimate of the child's disposition[93]. Any other observer might have seen few but unamiable traits[94], and have given them a far darker coloring[95]. But now the idea came strongly into Hester's mind, {that Pearl, [with her remarkable precocity[96] and acuteness[97]], might already have approached the age [when she could

---

기대하지 않도록

89 petulant: 심술을 부리는, 심통 사나운

90 chills oftener than caresses you, when you take it to your bosom: 품에 안으면 어루만져 주기보다는 더 자주 냉기를 주는

91 in requital of: ~의 보답으로

92 misdemeanours: 〈격식〉 (아주 심각하지는 않은) 비행, 못된 행실. *in requital of which misdemeanours: 이와 같은 못된 행실에 보답이라도 하듯이

93 the child's disposition: 아이의 (타고난) 기질[성격], 성향

94 unamiable traits: 붙임성 없는 특징들, 퉁명스러운 특성들

95 might ... have given them a far darker coloring: 이 특징들을 훨씬 더 어둡게 채색할지도 몰랐다. *이 앞뒤 맥락은 헤스터가 늘 자신의 과거 행위를 의식하면서 펄을 바라보기 때문에 다른 사람들과는 달리 착잡하면서 이중적이기도 한 시선을 딸에게 보낼 수밖에 없는 정황을 묘사하고 있다.

96 precocity: 조숙, 일됨, 올됨(=precociousness)

97 acuteness: 날카로움, 신랄함

have been made a friend, and intrusted with[98] as much of her mother's sorrows as could be imparted, without irreverence either to the parent or the child]}. In the little chaos of Pearl's character, there might be seen emerging—{and could have been from the very first}—the steadfast principles of an unflinching courage,—an uncontrollable will,—a sturdy pride, {which might be disciplined into self-respect},—and a bitter scorn of many things, {which, [when examined], might be found to have the taint of falsehood in them}. She possessed affections, too, [though hitherto acrid[99] and disagreeable[100], {as are the richest flavors of unripe fruit}]. With all these sterling attributes, {thought Hester}, the evil {which she inherited from her mother} must be great indeed, {if a noble woman do not grow out of this elfish child}.

Pearl's inevitable tendency to hover about[101] the enigma of the scarlet letter seemed an innate quality of her being. From the earliest epoch[102] of her conscious life, she had entered upon this as her appointed mission. Hester had often fancied {that Providence had a design of justice and retribution[103], in

---

98 intrusted with: B에게 A(일 따위)를 맡기다(=entrust A to B=entrust B with A)

99 acrid: 콕 쏘는, 얼얼한

100 disagreeable: 불쾌한

101 hover about: 주변을 맴돌다

102 epoch: 중요한 사건, 변화들이 일어난 시대

103 that Providence had a design of justice and retribution: 신의 섭

endowing the child with this marked propensity[104]}; but never, until now, had she bethought herself[105] to ask, {whether, [linked with that design], there might not likewise be a purpose of mercy and beneficence}. {If little Pearl were entertained with faith and trust, as a spirit-messenger no less than an earthly child}, might it not be her errand to soothe away the sorrow {that lay cold in her mother's heart, and converted it[106] into a tomb}? — and to help her to overcome the passion, [once so wild, and even yet neither dead nor asleep, but only imprisoned within the same tomb-like heart]?

Such were some of the thoughts {that now stirred in Hester's mind, with as much vivacity[107] of impression [as if they had actually been whispered into her ear]}. And there was little Pearl, all this while, holding her mother's hand in both her own, and turning her face upward, {while she put these searching questions, once, and again, and still a third time}.

"What does the letter mean, mother? — and why dost thou wear it? — and why does the minister keep his hand over his

---

리가 심판과 응징의 구도로 되어 있다는 것

104 in endowing the child with this marked propensity: 이 아이가 이런 두드러진 성향을 부여받았음에

105 bethought herself: 생각해 냈다

106 it: = her mother's heart

107 vivacity: 생기, 활기, 활발, 쾌활, 활달, 까불기, 장난, 〈보통 복수〉 쾌활한 행위[말]

heart?"

"What shall I say?" thought Hester to herself. — "No! If this be the price of the child's sympathy[108], I cannot pay it!"

Then she spoke aloud.

"Silly Pearl," said she, "what questions are these? There are many things in this world {that a child must not ask about}. What know I of the minister's heart? And as for the scarlet letter, I wear it for the sake of[109] its gold thread!"

In all the seven bygone years[110], Hester Prynne had never before been false to the symbol on her bosom. It may be that it was the talisman[111] of a stern and severe, but yet a guardian spirit, who now forsook her; as recognizing {that, [in spite of his strict watch over her heart], some new evil had crept into it, or some old one had never been expelled}. As for little Pearl, the earnestness soon passed out of her face.

But the child did not see fit [to let the matter drop]. Two or three times, {as her mother and she went homeward}, and

---

108 If this be the price of the child's sympathy: 이런 게 아이의 공감을 얻기 위해 치러야 하는 대가라면

109 for the sake of: ~ 때문에, ~을 좋아해서

110 In all the seven bygone years: 지난 7년 내내

111 talisman: (행운을 가져다준다고 여겨지는) 부적(符籍)

as often [at supper-time], and {while Hester was putting her to bed}, and once {after she seemed to be fairly asleep}, Pearl looked up, with mischief gleaming in her black eyes.

"Mother," said she, "what does the scarlet letter mean?"

And the next morning, the first indication {the child gave of[112] being awake} was by popping up her head from the pillow, and making that other inquiry, {which she had so unaccountably connected with her investigations about the scarlet letter}:—

"Mother!—Mother!—Why does the minister keep his hand over his heart?"

"Hold thy tongue, naughty child!" answered her mother, with an asperity[113] {that she had never permitted to herself before}. "Do not tease me; else I shall shut thee into the dark closet!"

---

112 give of: ~을 아낌없이 바치다[주다], 선뜻 내놓다
113 with an asperity: 호되게, 퉁명스럽게

102

The Scarlet Letter 16장

A Forest Walk

Hester Prynne remained constant in her resolve [to make known to Mr. Dimmesdale, {at whatever risk of present pain or ulterior consequences[1]}, the true character of the man {who had crept into his intimacy}]. For several days, however, she vainly sought an opportunity of addressing him in some of the meditative walks {which she knew him to be in the habit of taking, along the shores of the peninsula, or on the wooded hills of the neighbouring country}. There would have been no scandal, indeed, nor peril to the holy whiteness of the clergyman's good fame, {had she visited him in his own study; where many a penitent[2], ere now[3], had confessed sins of [perhaps as deep a dye[4] as the one betokened by the scarlet letter]}. But, partly {that she dreaded the secret[5] or undisguised interference[6] of old Roger Chillingworth}, and partly {that her conscious heart imputed[7] suspicion [where none could have been felt]}, and partly {that both the minister and she would need the whole wide world to breathe in, while they talked

---

1 at whatever risk of present pain or ulterior consequences: 당장의 고통 혹은 이후의 결과가 무엇이든 그 위험을 무릅쓰고

2 many a penitent: 많은 고해자들

3 ere now: 〈고어〉 지금까지

4 dye: 물든 색. *of the deepest[or blackest] dye: 극악무도한, 가장 악질의. 판본에 따라 'die'로 표기된 것이 있으나 dye로 보아야 한다.

5 secret: 비밀의. *undisguised와 함께 interference를 꾸민다.

6 undisguised interference: 노골적인 간섭, 참견

7 impute: 씌우다. *imparted(impart: 주다, 전하다)로 표시된 판본 도 있으나 표준판에는 imputed로 되어 있다.

together},—for all these reasons, Hester never thought of meeting him in any narrower privacy than beneath the open sky.

At last, {while attending in a sick-chamber[8], whither the Reverend Mr. Dimmesdale had been summoned to make a prayer}, she learnt {that he had gone, the day before, to visit the Apostle Eliot[9], among his Indian converts}. He would probably return, by a certain hour, in the afternoon of the morrow[10]. Betimes[11], therefore, the next day, Hester took little Pearl,— {who was necessarily the companion of all her mother's expeditions[12], however inconvenient her presence},—and set forth[13].

The road, {after the two wayfarers[14] had crossed from the peninsula to the mainland}, was no other than a footpath.[15]

---

8 a sick-chamber: 환자의 침실(방)

9 John Eliot(1604~1690). 영국의 케임브리지 대학에서 수학하고 1631년 신대륙 보스턴으로 이주하였다. 신대륙 인디언들에게 그들의 언어로 설교한 첫 번째 목사로 매사추세츠 인디언들을 개종시키려고 노력하였으며 성서를 알곤킨족(Algonquin) 인디언의 언어로 번역하였다. 이후로 '인디언 사도'로 알려졌다.

10 morrow: 그 다음 날, 내일

11 betimes: 〈문어〉 때마침, 늦기 전에, 일찍(=early), 〈고어〉 곧

12 expedition: (필요한 일을 하기 위한 짧은) 여행, 원정

13 set forth: 출발하다

14 the two wayfarers: 두 여행자(헤스터와 펄을 가리킴)

15 The road ... was no other than a footpath: 그 길은 오솔길에 지

It straggled[16] onward into the mystery of the primeval forest. This hemmed it in so narrowly, and stood so black and dense on either side, and disclosed such imperfect glimpses of the sky above, {that, to Hester's mind, it imaged not amiss[17] the moral wilderness [in which she had so long been wandering[18]]}. The day was chill and sombre. Overhead was a gray expanse of cloud, slightly stirred, however, by a breeze; {so that a gleam of flickering sunshine might now and then be seen at its solitary play[19] along the path}. This flitting cheerfulness was always at the farther extremity of some long vista[20] through the forest. The sportive sunlight — [feebly sportive, at best[21], in the predominant pensiveness of the day and scene] — withdrew itself {as they came nigh[22]}, and left the spots {where it had danced} the drearier, because they had hoped to find them bright.

"Mother," said little Pearl, "the sunshine does not love you. It runs away and hides itself, because it is afraid of something

---

나지 않았다

16 straggle: 제멋대로 뻗어 나가다, 퍼지다
17 amiss: 정상상태에서 벗어나, 부적당하게
18 the moral wilderness in which she had so long been wandering: 그녀가 이다지도 오래 방황해 왔던 도덕의 황무지
19 at its solitary play: 그것이 혼자 놀고 있는. *at play: 놀고 있는
20 vista: 〈문예체〉 (아름다운) 경치, 풍경, 〈격식〉 전망, 앞날
21 at best: 기껏[잘 해야][=at (the) most]
22 came nigh: =came near

on your bosom. Now, see! There it is, playing, a good way off[23]. Stand you here, and let me run and catch it. I am but a child. It will not flee from me; for I wear nothing on my bosom yet!"

"Nor ever will, my child, I hope," said Hester.

"And why not, mother?" asked Pearl, stopping short, just at the beginning of her race. "Will not it come of its own accord[24], when I am a woman grown?"

"Run away, child," answered her mother, "and catch the sunshine! It will soon be gone."

Pearl set forth, at a great pace[25], and, {as Hester smiled to perceive}, did actually catch the sunshine, and stood laughing in the midst of it, [all brightened by its splendor], and scintillating with[26] the vivacity[27] [excited by rapid motion]. The light lingered about the lonely child, {as if glad of such a

---

23 a good way off: 꽤 떨어져서[멀리서]

24 come of its own accord: 저절로 생기다. *of its own accord: 자청해서(저절로)=of one's own free will[free choice]=willingly= voluntarily

25 at a great pace: 빠른 속도로. *at a steady/gentle/leisurely pace: 안정된/차분한/느긋한 속도로

26 scintillate with: 반짝거리다, (재치, 기지가) 번득이다

27 vivacity: 생기, 활기, 활발, 쾌활, 활달; 까불기, 장난, 〈보통 복수〉 쾌활한 행위[말]

playmate}, {until her mother had drawn almost nigh enough to step into the magic circle too}.

"It will go now!" said Pearl, shaking her head.

"See!" answered Hester, smiling. "Now I can stretch out my hand, and grasp some of it."

{As she attempted to do so}, the sunshine vanished; or, to judge from[28] the bright expression {that was dancing on Pearl's features}, her mother could have fancied {that the child had absorbed it into herself, and would give it forth[29] again, with a gleam about her path, as they should plunge into[30] some gloomier shade}. There was no other attribute {that so much <u>impressed</u> her <u>with</u> a sense of new and untransmitted vigor in Pearl's nature[31], as this never-failing vivacity of spirits}; she had not the disease of sadness, {which almost all children, in these latter days, inherit, with the scrofula[32], from the troubles

---

28 to judge from: ~로 판단컨대, ~로 미루어 보면

29 give it forth: (소리, 냄새 따위)를 내다, 발하다

30 plunge into: 벌컥 뛰어들다[맹렬히 돌진하다]. *plunge into something: (불쾌한 일 속으로) 빠지다

31 that so much impressed her with a sense of new and untransmitted vigor in Pearl's nature: 펄의 본성에 내재된 새로운 유전되지 않은(untransmitted) 활력감이 헤스터에게 그렇게나 많은 인상을 남긴

32 scrofula: 〈의학〉 연주창(림프샘의 결핵성 부종인 갑상선종이 헐어

of their ancestors}. Perhaps this too was a disease, and but the reflex of the wild energy {with which Hester had fought against her sorrows, before Pearl's birth}. It was certainly a doubtful charm, imparting a hard, metallic lustre to the child's character[33]. She wanted — {what some people want throughout life[34]} — a grief {that should deeply touch her, and thus humanize and make her capable of sympathy}. But there was time enough yet for little Pearl!

"Come, my child!" said Hester, looking about her, from the spot {where Pearl had stood still in the sunshine}. "We will sit down a little way within the wood, and rest ourselves."

"I am not aweary[35], mother," replied the little girl. "But you may sit down, if you will tell me a story meanwhile."

"A story, child!" said Hester. "And about what?"

"O, a story about the Black Man!" answered Pearl, taking hold of her mother's gown, and looking up, half earnestly, half

---

서 터지는 병)

33 imparting a hard, metallic lustre to the child's character: 이 아이의 성격에 단단한 금속의 광택을 부여하는. *impart sth (to sth): (특정한 특성을) 주다

34 throughout life: 일생을 통해, 평생

35 aweary(=weary): (몹시) 지친, 피곤한, ~에 싫증난

mischievously[36], into her face. "{How he haunts this forest, and carries a book with him, — a big, heavy book, with iron clasps[37]}; and {how this ugly Black Man offers his book and an iron pen to every body [that meets him here among the trees]; and they are to write their names with their own blood}. And then he sets his mark on their bosoms! Didst thou ever meet the Black Man, mother?"

"And who told you this story, Pearl?" asked her mother, recognizing a common superstition of the period[38].

"It was the old dame in the chimney-corner[39], at the house {where you watched last night}," said the child. "But she fancied me asleep {while she was talking of it}. She said {that a thousand and a thousand people had met him here, and had written in his book, and have his mark on them}. And that ugly-tempered lady, old Mistress Hibbins, was one. And, mother, the old dame said {that this scarlet letter was the Black Man's mark on thee}, and {that it glows like a red flame when thou meetest him at midnight, here in the dark wood}. Is it true, mother? And dost thou go to meet him in the night-

---

36 mischievously: 짓궂게
37 with iron clasps: 쇠 걸쇠[잠금쇠]가 달린
38 recognizing a common superstition of the period: 요즘 흔히 퍼진 미신이라는 것을 알아채고는
39 chimney-corner: 벽난로 구석(따뜻하고 안락한 자리)

time?"

"Didst thou ever awake, and find thy mother gone?" asked ★MP3
16장 [2]
시작
Hester.

"Not that I remember," said the child. "{If thou fearest to leave me in our cottage}, thou mightest take me along with thee. I would very gladly go! But, mother, tell me now! Is there such a Black Man? And didst thou ever meet him? And is this his mark?"

"Wilt thou let me be at peace, if I once tell thee?" asked her mother.

"Yes, if thou tellest me all," answered Pearl.

"Once in my life I met the Black Man!" said her mother. "This scarlet letter is his mark!"

Thus conversing, they entered sufficiently deep into the wood to secure themselves from the observation of any casual passenger along the forest-track. Here they sat down on a luxuriant heap of moss; which, [at some epoch of the preceding century[40]], had been a gigantic pine, [with its roots

---

40 at some epoch of the preceding century: 이전 세기의 어떤 시대에

and trunk in the darksome shade, and its head aloft in the upper atmosphere]. It was a little dell[41] {where they had seated themselves}, with a leaf-strewn bank rising gently on either side[42], and a brook flowing through the midst, over a bed of fallen and drowned leaves[43]. The trees [impending over[44] it] had flung down[45] great branches, from time to time, {which choked up[46] the current, and compelled it to form eddies[47] and black depths at some points}; while, in its swifter and livelier passages, there appeared a channel-way[48] of pebbles, and brown, sparkling sand. [Letting the eyes follow along the course of the stream[49]], they could catch the reflected light from its water, at some short distance within the forest, but soon lost all traces of it [amid the bewilderment of tree-trunks and underbrush[50], and here and there a huge rock, covered

---

41 dell: 〈문예체〉 (나무가 우거진) 작은 골짜기[계곡]

42 with a leaf-strewn bank rising gently on either side: 나뭇잎으로 뒤덮인 제방(둑)이 완만하게 양쪽에서 기복을 이루고 있는[아늑하게 솟아 있는]

43 over a bed of fallen and drowned leaves: 낙엽들이 가라앉은 바닥 위로

44 impend over: ~위에 걸리다, 드리워지다

45 fling down: 넘어뜨리다, 메어치다, 내팽개치다

46 choke up: 제지하다, 방해하다

47 eddy: 소용돌이

48 channel-way: 수로, 강바닥

49 Letting the eyes follow along the course of the stream: 눈길이 시냇물의 흐름을 따라가도록 놔 두면

50 underbrush: 큰 나무 밑에 자라는 잡목 덤불

over with gray lichens[51]. All these giant trees and boulders
of granite[52] seemed intent on making a mystery of the course
of this small brook[53]; fearing, perhaps, {that, [with its never-
ceasing loquacity[54]], it should whisper tales out of the heart
of the old forest [whence it flowed], or mirror its revelations
on the smooth surface of a pool}. Continually, indeed, {as
it stole onward[55]}, the streamlet[56] kept up a babble[57], kind,
quiet, soothing, but melancholy, like the voice of a young child
{that was spending its infancy without playfulness, and knew
not how to be merry among sad acquaintance and events of
sombre hue[58]}.

"O brook! O foolish and tiresome little brook!" cried Pearl,
after listening awhile to its talk. "Why art thou so sad? Pluck up
a spirit[59], and do not be all the time sighing and murmuring!"

---

51 covered over with gray lichens: (물에 젖어) 회색빛 이끼들로 뒤
    덮인
52 boulders of granite: 화강암 성분의 반들반들한 바위들. *boulder:
    큰 바위, 거석
53 seemed intent on making a mystery of the course of this small
    brook: 이 작은 개울이 흘러가는 길의 신비를 만들어 내는 데 여념
    이 없는 듯했다. *make a mystery: 비밀로 하다, 신비화하다
54 with its never-ceasing loquacity: 그칠 줄 모르는 재잘거림으로
55 as it stole onward: 계속해서 앞으로 살며시 흘러가듯
56 streamlet: 작은 개천[시내], 개울
57 babble: (물이) 소리 내며 흐르다
58 sombre hue: 침울한 색조
59 pluck up a spirit: 힘을 내다

But the brook, in the course of its little lifetime among the forest-trees, had gone through so solemn an experience {that it could not help talking about it, and seemed to have nothing else to say}. Pearl resembled the brook, inasmuch as the current of her life gushed from a well-spring as mysterious, and had flowed through scenes shadowed as heavily with gloom. But, unlike the little stream, she danced and sparkled[60], and prattled[61] airily[62] along her course.

"What does this sad little brook say, mother?" inquired she.

"If thou hadst a sorrow of thine own, the brook might tell thee of it," answered her mother, "even as it is telling me of mine! But now, Pearl, I hear a footstep along the path, and the noise of one putting aside the branches. I would have thee betake thyself to play, and leave me to speak with him that comes yonder."

"Is it the Black Man?" asked Pearl.

"Wilt thou go and play, child?" repeated her mother. "But do not stray far into the wood. And take heed[63] that thou come

---

60 sparkle: 생기 넘치다, 재기 발랄하다
61 prattle: 마구 지껄이다, 떠들다
62 airily: 즐겁게, 명랑하게
63 take heed: 귀를 기울이다, ~을 주의하다, 조심하다, 중시하다

at my first call."

"Yes, mother," answered Pearl. "But, if it be the Black Man, wilt thou not let me stay a moment, and look at him, with his big book under his arm?"

"Go, silly child!" said her mother, impatiently. "It is no Black Man! Thou canst see him now through the trees. It is the minister!"

"And so it is!" said the child. "And, mother, he has his hand over his heart! Is it because, {when the minister wrote his name in the book}, the Black Man set his mark in that place? But why does he not wear it outside his bosom, as thou dost, mother?"

"Go now, child, and thou shalt tease me as thou wilt another time," cried Hester Prynne. "But do not stray far. Keep where thou canst hear the babble of the brook."

The child went singing away, following up the current of the brook, and striving to mingle a more lightsome cadence[64] with its melancholy voice. But the little stream would not be comforted, and still kept telling its unintelligible secret

---

64 cadence: 억양, 어조

of some very mournful mystery {that had happened — [or making a prophetic lamentation about something that was yet to happen] — within the verge of the dismal forest}. So Pearl, {who had enough of shadow in her own little life}, chose to break off[65] all acquaintance with this repining[66] brook. She set herself, therefore, to gathering violets and wood-anemones[67], and some scarlet columbines[68] {that she found growing in the crevices[69] of a high rock}.

When her elf-child had departed, Hester Prynne made a step or two towards the track that led through the forest, but still remained under the deep shadow of the trees. She beheld[70] the minister advancing along the path, entirely alone, and leaning on a staff {which he had cut by the way-side}. He looked haggard[71] and feeble, and betrayed a nerveless[72] despondency[73] in his air, {which had never so remarkably characterized him in his walks about the settlement, nor in any other situation [where he deemed himself liable to notice]}.

---

65 break off: 연분을 끊다
66 repining: 투덜거리는, 푸념하는, 불평하는
67 wood-anemones: 〈식물〉 아네모네속(屬)의 초본, (특히) 유럽산 (産) 숲바람꽃
68 columbine: 매발톱꽃
69 crevice: (바위나 담에 생긴) 틈
70 behold: 바라보다(= see)
71 haggard: 초췌한
72 nerveless: 힘없는
73 despondency: 낙담, 의기소침

Here it was wofully[74] visible, in this intense seclusion of the forest, {which of itself would have been a heavy trial to the spirits[75]}. There was a listlessness in his gait[76]; {as if he saw no reason for taking one step farther, nor felt any desire to do so, but would have been glad, [could he be glad of any thing], to fling himself down at the root of the nearest tree, and lie there passive for evermore[77]}. The leaves might bestrew[78] him, and the soil gradually accumulate and form a little hillock[79] over his frame, {no matter whether there were life in it or no}. Death was too definite an object to be wished for, or avoided.

To Hester's eye, the Reverend Mr. Dimmesdale exhibited no symptom of positive and vivacious suffering, except {that, [as little Pearl had remarked], he kept his hand over his heart}.

---

74 wofully: woeful의 고어. 비참하게

75 a heavy trial to the spirits: 영혼에 대한 무거운 시험(시련)

76 There was a listlessness in his gait: 그의 걸음에는 힘이 없었다

77 to fling himself down at the root of the nearest tree, and lie there passive for evermore: 지척의 나무 밑동에 몸을 던져서 그대로 영원히 거기에 눕는다면

78 bestrew: (장소를 ~으로) 뒤덮다, (장소에 ~을) 흩뿌리다(with)

79 a little hillock: 작은 언덕

The Scarlet Letter 17장

The Pastor and His Parishioner[1]

{Slowly as the minister walked}, he had almost gone by, before Hester Prynne could gather voice enough to attract his observation. At length, she succeeded.

"Arthur Dimmesdale!" she said, faintly at first; then louder, but hoarsely. "Arthur Dimmesdale!"

"Who speaks?" answered the minister.

Gathering himself quickly up[2], he stood more erect, like a man taken by surprise in a mood {to which he was reluctant to have witnesses}. Throwing his eyes anxiously in the direction of the voice, he indistinctly beheld a form [under the trees], clad in garments so sombre[3], and so little relieved[4] from the gray twilight {into which the clouded sky and the heavy foliage[5] had darkened the noontide[6]}, that he knew not whether it were a woman or a shadow. It may be, that his pathway through life was haunted thus, by a spectre[7] {that had stolen out from among his thoughts}.

---

1 parishioner: 교구민
2 Gathering himself quickly up: 재빨리 정신을 가다듬으며
3 clad in garments so sombre: 칙칙한 빛깔의 옷을 입은
4 relieved: ~에서 벗어난, 해방된
5 the heavy foliage: 울창한 나뭇잎
6 noontide: 한낮 (무렵)
7 spectre: (of sth) 불안[공포](의 원인이 되는 것), 〈문예체〉 유령

He made a step nigher, and discovered the scarlet letter.

"Hester! Hester Prynne!" said he. "Is it thou? Art thou in life?"

"Even so!"[8] she answered. "In such life {as has been mine these seven years past}! And thou, Arthur Dimmesdale, dost thou yet live?"

It was no wonder {that they thus questioned one another's actual and bodily existence, and even doubted of their own}. So strangely did they meet, in the dim wood, that it was like the first encounter, in the world beyond the grave, of two spirits {who had been intimately connected in their former life, but now stood coldly shuddering, in mutual dread; as not yet familiar with their state, nor wonted to the companionship of disembodied beings[9]}. Each a ghost, and awe-stricken[10] at the other ghost! They were awe-stricken likewise at themselves; because the crisis flung back to them [their consciousness], and revealed to each heart [its history and experience], {as life never does, except at such breathless[11] epochs}. The soul

---

8 Even so: 많은 경우 '그렇기는 하지만', '그렇다고 하더라도'의 의미를 띠지만 여기서는 '바로 그렇지요'의 뜻으로 쓰였다.

9 disembodied beings: 육신을 떠난, 육체에서 분리된 존재들

10 awe-stricken: 경이로워하는(=awe-struck)

11 breathless: 숨이 찬, 절박한, 숨이 끊어진

beheld its features in the mirror of the passing moment. It was with fear, and tremulously, and, as it were, by a slow, reluctant necessity, {that Arthur Dimmesdale put forth his hand[12], chill as death, and touched the chill hand of Hester Prynne}. The grasp, {cold as it was}, took away {what was dreariest in the interview}. They now felt themselves, at least, inhabitants of the same sphere.

Without a word more spoken,—neither he nor she assuming the guidance, but with an unexpressed consent,—they glided back into the shadow of the woods, {whence Hester had emerged}, and sat down on the heap of moss {where she and Pearl had before been sitting}. {When they found voice to speak}, it was, at first, only to utter remarks and inquiries {such as any two acquaintance might have made, about the gloomy sky, the threatening storm, and, next, the health of each}. Thus they went onward, not boldly, but step by step, into the themes {that were brooding deepest in their hearts}. So long estranged by fate and circumstances, they needed [something slight and casual] to run before, and throw open the doors of intercourse, {so that their real thoughts might be led across the threshold}.

After a while, the minister fixed his eyes on Hester Prynne's.

---

12 put forth one's hand: 손을 내밀다, 뻗다

"Hester," said he, "hast thou found peace?"

She smiled drearily, looking down upon her bosom.

"Hast thou?" she asked.

"None!—nothing but despair!" he answered. "What else could I look for, being what I am, and leading such a life as mine? Were I an atheist[13],—a man {devoid of conscience,}—a wretch with coarse and brutal instincts,—I might have found peace, long ere now. Nay, I never should have lost it! But, {as matters stand with my soul}, {whatever of good capacity there originally was in me}, all of God's gifts {that were the choicest} have become the ministers of spiritual torment. Hester, I am most miserable!"

"The people reverence thee," said Hester. "And surely thou workest good among them! Doth this bring thee no comfort?"

"More misery, Hester!—only the more misery!" answered the clergyman, with a bitter smile. "{As concerns the good [which I may appear to do]}, I have no faith in it. It must needs be a delusion. What can a ruined soul, like mine, effect towards the redemption of other souls?—or a polluted soul, towards

---

13 atheist: 무신론자

their purification? And [as for the people's reverence], would that it were turned to scorn and hatred! Canst thou deem it, Hester, a consolation[14], {that I must stand up in my pulpit, and meet so many eyes turned upward to my face, [as if the light of heaven were beaming from it!] — must see my flock[15] hungry for the truth, and listening to my words [as if a tongue of Pentecost[16] were speaking!] — and then look inward, and discern the black reality of [what they idolize]}? I have laughed, in bitterness and agony of heart, at the contrast between {what I seem} and {what I am}! And Satan laughs at it!"

"You wrong yourself in this," said Hester gently. "You have deeply and sorely repented. Your sin is left behind you, in the days long past. Your present life is not less holy, in very truth, {than it seems in people's eyes}. Is there no reality in the penitence[17] [thus sealed and witnessed by good works]? And wherefore should it not bring you peace?"

"No, Hester, no!" replied the clergyman. "There is no substance in it![18] It is cold and dead, and can do nothing

---

14 consolation: 위안[위로](을 주는 사람 · 것)

15 flock: (특정 교회의) 신도들

16 Pentecost: (기독교에서) 성령 강림절(부활절 뒤 7번째 일요일)

17 penitence: 뉘우침, 참회(懺悔)

18 There is no substance in it!: 그것[참회]에는 아무런 실체[내용]도 없어요!

for me! [Of penance] I have had enough![19] [Of penitence] there has been none! Else, I should long ago have thrown off these garments of mock holiness[20], and have shown myself to mankind {as they will see me at the judgment-seat[21]}. Happy are you, Hester, {that wear the scarlet letter openly upon your bosom}! Mine burns in secret![22] Thou little knowest {what a relief it is, after the torment of a seven years' cheat, [to look into an eye that recognizes me for what I am]}! Had I one friend, — or were it my worst enemy! — {to whom, [when sickened with the praises of all other men], I could daily betake myself, and be known as the vilest of all sinners}, methinks my soul might keep itself alive thereby. Even thus much of truth would save me! But now, it is all falsehood! — all emptiness! — all death!"

Hester Prynne looked into his face, but hesitated to speak. Yet, [uttering his long-restrained emotions[23] so vehemently[24] as he did], his words here offered her the very point of

---

19 Of penance I have had enough: 속죄는 충분히 했다. *have had (quite) enough of: ~으로 족하다, 충분하다; ~은 질색이다, ~은 더 이상 못 참다

20 should long ago have thrown off these garments of mock holiness: 신성을 기만하는—신성을 가장한—이 옷을 오래전에 벗어 버려야 했다

21 judgment-seat: 판사석, 법정, 최후의 심판대

22 Mine burns in secret!: 내 가슴은 비밀리에 타들어 가고 있소!

23 long-restrained emotions: 오랫동안 억눌러 왔던 감정

24 vehemently: 격렬하게, 맹렬히

circumstances [in which to interpose[25] {what she came to say}]. She conquered her fears, and spoke.

"Such a friend {as thou hast even now wished for}," said she, "[with whom to weep over thy sin], thou hast in me, the partner of it!" —Again she hesitated, but brought out the words with an effort.— "Thou hast long had such an enemy, and dwellest with him under the same roof!"

MP3 ★
17장 (2)
시작 The minister started to his feet, gasping for breath[26], and clutching at his heart {as if he would have torn it out of his bosom}.

"Ha! What sayest thou?" cried he. "An enemy! And under mine own roof! What mean you?"

Hester Prynne was now fully sensible of the deep injury[27] {for which she was responsible to this unhappy man, in permitting him to lie for so many years, or, indeed, for a single moment, at the mercy of[28] one, [whose purposes could not be other than malevolent[29]]}. The very contiguity[30] of his enemy,

---

25 interpose: (대화 중에 질문이나 발언을) 덧붙이다, 끼어들다
26 gasping for breath: 숨이 가빠서 헐떡거리며
27 the deep injury: 깊은 마음의 상처
28 at the mercy of: ~에 휘둘리는[~ 앞에서 속수무책인]
29 malevolent: 악의 있는, 악의적인

126

{beneath whatever mask the latter might conceal himself}, was enough to disturb the magnetic sphere of a being so sensitive as Arthur Dimmesdale. There had been a period {when Hester was less alive to this consideration}; or, perhaps, [in the misanthropy[31] of her own trouble], she left the minister to bear {what she might picture to herself as a more tolerable doom}. But of late[32], [since the night of his vigil[33]], all her sympathies towards him had been both softened and invigorated[34]. She now read his heart more accurately. She doubted not, {that the continual presence of Roger Chillingworth, — the secret poison of his malignity[35], infecting all the air about him, — and his authorized interference[36], as a physician, with the minister's physical and spiritual infirmities[37]}, — {that these bad opportunities had been turned to a cruel purpose}. By means of[38] them, the sufferer's conscience had been kept in[39] an irritated state, {the tendency of which was, not to cure by

---

30 contiguity: 접근, 접촉, 인접(=proximity), 〈심리〉 (시공간상의) 접근, 관념 연상
31 misanthropy: 사람을 싫어함, 염세. cf) philanthropy: 박애
32 of late: 최근에
33 vigil: (밤샘) 간호, (철야) 기도
34 invigorate: 〈동사〉 (흔히 수동태로) 기운 나게 하다, 활기를 북돋우다
35 malignity: 악의, 앙심, 원한
36 authorized interference: 권한을 부여받은 간섭
37 infirmity: (장기적인) 병약[질환]
38 by means of: ~의 도움으로[~을 통하여]
39 be kept in: ~한 상태로 되어 있다

wholesome pain, but to disorganize and corrupt his spiritual being}. Its result, on earth[40], could hardly fail to be insanity[41], and hereafter[42], that eternal alienation from the Good and True, {of which madness is perhaps the earthly type}.

Such was the ruin {to which she had brought the man, [once,—nay, why should we not speak it?—still so passionately loved]}! Hester felt {that the sacrifice of the clergyman's good name, and death itself, [as she had already told Roger Chillingworth], would have been infinitely preferable to the alternative [which she had taken upon herself to choose]}. And now, [rather than have had this grievous wrong to confess], she would gladly have laid down on the forest-leaves, and died there, at Arthur Dimmesdale's feet.

"O Arthur," cried she, "forgive me! In all things else, I have striven to be true! Truth was the one virtue {which I might have held fast, and did hold fast through all extremity; save [when thy good,—thy life,—thy fame,—were put in question]}! Then I consented to a deception. But a lie is never good, {even though death threaten on the other side}! Dost thou not see {what I would say}? That old man!—the physician!—he {whom they call Roger Chillingworth}!—he

---

40 on earth: 도대체, 어떻게, 왜, 어디서
41 insanity: 정신 이상, 미친[무모한] 짓
42 hereafter: 장차, 이후로, 이후 내용에서

was my husband!"

The minister looked at her, for an instant, with all that violence of passion, {which—intermixed, in more shapes than one, with his higher, purer, softer qualities—was, in fact, the portion of him [which the Devil claimed], and [through which he sought to win the rest]}. Never was there a blacker or a fiercer frown, {than Hester now encountered}. For the brief space {that it lasted}, it was a dark transfiguration[43]. But his character had been so much enfeebled[44] by suffering, {that even its lower energies were incapable of more than a temporary struggle}. He sank down on the ground, and buried his face in his hands.

"I might have known it!" murmured he. "I did know it! Was not the secret told me in the natural recoil[45] of my heart, [at the first sight of him], and [as often as I have seen him since]? Why did I not understand? O Hester Prynne, thou little, little knowest all the horror of this thing! And the shame!— the indelicacy[46]!—the horrible ugliness of this exposure of a sick and guilty heart to the very eye {that would gloat over[47]

---

43 transfiguration: 변형, 변신(變身)
44 enfeeble: 약화시키다, 쇠약하게 만들다
45 recoil: (무섭거나 불쾌한 것을 보고) 움찔하다[흠칫 놀라다]
46 indelicacy: 상스러움, 야비함, 버릇없음, 외설, 상스러운 언동
47 gloat over: 침을 흘리며 바라보다, 고소한 듯 바라보다

it}! Woman, woman, thou art accountable for[48] this! I cannot forgive thee!"

"Thou shalt forgive me!" cried Hester, flinging herself on the fallen leaves beside him[49]. "Let God punish! Thou shalt forgive!"

With sudden and desperate tenderness[50], she threw her arms around him, and pressed his head against her bosom; little caring[51] {though his cheek rested on the scarlet letter}. He would have released himself, but strove in vain to do so. Hester would not set him free, {lest he should look her sternly in the face}. All the world had frowned on her, — [for seven long years] had it frowned upon this lonely woman, — and still she bore it all, nor ever once turned away her firm, sad eyes. Heaven, likewise, had frowned upon her, and she had not died. But the frown of this pale, weak, sinful, and sorrow-stricken man was {what Hester could not bear, and live}!

"Wilt thou yet forgive me?" she repeated, over and over

---

48 accountable for: ~에 대한 책임이 있다
49 flinging herself on the fallen leaves beside him: 딤즈데일 곁의 낙엽에 몸을 던지며
50 With sudden and desperate tenderness: 갑작스럽고 필사적인 부드러움으로
51 little caring: 개의치 않고

again. "Wilt thou not frown? Wilt thou forgive?"

"I do forgive you, Hester," replied the minister, at length, with a deep utterance out of an abyss of sadness[52], but no anger. "I freely forgive you now. May God forgive us both! We are not, Hester, the worst sinners in the world. There is one worse than even the polluted priest![53] That old man's revenge has been blacker than my sin. He has violated, in cold blood[54], the sanctity[55] of a human heart. Thou and I, Hester, never did so!"

"Never, never!" whispered she. "{What we did} had a consecration[56] of its own. We felt it so! We said so to each other! Hast thou forgotten it?"

"Hush, Hester!" said Arthur Dimmesdale, rising from the ground. "No; I have not forgotten!"

They sat down again, side by side, and hand clasped in

---

52 with a deep utterance out of an abyss of sadness: 슬픔의 심연에서 나오는 낮은 어조로

53 There is one worse than even the polluted priest!: 타락한 목사보다 더 최악인 사람이 있다니!

54 in cold blood: 냉혈의, 냉혹한

55 sanctity: 성스러움

56 consecration: 신성화, 정화, 헌신(= devotion)

hand[57], on the mossy trunk of the fallen tree. Life had never brought them a gloomier hour; it was the point {whither their pathway had so long been tending, and darkening ever, as it stole along[58];—and yet it inclosed a charm [that made them linger upon it, and claim another, and another, and, after all, another moment]}. The forest was obscure around them, and creaked with a blast {that was passing through it}. The boughs were tossing heavily above their heads; {while one solemn old tree groaned dolefully[59] to another, [as if telling the sad story of the pair {that sat beneath}, or constrained to forbode evil to come]}.

And yet they lingered. How dreary[60] looked the forest-track {that led backward to the settlement, [where Hester Prynne must take up again the burden of her ignominy[61], and the minister the hollow mockery of his good name]}! So they lingered an instant longer. No golden light had ever been so precious as the gloom of this dark forest. Here, [seen only by his eyes], the scarlet letter need not burn into the bosom of the fallen woman! Here, [seen only by her eyes], Arthur Dimmesdale, [false to God and man], might be, for one

---

57 hand clasped in hand: 손을 꼭 움켜잡고
58 steal along: 덧없이 (슬그머니) 가 버리다
59 dolefully: 애절하게
60 dreary: 음울한, 따분한
61 ignominy: 불명예, 수치

moment, true!

He started at a thought {that suddenly occurred to him}.

"Hester!" cried he, "here is a new horror! Roger Chilling-worth knows your purpose to reveal his true character. Will he continue, then, to keep our secret? What will now be the course of his revenge?"

"There is a strange secrecy in his nature," replied Hester, thoughtfully; "and it has grown upon him by the hidden practices of his revenge. I deem it not likely {that he will betray the secret}. He will doubtless seek other means of [satiating[62] his dark passion]."

"And I! — how am I to live longer, breathing the same air with this deadly enemy?" exclaimed Arthur Dimmesdale, shrinking within himself, and pressing his hand nervously against his heart, — a gesture {that had grown involuntary[63] with him}. "Think for me, Hester! Thou art strong. Resolve for me!"

"Thou must dwell no longer with this man," said Hester, slowly and firmly. "Thy heart must be no longer under his evil eye!"

---

62 satiate: 실컷 만족시키다
63 involuntary: 무의식적인, 자기도 모르게 하는

"It were far worse than death!" replied the minister. "But how to avoid it? What choice remains to me? Shall I lie down again on these withered leaves, {where I cast myself [when thou didst tell me {what he was}]}? Must I sink down there, and die at once?"

"Alas, what a ruin has befallen thee!" said Hester, with the tears gushing into her eyes. "Wilt thou die for very weakness? There is no other cause!"

"The judgment of God is on me," answered the conscience-stricken[64] priest. "It is too mighty for me to struggle with!"

"Heaven would show mercy," rejoined Hester, "{hadst thou but the strength to take advantage of it}."

"Be thou strong for me!" answered he. "Advise me [what to do]."

"Is the world then so narrow?" exclaimed Hester Prynne, fixing her deep eyes on the minister's, and instinctively exercising a magnetic power over a spirit [so shattered and subdued, {that it could hardly hold itself erect}]. "Doth the universe lie within the compass of yonder town, {which [only

---

64 conscience-stricken: 양심의 가책을 받는, 마음에 걸리는

a little time ago] was but a leaf-strewn desert, [as lonely as this around us]}? Whither leads yonder forest-track? Backward to the settlement, thou sayest! Yes; but onward, too! Deeper it goes, and deeper, into the wilderness, [less plainly to be seen at every step]; {until, some few miles hence, the yellow leaves will show no vestige[65] of the white man's tread}. There thou art free! So brief a journey would bring thee from a world {where thou hast been most wretched}, to one {where thou mayest still be happy}! Is there not shade enough [in all this boundless forest] to hide thy heart from the gaze of Roger Chillingworth?"

"Yes, Hester; but only under the fallen leaves!" replied the minister, with a sad smile.

"Then there is the broad pathway of the sea!" continued Hester. "It brought thee hither. If thou so choose, it will bear thee back again. In our native land, {whether in some remote rural village or in vast London}, — or, surely, in Germany, in France, in pleasant Italy, — thou wouldst be beyond his power and knowledge! And what hast thou to do with all these iron men, and their opinions? They have kept thy better part in bondage too long already!"

"It cannot be!" answered the minister, listening {as if he

---

65 vestige: 자취, 흔적

were called upon to realize a dream}. "I am powerless to go. {Wretched and sinful as I am}, I have had no other thought [than to drag on my earthly existence in the sphere {where Providence hath placed me}]. {Lost as my own soul is}, I would still do {what I may for other human souls}! I dare not quit my post, [though an unfaithful sentinel, {whose sure reward is death and dishonor, when his dreary watch shall come to an end}]!"

"Thou art crushed under this seven years' weight of misery," replied Hester, fervently resolved to buoy him up[66] with her own energy. "But thou shalt leave it all behind thee! It shall not cumber[67] thy steps, {as thou treadest along the forest-path}; neither shalt thou freight the ship with it, {if thou prefer to cross the sea}. Leave this wreck and ruin here {where it hath happened}! Meddle[68] no more with it! Begin all anew! Hast thou exhausted possibility in the failure of this one trial? Not so! The future is yet full of trial and success. There is happiness to be enjoyed! There is good to be done! Exchange this false life of thine for a true one. Be, {if thy spirit summon thee to such a mission}, the teacher and apostle of the red men. Or,— {as is more thy nature},— be a scholar and a sage among the wisest and the most renowned of the cultivated world. Preach! Write! Act! Do any thing, save to lie down and die! Give up this name

---

66 buoy up: 기분을 좋게[들뜨게] 하다
67 cumber: 방해하다
68 meddle (in/with sth): (남의 일에) 간섭하다[참견하다/끼어들다]

of Arthur Dimmesdale, and make thyself another, and a high one, such {as thou canst wear without fear or shame}. Why shouldst thou tarry[69] so much as one other day in the torments {that have so gnawed into[70] thy life}! — {that have made thee feeble to will and to do}! — {that will leave thee powerless even to repent}! Up, and away!"

"O Hester!" cried Arthur Dimmesdale, {in whose eyes a fitful light, [kindled by her enthusiasm], flashed up and died away}, "thou tellest of running a race to a man {whose knees are tottering beneath him}! I must die here. There is not the strength or courage [left me] to venture into the wide, strange, difficult world, alone!"

It was the last expression of the despondency of a broken spirit. He lacked energy to grasp the better fortune {that seemed within his reach}.

He repeated the word.

"Alone, Hester!"

"Thou shall not go alone!" answered she, in a deep whisper.

Then, all was spoken!

---

69 tarry: 지체하다
70 gnaw into: 갉아먹다

The Scarlet Letter 18장

A Flood of Sunshine

Arthur Dimmesdale gazed into Hester's face with a look {in which hope and joy shone out, indeed, but with fear betwixt them, and a kind of horror at her boldness, [who had spoken {what he vaguely hinted at, but dared not speak}]}.

But Hester Prynne, [with a mind of native courage and activity, and for so long a period not merely estranged, but outlawed, from society¹], had habituated herself to² such latitude³ of speculation {as was altogether foreign to the clergyman}. She had wandered, [without rule or guidance], in a moral wilderness; as vast, as intricate⁴ and shadowy⁵, as the untamed forest⁶, {amid the gloom of which they were now holding a colloquy⁷ [that was to decide their fate]}. Her intellect and heart had their home, as it were, in desert places, {where she roamed as freely as the wild Indian in his woods}. For years past she had looked [from this estranged point of view] at [human institutions, and whatever priests or

---

1 for so long a period not merely estranged, but outlawed, from society: 그토록 오랜 기간 사회에서 소외당했을 뿐만 아니라 범법자 취급을 당했던

2 habituate oneself to: ~에 습관을 들(이)다

3 latitude: (선택·행동 방식의) 자유

4 intricate: 복잡한

5 shadowy: 그늘이 진, 어둑어둑한, 잘 알려져 있지 않은, (어둑해서) 잘 보이지 않는, 어슴푸레한

6 untamed forest: 야성 그대로의 숲

7 colloquy: 대화

legislators had established]; criticizing all with hardly more reverence {than the Indian would feel for[8] the clerical[9] band, the judicial robe, the pillory[10], the gallows[11], the fireside, or the church}. The tendency of her fate and fortunes had been to set her free. The scarlet letter was her passport into regions {where other women dared not tread}. Shame, Despair, Solitude! These had been her teachers,—stern and wild ones,—and they had made her strong, but taught her much amiss[12].

The minister, on the other hand, had never gone through[13] an experience [calculated[14] to lead him beyond the scope of generally received laws]; although, [in a single instance], he had so fearfully transgressed[15] one of the most sacred of them. But this had been a sin of passion, not of principle, nor even purpose[16]. [Since that wretched epoch], he had watched, [with morbid zeal and minuteness[17]], not his acts,—for those it was

---

8　feel for: ~에 대한 (타고난) 감각이 있다

9　clerical: 성직자의

10　pillory: (옛날 죄인에게 씌우던) 칼

11　gallows: 교수대

12　amiss: 잘못된

13　go through: 겪어 보다

14　an experience calculated: 계획적인 일, 계산된 경험

15　transgress: (도덕적 · 법적 한계를) 넘어서다[벗어나다]

16　this had been a sin of passion, not of principle, nor even purpose: 이것은 열정의 죄였지 (개인의 도덕 · 신념과 관련된) 원칙상의 죄도 목적상의 죄도 아니었다

17　with morbid zeal and minuteness: 병적인 열성으로 주도면밀하게

easy to arrange,—but each breath of emotion, and his every thought. [At the head of the social system, {as the clergymen of that day stood}], he was only the more trammelled[18] by its regulations, its principles, and even its prejudices. As a priest, the framework of his order[19] inevitably hemmed him in[20]. As a man {who had once sinned}, but {who kept his conscience all alive and painfully sensitive by the fretting of an unhealed wound[21]}, he might have been supposed safer within the line of virtue, {than if he had never sinned at all}.

Thus, we seem to see[22] that, [as regarded Hester Prynne], the whole seven years of outlaw and ignominy had been little other than a preparation for this very hour[23]. But Arthur Dimmesdale! {Were such a man once more to fall}, what plea could be urged in extenuation of[24] his crime? None; unless it avail[25] him somewhat[26], that he was broken down by long and

---

18 trammel: (움직임 · 활동을) 구속[제한]하다

19 order: 체제, 계층, 교단

20 hem sb/sth in: ~을 (꼼짝 못하게) 둘러싸다

21 As a man who had once sinned, but who kept his conscience all alive and painfully sensitive by the fretting of an unhealed wound: 한때 죄를 지었지만 자신의 의식이 전적으로 깨어 있도록 그리고 치유되지 않는 상처에 극도로 예민하도록 유지해 온 한 남자로서

22 seem to see ...: 아무래도 ~라고 보게 된다

23 had been little other than a preparation for this very hour: 바로 이 시간에 대비한 준비과정과 다름없었다

24 in extenuation of: ~의 정상을 참작하여

25 avail: 도움이 되다, 소용에 닿다

exquisite suffering[27]; that his mind was darkened and confused by the very remorse {which harrowed it}[28]; that, [between fleeing as an avowed criminal, and remaining as a hypocrite], conscience might find it hard to strike the balance[29]; that it was human to avoid [the peril of death and infamy, and the inscrutable machinations of an enemy][30]; that, finally, {to this poor pilgrim, [on his dreary and desert path], [faint, sick, miserable]}, there appeared a glimpse of human affection and sympathy, a new life, and a true one, in exchange for the heavy doom {which he was now expiating}[31]. And be the stern and

---

26 이어지는 5개의 that 절이 그에게 소용이 없는 한, [그의 죄를 정상 참작할 어떤 청원도 있을 수] 없다.

27 that he was broken down by long and exquisite suffering: 길고 도 격렬한 고통으로 인해 그가 무너졌던 것

28 that his mind was darkened and confused by the very remorse which harrowed it: 그것으로 시달림을 당했던 바로 그 가책 때문 에 그의 마음이 어두워지고 혼란스러웠던 것

29 that, between fleeing as an avowed criminal, and remaining as a hypocrite, conscience might find it hard to strike the balance: 스 스로 인정한 범죄자로서 도피하는 것과 위선자로서 남아 있는 것 사이에서 양심이 대차를 결산하는 데(균형을 맞춘다는 데) 어려움 이 있다는 것을 알게 되리라는 것

30 that it was human to avoid the peril of death and infamy, and the inscrutable machinations of an enemy: 죽음과 오명의 위험과 적의 헤아리기 어려운 교묘한 책략을 피하고자 하는 존재가 인간 이었다는 것

31 that, finally, to this poor pilgrim, on his dreary and desert path, faint, sick, miserable, there appeared a glimpse of human affection and sympathy, a new life, and a true one, in exchange for the heavy doom which he was now expiating: 결국, 자신의

sad truth spoken, that the breach {which guilt has once made into the human soul} is never, in this mortal state, repaired. It may be watched and guarded; so that the enemy shall not force his way again into the citadel[32], and might even, in his subsequent assaults[33], select some other avenue, in preference to[34] that {where he had formerly succeeded}. But there is still the ruined wall, and, near it, the stealthy tread of the foe {that would win over again his unforgotten triumph}.

The struggle, {if there were one}, need not be described. Let it suffice, that the clergyman resolved to flee, and not alone.

"{If, in all these past seven years," thought he, "I could recall one instant of peace or hope}, I would yet endure, for the sake of[35] that earnest[36] of Heaven's mercy. But now,— since I am irrevocably[37] doomed,— wherefore should I not snatch the solace[38] [allowed to the condemned culprit[39] before

---

음울하고 황량한 길에서 어지럽고 병들고 비참한 상태에 이른 이 가여운 순례자에게, 지금 자신이 속죄하고 있는 무거운 운명 대신에, 인간적인 애정과 동정, 새로운 삶, 진실한 삶이 얼핏 보였다는 것

32 citadel: (과거 도시의 주민 피신용) 성채[요새]

33 subsequent assaults: 차후의 공격

34 in preference to: ~보다 우선적으로

35 for the sake of: ~ 때문에[~를 위해서]

36 earnest: 증표, 증거물

37 irrevocably: 돌이킬 수 없게, 변경할 수 없게

38 solace: 위안, 위로, 위안[위로](이 되는 사람, 것)

39 the condemned culprit: 비난을 받는 장본인, 유죄선고를 받은 범

his execution[40]]? Or, if this be the path to a better life[41], {as Hester would persuade me}, I surely give up no fairer prospect by pursuing it![42] Neither can I any longer live without her companionship; so powerful is she to sustain, — so tender to soothe[43]! O Thou {to whom I dare not lift mine eyes}, wilt Thou yet pardon me!"

"Thou wilt go!" said Hester calmly, as he met her glance.

{The decision once made}, a glow of strange enjoyment threw its flickering brightness over the trouble of his breast. It was the exhilarating effect — upon a prisoner [just escaped from the dungeon of his own heart] — of breathing the wild, free atmosphere of an unredeemed, unchristianized, lawless region. His spirit rose, {as it were}, with a bound, and attained a nearer prospect of the sky, than throughout all the misery {which had kept him grovelling on the earth}[44]. Of a deeply

---

인, 사형수

40 execution: 처형, 사형(집행)

41 if this be the path to a better life: 이것이 더 나은 삶으로 이어지는 길이라면

42 I surely give up no fairer prospect by pursuing it!: 그 길을 추구한다고 해서 더 좋은 장래를 포기하는 것은 정녕 아닐 것이다

43 so powerful is she to sustain, — so tender to soothe: 그녀는 목사 자신을 지탱해 줄 만큼 강력하고, 또 목사 자신을 달래 줄 만큼 매우 부드럽다. *sustain과 soothe의 목적어를 목사 자신으로 이해하는 게 자연스럽다.

44 which had kept him grovelling on the earth: 그를 땅으로 기어

religious temperament[45], there was inevitably a tinge of the devotional in his mood[46].

"Do I feel joy again?" cried he, wondering at himself. "Methought the germ of it was dead in me! O Hester, thou art my better angel! I seem to have flung myself—sick, sin-stained, and sorrow-blackened—down upon these forest-leaves, and to have risen up [all made anew], and [with new powers to glorify Him {that hath been merciful}]! This is already the better life! Why did we not find it sooner?"

MP3 ★
18장 [2]
시작
"Let us not look back," answered Hester Prynne. "The past is gone! Wherefore should we linger upon it now? See! With this symbol, I undo[47] it all, and make it {as if it had never been}!"

So speaking, she undid[48] the clasp {that fastened the scarlet letter}, and, [taking it from her bosom], threw it to a distance among the withered leaves. The mystic token alighted[49] on the hither verge of the stream. [With a hand's breadth farther flight[50]] it would have fallen into the water, and have given

---

다니게 했었던, 계속적으로 그를 비굴하게 만들었던

45 religious temperament: 종교적인 기질

46 there was inevitably a tinge of the devotional in his mood: 아니나 다를까[필연적으로] 그의 기분에는 종교적인 색채가 묻어났다

47 undo: 되물리다, 되돌리다

48 undo: 풀다, 끄르다, 뜯다

49 alight: ~에 내려 앉다

50 With a hand's breadth farther flight: 한 뼘 더 멀리 날아갔다면.

the little brook another woe to carry onward, besides the unintelligible tale {which it still kept murmuring about}. But there lay the embroidered letter, [glittering like a lost jewel], {which some ill-fated wanderer might pick up, and thenceforth be haunted by strange phantoms of guilt, sinkings[51] of the heart, and unaccountable misfortune}.

[The stigma[52] gone], Hester heaved[53] a long, deep sigh, {in which the burden of shame and anguish departed from her spirit}. O exquisite[54] relief! She had not known the weight, {until she felt the freedom}! By another impulse, she took off the formal[55] cap {that confined her hair}; and down it fell upon her shoulders, dark and rich, [with at once a shadow and a light in its abundance], and imparting the charm of softness to her features. There played around her mouth, and beamed out of her eyes, a radiant and tender smile, {that seemed gushing from the very heart of womanhood}. A crimson flush was glowing on her cheek, {that had been long so pale}. Her sex, her youth, and the whole richness of her beauty, came back from {what men call the irrevocable past}, and clustered

---

＊hand's breadth: 손의 폭, 손폭 치수, 뼘
51 sinking: 가라앉기, 의기소침, 쇠약
52 stigma: 오명, 치욕
53 heave: 가슴을 부풀리다, 내쉬다
54 exquisite: 강렬한, 격렬한
55 formal: 격식을 차린, 형식상의

themselves, with her maiden[56] hope, and a happiness [before unknown], within the magic circle of this hour. And, {as if the gloom of the earth and sky had been but the effluence[57] of these two mortal hearts}, it vanished with their sorrow. All at once, [as with a sudden smile of heaven], forth burst the sunshine, [pouring a very flood into the obscure forest, gladdening[58] each green leaf, transmuting the yellow fallen ones to gold, and gleaming adown[59] the gray trunks of the solemn trees]. The objects {that had made a shadow hitherto}, embodied the brightness now. The course of the little brook might be traced by its merry gleam afar[60] into the wood's heart of mystery, {which had become a mystery of joy}.

Such was the sympathy of Nature — that wild, heathen Nature of the forest, [never subjugated by human law, nor illumined by higher truth] — with the bliss of these two spirits! Love, {whether newly born, or aroused from a deathlike slumber}, must always create a sunshine, filling the heart so full of radiance, that it overflows upon the outward world. {Had the forest still kept its gloom}, it would have been bright in Hester's eyes, and bright in Arthur Dimmesdale's!

---

56 maiden: 소녀다운, 처녀다운
57 effluence: 내뿜음, 발산, 방출, 흘러나옴(=outflow)
58 gladden: 〈구식〉 기쁘게 하다
59 adown: =down
60 afar: =far

Hester looked at him with the thrill of another joy.

"Thou must know Pearl!" said she. "Our little Pearl! Thou hast seen her,—yes, I know it!—but thou wilt see her now with other eyes. She is a strange child! I hardly comprehend her! But thou wilt love her dearly, as I do, and wilt advise me how to deal with her."

"Dost thou think {the child will be glad to know me}?" asked the minister, somewhat uneasily. "I have long shrunk from children, because they often show a distrust,—a backwardness[61] to be familiar with me. I have even been afraid of little Pearl!"

"Ah, that was sad!" answered the mother. "But she will love thee dearly, and thou her. She is not far off. I will call her! Pearl! Pearl!"

"I see the child," observed the minister. "Yonder she is, standing in a streak of sunshine[62], a good way off[63], on the other side of the brook. So thou thinkest {the child will love me}?"

---

61 backward: 망설이는, 내성적인, 뒤로, 거꾸로의, 뒤진
62 in a streak of sunshine: 한 줄기의 햇살 속에
63 way off: 떨어진, 먼

Hester smiled, and again called to Pearl, {who was visible, at some distance, [as the minister had described her], like a bright-apparelled vision, in a sunbeam, [which fell down upon her through an arch of boughs]}. The ray quivered to and fro, making her figure dim or distinct, — now like a real child, now like a child's spirit, — {as the splendor went and came again}. She heard her mother's voice, and approached slowly through the forest.

Pearl had not found the hour pass wearisomely[64], {while her mother sat talking with the clergyman}. The great black forest — stern as it showed itself to those {who brought the guilt and troubles of the world into its bosom} — became the playmate of the lonely infant, as well as it knew how. {Sombre as it was[65]}, it put on the kindest of its moods to welcome her. It offered her the partridge-berries[66], the growth of the preceding[67] autumn, [but ripening only in the spring, and now red as drops of blood upon the withered leaves]. [These] Pearl gathered, and was pleased with their wild flavor. The small

---

64 wearisomely: (아주) 지루하게

65 Sombre as it was: 숲은 음산하기는 했지만

66 partridge-berries: 〈식물〉 호자덩굴(twinberry)[북미산(産)의 흰 꽃이 피는 다년초], 그 열매

67 preceding: (시간·장소의) 이전의(=previous), 앞선, 선행하는, 바로 앞의

denizens[68] of the wilderness hardly took pains[69] to move out of[70] her path. A partridge[71], indeed, [with a brood of ten[72] behind her], ran forward threateningly[73], but soon repented of her fierceness, and clucked[74] to her young ones [not to be afraid]. A pigeon, alone on a low branch, allowed Pearl to come beneath, and uttered a sound as much of greeting as alarm. A squirrel, [from the lofty depths of his domestic[75] tree], chattered either in anger or merriment, — {for a squirrel is such a choleric[76] and humorous little personage that it is hard to distinguish between his moods}, — so he chattered at the child, and flung down a nut upon her head. It was a last year's nut, and already gnawed by his sharp tooth. A fox, [startled from his sleep by her light footstep on the leaves], looked inquisitively[77] at Pearl, [as doubting whether it were better to steal off, or renew his nap on the same spot]. A wolf, {it is said}, — {but here the tale has surely lapsed into the improbable}, — came up, and smelt of Pearl's robe, and offered

---

68 denizens: [특정 지역에서 사는(흔히 발견되는)] 사람[생물]
69 take pain: 고심하다, 둥개다(쩔쩔매다), 힘들이다
70 move out of: 벗어나다
71 partridge: 자고새(꿩과의 새 또는 그 고기)
72 with a brood of ten: 열 마리의 새끼를 거느린. *brood: 한배 병아리, 한배 새끼
73 threateningly: 위협적으로
74 cluck: (암탉이) 꼬꼬하고 울다
75 domestic: 가정용, 가정을 꾸리고 있는
76 choleric: 화를 잘 내는, 걸핏하면 화를 내는
77 inquisitively: 호기심에 어려

his savage head [to be patted by her hand]. The truth seems to be, however, that the mother-forest, and these wild things {which it nourished}, all recognized a kindred wildness in the human child.

And she was gentler here than in the grassy-margined streets of the settlement, or in her mother's cottage. The flowers appeared to know it; and one and another whispered, as she passed, "Adorn[78] thyself with me, thou beautiful child, adorn thyself with me!"—and, to please them, Pearl gathered the violets[79], and anemones[80], and columbines[81], and some twigs of the freshest green, {which the old trees held down before her eyes[82]}. [With these] she decorated her hair, and her young waist, and became a nymph-child, or an infant dryad[83], or whatever else was in closest sympathy with the antique wood. [In such guise] had Pearl adorned herself, when she heard her mother's voice, and came slowly back.

Slowly; for she saw the clergyman!

---

78 adorn: 치장하다

79 violets: 제비꽃

80 anemones: 아네모네

81 columbines: 매발톱꽃

82 which the old trees held down before her eyes: 해묵은 나무들이 그녀의 눈앞에 늘어뜨린

83 dryad: (신화 속의) 드라이어드, 나무의 요정

The Scarlet Letter 19장

The Child at the Brook-Side

"Thou wilt love her dearly," repeated Hester Prynne, {as she and the minister sat watching little Pearl}. "Dost thou not think her beautiful? And see {with what natural skill she has made those simple flowers adorn her}! {Had she gathered pearls, and diamonds, and rubies, in the wood}, they could not have become her better. She is a splendid child! But I know {whose brow she has}!"

"Dost thou know, Hester," said Arthur Dimmesdale, with an unquiet smile, "that this dear child, [tripping[1] about always at thy side], hath caused me many an alarm? Methought— O Hester, {what a thought is that[2]}, and {how terrible to dread it}!—that my own features were partly repeated in her face, and so strikingly {that the world might see them}! But she is mostly thine!"

"No, no! Not mostly!" answered the mother with a tender smile. "A little longer[3], and thou needest not to be afraid to trace {whose child she is}. But how strangely beautiful she looks, with those wild flowers in her hair! It is as if one of the fairies, {whom we left in dear old England}, had decked her out to meet us."

---

1 trip: 경쾌하게 걷다[달리다, 춤추다]
2 what a thought is that: 그것은 얼마나 끔찍한 생각인가
3 a little longer: 좀 더. *a little bit later on: 좀 더 있으면

It was with a feeling {which neither of them had ever before experienced}, that they sat and watched Pearl's slow advance. In her was visible the tie {that united them}. She had been offered to the world, these seven past years, as the living hieroglyphic[4], {in which was revealed the secret [they so darkly sought to hide]},—all written in this symbol,—all plainly manifest,—{had there been a prophet or magician skilled to read the character of flame}! And Pearl was the oneness[5] of their being. Be the foregone evil {what it might}, how could they doubt {that their earthly lives and future destinies were conjoined[6]}, {when they beheld at once the material union, and the spiritual idea, [in whom they met, and were to dwell immortally together]}? Thoughts like these—and perhaps other thoughts, {which they did not acknowledge or define}— threw an awe about the child, {as she came onward}.

"Let her see nothing strange—no passion or eagerness— in thy way of accosting[7] her," whispered Hester. "Our Pearl is a fitful[8] and fantastic little elf, sometimes. Especially, she

---

4 hieroglyphic: (고대 이집트의) 성각(聖刻)[신성] 문자, 상형 문자, 〈보통 복수〉 상형 문자 표기법, 상형 문자의 문서, 비밀 문자. *the living hieroglyphic: 살아 있는 표식, 상징

5 oneness: (완전한) 일체[일치]

6 conjoin: 결합하다[시키다]

7 accost: (특히 위협적으로) 다가가 말을 걸다

8 fitful: 잠깐씩 하다가 마는, 변덕스러운

is seldom tolerant of emotion[9], {when she does not fully comprehend [the why and wherefore]}. But the child hath strong affections! She loves me, and will love thee!"

"Thou canst not think," said the minister, [glancing aside at Hester Prynne], "{how my heart dreads this interview, and yearns for it}! But, in truth, {as I already told thee}, children are not readily won to be familiar with me. They will not climb my knee, nor prattle[10] in my ear, nor answer to my smile; but stand apart, and eye me strangely. Even little babes, {when I take them in my arms}, weep bitterly. Yet Pearl, twice in her little lifetime, hath been kind to me! The first time, — {thou knowest it well}! The last was {when thou ledst her with thee to the house of yonder stern old Governor}."

"And thou didst plead so bravely in her behalf and mine!" answered the mother. "I remember it; and so shall little Pearl. Fear nothing! She may be strange and shy at first, but will soon learn to love thee!"

By this time Pearl had reached the margin of the brook, and stood on the farther side, [gazing silently at Hester and the clergyman], {who still sat together on the mossy tree-trunk,

---

9 is seldom tolerant of emotion: 감정을 견디지 못하다
10 prattle: (쓸데없이 마구) 지껄이다

waiting to receive her}. {Just where she had paused} the brook chanced to form a pool, so smooth and quiet {that it reflected a perfect image of her little figure, [with all the brilliant picturesqueness[11] of her beauty], [in its adornment of flowers and wreathed[12] foliage], but [more refined and spiritualized than the reality]}. This image, [so nearly identical with the living Pearl], seemed to communicate [somewhat of its own shadowy and intangible quality] to the child herself. It was strange, {the way in which Pearl stood, [looking so steadfastly at them through the dim medium of the forest-gloom]; herself, meanwhile, [all glorified with a ray of sunshine, {that was attracted thitherward as by a certain sympathy}]}. In the brook beneath stood another child,— another and the same, — [with likewise its ray of golden light]. Hester felt herself, [in some indistinct and tantalizing[13] manner], estranged from Pearl; {as if the child, [in her lonely ramble through the forest], had strayed out of the sphere [in which she and her mother dwelt together], and was now vainly seeking to return to it}.

There were both truth and error in the impression; the child and mother were estranged, but through Hester's fault, not Pearl's. {Since the latter rambled from her side}, another inmate had been admitted within the circle of the mother's

---

11 picturesque: 그림 같은(특히 고풍스러운)
12 wreathe: 둘러싸다, 에워싸다
13 tantalizing: 애타게 하는, 감질나게 하는

feelings, and so modified the aspect of them all, {that Pearl, [the returning wanderer], could not find her wonted place, and hardly knew [where she was]}.

"I have a strange fancy," observed the sensitive minister, "{that this brook is the boundary between two worlds}, and {that thou canst never meet thy Pearl again}. Or is she an elfish spirit, {who, [as the legends of our childhood taught us], is forbidden to cross a running stream}? Pray hasten[14] her; {for this delay has already imparted a tremor to my nerves}."

"Come, dearest child!" said Hester encouragingly, and stretching out both her arms. "How slow thou art! When hast thou been so sluggish before now? Here is a friend of mine, {who must be thy friend also}. Thou wilt have twice as much love, henceforward, {as thy mother alone could give thee}! Leap across the brook and come to us. Thou canst leap like a young deer!"

Pearl, [without responding in any manner to these honey-sweet expressions], remained on the other side of the brook. Now she fixed her bright, wild eyes on her mother, now on the minister, and now included them both in the same glance; [as if to detect and explain to herself the relation {which

---

14 hasten: 재촉하다

they bore to one another}]. For some unaccountable reason, {as Arthur Dimmesdale felt the child's eyes upon himself}, his hand—with that gesture [so habitual as to have become involuntary]—stole over his heart[15]. At length, [assuming a singular air of authority], Pearl stretched out her hand, [with the small forefinger extended], and [pointing evidently towards her mother's breast]. And beneath, [in the mirror of the brook], there was the flower-girdled[16] and sunny image of little Pearl, [pointing her small forefinger too].

"Thou strange child, why dost thou not come to me?" exclaimed Hester.

Pearl still pointed with her forefinger; and a frown gathered on her brow; the more impressive[17] from[18] the childish, the almost baby-like aspect of the features {that conveyed it}. {As her mother still kept beckoning to her, and arraying her face in a holiday suit[19] of unaccustomed smiles}, the child stamped her foot with a yet more imperious look[20] and gesture. In the

---

15 his hand ... stole over his heart: 자신도 모르게 가슴에 손을 얹었다
16 girdle: 둘러싸는 것, 둘러싸다
17 the more impressive(=the more impressive frown): 더 인상적인 찡그림
18 from: ~의 이유로 인해
19 suit: 옷 한 벌, 세트
20 imperious look: 고압적인 표정, 도도한 표정

brook, again, was the fantastic beauty of the image, [with its reflected frown, its pointed finger, and imperious gesture, giving emphasis to the aspect of little Pearl].

MP3★
18장 (2)
시작

"Hasten, Pearl; or I shall be angry with thee!" cried Hester Prynne, {who, [however inured to[21] such behaviour on the elf-child's part at other seasons[22]], was naturally anxious for a more seemly deportment[23] now}. "Leap across the brook, naughty child, and run hither! Else I must come to thee!"

But Pearl, [not a whit[24] startled at her mother's threats, any more than mollified by her entreaties[25]], now suddenly burst into a fit of passion, [gesticulating violently, and throwing her small figure into the most extravagant contortions[26]]. She accompanied this wild outbreak with piercing shrieks[27], {which the woods reverberated on all sides[28]}; so that, [alone as she was in her childish and unreasonable wrath], it seemed

---

21 inured to: 익숙해져 있다

22 at other seasons: 다른 때 같으면

23 deportment: 몸가짐, 행실, 행동거지

24 not a whit: 전혀, 조금도, 터럭만큼도

25 Pearl, not a whit startled at her mother's threats, any more than mollified by her entreaties: 그녀[헤스터]의 간청에 누그러들지 않았듯이 엄마의 협박에도 조금도 놀라지 않았던 펄

26 contortions: 뒤틀림, 일그러짐

27 with piercing shrieks: 째지는 비명소리로

28 which the woods reverberated on all sides: 그 소리는 숲 전체에 울려 퍼졌다

as if a hidden multitude[29] were lending her their sympathy and encouragement. [Seen in the brook], once more, was the shadowy wrath of Pearl's image, [crowned and girdled with flowers], but [stamping its foot, wildly gesticulating[30], and, in the midst of all, still pointing its small forefinger at Hester's bosom]!

"I see {what ails[31] the child}," whispered Hester to the clergyman, and [turning pale in spite of a strong effort to conceal her trouble and annoyance]. "Children will not abide[32] any, the slightest, change in the accustomed aspect of things {that are daily before their eyes}. Pearl misses something {which she has always seen me wear}!"

"I pray you," answered the minister, "{if thou hast any means of pacifying the child[33]}, do it forthwith[34]! Save[35] {it were the cankered wrath[36] of an old witch, like Mistress Hibbins}," added he, attempting to smile, "I know nothing {that

---

29 a hidden multitude: 숨어 있는 무리, 군중
30 gesticulate: 몸짓[손짓]으로 가리키다[나타내다]
31 ails: 괴롭히다
32 abide: 감수하다, 참다. *can not/will not abide ∼: ∼이라면 질색을 하다, ∼을 못 견디다
33 if thou hast any means of pacifying the child: 당신이 저 아이를 달랠 방법이 있다면
34 forthwith: 곧, 당장
35 Save: =Except
36 cankered wrath: 성미 고약한 노여움

I would not sooner[37] encounter than this passion in a child}. In Pearl's young beauty, [as in the wrinkled witch], it has a preternatural[38] effect. Pacify her, {if thou lovest me}!"

Hester turned again towards Pearl, [with a crimson blush upon her cheek, a conscious glance aside at the clergyman, and then a heavy sigh]; while, [even before she had time to speak], the blush yielded to a deadly pallor[39].

"Pearl," said she, sadly, "look down at thy feet! There! — before thee! — on the hither side of the brook!"

The child turned her eyes to the point [indicated]; and there lay the scarlet letter, so close upon the margin of the stream, {that the gold embroidery was reflected in it}.

"Bring it hither!" said Hester.

"Come thou and take it up!" answered Pearl.

"Was ever such a child!" observed Hester aside to the minister. "O, I have much to tell thee about her. But, in very

---

37 would sooner: 차라리 ~하겠다
38 preternatural: 이상한, 기이한, 초자연적인
39 pallor: (얼굴 색깔이 특히 병·두려움으로) 창백함[파리함]

truth, she is right as regards this hateful token. I must bear its torture yet a little longer, — only a few days longer, — {until we shall have left this region, and look back hither as to a land [which we have dreamed of]}. The forest cannot hide it! The mid-ocean shall take it from my hand, and swallow it up for ever!"

[With these words], she advanced to the margin of the brook, took up the scarlet letter, and fastened it again into her bosom. {Hopefully, but a moment ago, as Hester had spoken of drowning it in the deep sea}, there was a sense of inevitable doom upon her, {as she thus received back this deadly symbol from the hand of fate}. She had flung it into infinite space! — she had drawn an hour's free breath! — and here again was the scarlet misery, [glittering on the old spot]! So it ever is, {whether thus typified or no}, that an evil deed invests itself with the character of doom. Hester next gathered up the heavy tresses[40] of her hair, and confined them beneath her cap. {As if there were a withering spell in the sad letter}, her beauty, the warmth and richness of her womanhood, departed, like fading sunshine; and a gray shadow seemed to fall across her.

{When the dreary change was wrought[41]}, she extended her

---

40 tresses: 〈문예체〉 (여성의) 긴 머리, 삼단 같은 머리
41 wrought: work의 과거형을 나타내는 고어. (변화 등을) 초래하다,

hand to Pearl.

"Dost thou know thy mother now, child?" asked she, reproachfully[42], but with a subdued tone. "Wilt thou come across the brook, and own thy mother, {now that she has her shame upon her}, — {now that she is sad}?"

"Yes; now I will!" answered the child, bounding across the brook, and clasping Hester in her arms. "Now thou art my mother indeed! And I am thy little Pearl!"

In a mood of tenderness {that was not usual with her}, she drew down her mother's head, and kissed her brow and both her cheeks. But then — by a kind of necessity {that always impelled this child to alloy [whatever comfort she might chance to give] with a throb[43] of anguish} — Pearl put up her mouth, and kissed the scarlet letter, too!

"That was not kind!" said Hester. "When thou hast shown me a little love, thou mockest me!"

"Why doth the minister sit yonder?" asked Pearl.

_____

일으키다

42 reproachfully: 나무라는 듯이, 책망하듯이
43 throb: 진동, 욱신[지끈]거림

"He waits to welcome thee," replied her mother. "Come thou, and entreat his blessing! He loves thee, my little Pearl, and loves thy mother too. Wilt thou not love him? Come! he longs to greet thee!"

"Doth he love us?" said Pearl, looking up [with acute intelligence] into her mother's face. "Will he go back with us, hand in hand, we three together, into the town?"

"Not now, dear child," answered Hester. "But in days to come he will walk hand in hand with us. We will have a home and fireside of our own; and thou shalt sit upon his knee; and he will teach thee many things, and love thee dearly. Thou wilt love him; wilt thou not?"

"And will he always keep his hand over his heart?" inquired Pearl.

"Foolish child, what a question is that!" exclaimed her mother. "Come and ask his blessing!"

But, {whether influenced by the jealousy [that seems instinctive with every petted[44] child towards a dangerous

---

44 petted: 응석받이의

rival], or from whatever caprice of her freakish[45] nature},
Pearl would show no favor to the clergyman. It was only by
an exertion of force[46] {that her mother brought her up to him,
[hanging back[47], and manifesting her reluctance[48] by odd
grimaces[49]]}; {of which, [ever since her babyhood], she had
possessed a singular variety, and could transform her mobile
physiognomy[50] into a series of different aspects, [with a new
mischief in them, each and all]}. The minister — [painfully
embarrassed, but hoping {that a kiss might prove a talisman[51]
to admit him into the child's kindlier regards[52]}] — bent
forward, and impressed one on her brow. Hereupon[53], Pearl
broke away from[54] her mother, and, [running to the brook],
stooped over it, and bathed her forehead, {until the unwelcome
kiss was quite washed off, and diffused through a long lapse of
the gliding water}. She then remained apart, [silently watching
Hester and the clergyman]; while they talked together, and
made such arrangements {as were suggested by [their new

---

45 freakish: 변덕스러운, 기이한
46 by an exertion of force: 물리적 힘을 사용하여, 억지로
47 hanging back: 망설이면서
48 manifesting her reluctance: 마음이 내키지 않는다는 것을 분명하
   게 드러내 보이면서
49 by odd grimaces: 이상야릇하게 찡그린 표정으로
50 physiognomy: (어떤 사람의) 얼굴 모습[생김새], 골상
51 talisman: (행운을 가져다 준다고 여겨지는) 부적(符籍)
52 kind regard: 다정한 배려, 관심
53 hereupon: 지금 이후로는, 바로 이것의 결과로, 그러자
54 break away from: ~에서 벗어나다, ~로부터 떨어지다

position, and the purposes soon to be fulfilled]}.

And now this fateful interview had come to a close. The dell was to be left a solitude[55] among its dark, old trees, {which, [with their multitudinous tongues], would whisper long of [what had passed there], and no mortal be the wiser}. And the melancholy brook would add this other tale to the mystery {with which its little heart was already overburdened}, and {whereof it still kept up a murmuring babble, with not a whit more cheerfulness of tone than for ages heretofore[56]}.

---

55 solitude: 고독, 외딴 장소, 한적한 곳. *in solitude: 고독하게
56 with not a whit more cheerfulness of tone than for ages here-
    tofore: 지금까지의 세월 동안 그랬듯이 조금도 활기차지 않은 곡
    조로, 이제껏 그래 왔듯이 생기라고는 없는 음조로

The Minister in a Maze

{As the minister departed, in advance of Hester Prynne and little Pearl}, he threw a backward glance; [half expecting {that he should discover only some faintly traced features or outline of the mother and the child, slowly fading into the twilight of the woods}]. So great a vicissitude[1] in his life could not at once be received as real. But there was Hester, [clad in her gray robe], [still standing beside the tree-trunk[2], {which some blast[3] had overthrown a long antiquity ago[4]}, and {which time had ever since been covering with moss[5], [so that these two fated ones, with earth's heaviest burden on them, might there sit down together, and find a single hour's rest and solace]}]. And there was Pearl, too, [lightly dancing from the margin of the brook, — {now that the intrusive[6] third person was gone}, — and taking her old place by her mother's side]. So the minister had not fallen asleep, and dreamed!

In order to free his mind from this indistinctness[7] and duplicity of impression[8], {which vexed it with a strange

---

1 vicissitude: 변화, 인생의 영고성쇠(인생의 번성함과 쇠락함이 서로 바뀜)

2 the tree-trunk: 나무줄기

3 blast: 센 바람, 돌풍

4 a long antiquity ago: 까마득히 먼 옛날

5 moss: 이끼

6 intrusive: 방해하는, 끼어드는

7 indistinctness: 희미함

8 duplicity of impression: 인상의 이중성

170

disquietude[9]}, he recalled and more thoroughly defined[10] the plans {which Hester and himself had sketched for their departure}. It had been determined between them, {that the Old World, [with its crowds and cities], offered them a more eligible[11] shelter and concealment[12] than the wilds of New England, or all America, [with its alternatives of an Indian wigwam[13], or the few settlements of Europeans, scattered thinly along the sea-board]. Not to speak of the clergyman's health, [so inadequate to sustain the hardships of a forest life[14]], his native gifts, his culture, and his entire development would secure him a home only in the midst of civilization and refinement; the higher [the state], the more delicately adapted to it [the man]. In furtherance of this choice[15], it so happened {that a ship lay in the harbour}; one of those questionable cruisers[16], [frequent at that day], {which, [without being absolutely outlaws of the deep], yet roamed over its surface with a remarkable irresponsibility of character}. This vessel had

---

9 disquietude: 불안한 상태
10 define: 정의하다, 분명히 하다
11 eligible: 적격의, 적합한
12 concealment: 은폐
13 wigwam: 북미 인디언의 오두막집
14 Not to speak of the clergyman's health, so inadequate to sustain the hardships of a forest life: 숲 생활의 고통스러움을 견디기에 부적합한 목사의 건강은 두말할 필요도 없겠고
15 In furtherance of this choice: 이 선택을 촉진시켜 주려는 듯이
16 cruiser: 순양함

recently arrived from the Spanish Main[17], and, [within three days' time], would sail for Bristol[18]. Hester Prynne — {whose vocation[19], [as a self-enlisted[20] Sister of Charity[21]], had brought her acquainted with the captain and crew} — could take upon herself to secure the passage of two individuals and a child, with all the secrecy {which circumstances rendered more than desirable}.

The minister had inquired of Hester, [with no little interest], the precise time {at which the vessel might be expected to depart}. It would probably be on the fourth day from the present. "This is most fortunate!" he had then said to himself. Now, {why the Reverend Mr. Dimmesdale considered it so very fortunate}, we hesitate to reveal. Nevertheless, — to hold nothing back from the reader, — it was because, [on the third day from the present], he was to preach the Election Sermon[22]; and, {as such an occasion formed an honorable epoch in the

---

17 Spanish Main: 카리브 해 연안의 남미 북부지역

18 Bristol: 영국 잉글랜드 서남부의 무역항

19 vocation: 직업

20 enlist: 입대하다, ~을 병적에 넣다, 징모하다

21 Sister of Charity: 애덕회 수녀[1634년 성 뱅상 드 폴(St. Vincent de Paul)이 창립한 수녀회의 회원, 환자 간호에 종사], 자선 수녀회의 회원

22 Election Sermon: 선거일 설교는 새로 선출된 총독의 취임식과 의회의 개원이 동시에 이루어지는 날에 행해진 설교로 목사에게 주어지는 최고의 영예였다.

life of a New England clergyman}, he could not have chanced upon[23] a more suitable mode and time of terminating his professional career. "At least, they shall say of me," thought this exemplary man, "that I leave [no public duty] unperformed, nor ill performed!" Sad, indeed, that an introspection[24] [so profound and acute[25] as this poor minister's] should be so miserably deceived! We have had, and may still have, worse things to tell of him; but none, we apprehend, so pitiably weak[26]; no evidence, [at once so slight and irrefragable[27]], of a subtle disease, {that had long since begun to eat into the real substance of his character}. No man, for any considerable period, can wear one face to himself, and another to the multitude, [without finally getting bewildered as to which may be the true.

The excitement of Mr. Dimmesdale's feelings, {as he returned from his interview with Hester}, lent him unaccustomed physical energy, and hurried him townward at a rapid pace. The pathway [among the woods] seemed wilder, more uncouth[28] [with its rude natural obstacles], and

---

23 chance upon: 우연히 발견하다
24 introspection: 자기반성
25 profound and acute: 깊고도 예리한
26 pitiably weak: 가엾을 만큼 약한
27 irrefragable: 논쟁의 여지가 없는
28 uncouth: 거친

less trodden [by the foot of man], {than he remembered it on his outward journey}. But he leaped across the plashy places, thrust himself through the clinging underbrush, climbed the ascent, plunged into the hollow, and overcame, in short, all the difficulties of the track, [with an unweariable activity {that astonished him}]. He could not but recall {how feebly, and with what frequent pauses for breath, he had toiled over the same ground only two days before}. As he drew near the town, he took an impression of change from the series of familiar objects {that presented themselves}. It seemed not yesterday, not one, nor two, but many days, or even years ago, {since he had quitted them}. There, indeed, was each former trace of the street, {as he remembered it}, and all the peculiarities[29] of the houses, [with the due[30] multitude of gable-peaks], and a weathercock [at every point {where his memory suggested one}]. Not the less, however, came this importunately[31] obtrusive sense of change.[32] The same was true [as regarded the acquaintances {whom he met}, and all the well-known shapes of human life, about the little town]. They looked neither older nor younger, now; the beards of the aged were no whiter, nor

---

29 peculiarities: 특징들

30 due: 적절한, 응당, 상응하는, 옳은, 같은 수의

31 importunately: 끈덕지게, 끈질기게

32 Not the less, however, came this importunately obtrusive sense of change: 그러나 그럼에도 불구하고 인상이 달라졌다는 생각이 성가시게 자꾸 떠오르는 것이었다

could the creeping babe of yesterday walk on his feet to-day; it was impossible to describe [in what respect they differed from the individuals {on whom he had so recently bestowed a parting glance}]; and yet the minister's deepest sense seemed to inform him of their mutability[33]. A similar impression struck him most remarkably, {as he passed under the walls of his own church}. The edifice had so very strange, and yet so familiar, an aspect, {that Mr. Dimmesdale's mind vibrated between two ideas; either [that he had seen it only in a dream hitherto], or [that he was merely dreaming about it now]}.

This phenomenon, [in the various shapes {which it assumed}], indicated no external[34] change, but [so sudden and important a change in the spectator of the familiar scene], {that the intervening space of a single day had operated on his consciousness like the lapse of years}. The minister's own will, and Hester's will, and the fate {that grew between them}, had wrought this transformation. It was the same town [as heretofore]; but the same minister returned not from the forest. He might have said to the friends {who greeted him}, — "I am not the man {for whom you take me}! I left him yonder in the forest, [withdrawn[35] into a secret dell], by a mossy tree-trunk, and near a melancholy brook! Go, seek your minister,

---

33 mutability: 변화
34 external: 외부의, 외면적인
35 withdrawn: 내향적인, 깊숙이 들어간

and see {if his emaciated[36] figure, his thin cheek, his white, heavy, pain-wrinkled brow, be not flung down[37] there like a cast-off garment[38]}!" His friends, no doubt, would still have insisted with him, — "Thou art thyself the man!" — but the error would have been their own, not his.

{Before Mr. Dimmesdale reached home}, his inner man gave him other evidences of a revolution[39] in the sphere of thought and feeling. In truth, nothing [short of a total change of dynasty and moral code, in that interior kingdom], was adequate to account for the impulses [now communicated to the unfortunate and startled minister]. At every step he was incited to do [some strange, wild, wicked thing or other], with a sense {that it would be at once involuntary[40] and intentional; in spite of himself, yet growing out of a profounder self[41] than that [which opposed the impulse]}. For instance, he met one of his own deacons. The good old man addressed him with the paternal affection and patriarchal privilege[42], {which [his venerable age[43], his upright[44] and holy character, and his

---

36 emaciated: 수척한
37 fling down: 내동댕이치다
38 like a cast-off garment: 벗어던진 옷가지처럼
39 revolution: 혁명
40 involuntary: 본의 아닌, 부지불식간의
41 a profounder self: 더 심오한 자아
42 patriarchal privilege: 원로의 특권
43 venerable age: 고령

station in the Church], entitled him to use}; and, conjoined[45] with this[46], the deep, almost worshipping respect, {which the minister's professional and private claims[47] alike demanded}. Never was there a more beautiful example of {how the majesty of age and wisdom may comport with[48] the obeisance[49] and respect [enjoined upon it, as from a lower social rank and inferior order of endowment, towards a higher]}. Now, during a conversation of some two or three moments [between the Reverend Mr. Dimmesdale and this excellent and hoary-bearded deacon], it was only by the most careful self-control {that the former could refrain from uttering certain blasphemous suggestions [that rose into his mind, respecting the communion-supper]}. He absolutely trembled and turned pale as ashes, {lest his tongue should wag itself, [in utterance of these horrible matters, and plead his own consent for so doing, [without his having fairly given it[50]]}. And, [even with this terror in his heart], he could hardly avoid laughing to imagine {how the sanctified old patriarchal deacon would have been petrified[51] by his minister's impiety}!

---

44 upright: 고결한
45 conjoin: 결합하다
46 this: =the paternal affection and patriarchal privilege
47 claim: 주장, 권리, 자격
48 comport with: 어울리다, 적합하다
49 obeisance: 복종
50 it: =his own consent
51 petrify: 깜짝 놀라게 하다

Again, another incident of the same nature. Hurrying along the street, the Reverend Mr. Dimmesdale encountered[52] the eldest female member of his church; a most pious and exemplary[53] old dame; poor, widowed, lonely, and with a heart [as full of reminiscences[54] about her dead husband and children, and her dead friends of long ago, as a burial-ground is full of storied gravestones[55]]. Yet all this, {which would else have been such heavy sorrow}, was made almost a solemn joy to her devout[56] old soul [by religious consolations[57] and the truths of Scripture], {wherewith she had fed herself continually for more than thirty years}. And, {since Mr. Dimmesdale had taken her in charge}, the good grandam's[58] chief earthly comfort—{which, [unless it had been likewise a heavenly comfort], could have been none at all}—was to meet her pastor, [whether casually, or of set purpose], and be refreshed with a word of warm, fragrant[59], heaven-breathing Gospel truth [from his beloved lips into her dulled, but rapturously[60]

---

52 encounter: 만나다

53 exemplary: 모범적인

54 reminiscences: 회상, 추억

55 as a burial-ground is full of storied gravestones: 유서 깊은 비석
    으로 가득 찬 무덤처럼

56 devout: 믿음이 깊은, 독실한

57 consolations: 위로, 위안

58 grandam: 조모, 할머니, 아줌마

59 fragrant: 향기로운

60 rapturously: 미칠 듯이 기쁘게

attentive ear]. But, on this occasion, up to the moment of putting his lips to the old woman's ear, Mr. Dimmesdale, {as the great enemy of souls would have it}, could recall no text of Scripture, nor aught else, except [a brief, pithy[61], and, {as it then appeared to him}, unanswerable argument against the immortality of the human soul]. The instilment[62] thereof[63] into her mind would probably have caused this aged sister to drop down dead, at once, as by the effect of an intensely poisonous infusion. {What he really did whisper}, the minister could never afterwards recollect. There was, perhaps, a fortunate disorder in his utterance, {which failed to impart any distinct idea to the good widow's comprehension}, or {which Providence interpreted after a method of its own}. Assuredly, {as the minister looked back}, he beheld an expression of divine gratitude and ecstasy {that seemed like the shine of the celestial city on her face, [so wrinkled and ashy pale]}.

Again, a third instance. [After parting from the old church-member], he met the youngest sister of them all. It was a maiden [newly won—and won by the Reverend Mr. Dimmesdale's own sermon, on the Sabbath after his vigil—to[64] barter the transitory pleasures of the world for the heavenly

---

61 pithy: 핵심을 찌른
62 instil: 불어넣다
63 thereof: (앞에 언급된) 그것의
64 win ... to ...: ～을 ～하도록 설득하다

hope[65], that was to assume brighter substance {as life grew dark around her}, and {which would gild the utter gloom with final glory}. She was fair and pure as a lily {that had bloomed in Paradise}. The minister knew well that he was himself enshrined within the stainless[66] sanctity of her heart, {which hung its snowy curtains about his image, imparting to religion [the warmth of love], and to love [a religious purity]}. Satan, that afternoon, had surely led the poor young girl away from her mother's side, and thrown her into the pathway of this sorely[67] tempted, or—shall we not rather say?—this lost and desperate man. {As she drew nigh}, the arch-fiend whispered him to condense into small compass and drop into her tender bosom [a germ of evil {that would be sure to blossom darkly soon, and bear black fruit betimes}]. Such was his sense of power over this virgin soul, [trusting him as she did], that the minister felt potent[68] to blight[69] all the field of innocence with but one wicked look, and develop all its opposite with but a word. So—[with a mightier struggle than he had yet sustained]—he held his Geneva cloak before his face[70], and

---

65 to barter the transitory pleasures of the world for the heavenly hope: 이 세상의 일시적인 쾌락을 성스러운 희망으로 바꾸다.
  *barter for: ~로 교환하다

66 stainless: 흠 없는, 깨끗한

67 sorely: 몹시, 심하게

68 potent: 강한, 강력한

69 blight: 시들게 하다, 파괴하다

70 he held his Geneva cloak before his face: 제네바산 망토를 얼굴

hurried onward, making no sign of recognition, and leaving the young sister to digest his rudeness as she might. She ransacked[71] her conscience, — {which was full of harmless little matters, like her pocket or her work-bag}, — and took herself to task[72], poor thing, for a thousand imaginary faults; and went about her household duties with swollen[73] eyelids the next morning.

{Before the minister had time to celebrate his victory over this last temptation}, he was conscious of another impulse, [more ludicrous[74], and almost as horrible]. It was, — {we blush to tell it}, — it was to stop short in the road, and teach some very wicked words to a knot of little Puritan children {who were playing there, and had but just begun to talk}. [Denying himself this freak[75], as unworthy of his cloth], he met a drunken seaman, one of the ship's crew from the Spanish Main. And, here, {since he had so valiantly[76] forborne all other wickedness}, poor Mr. Dimmesdale longed, at least, to shake hands with the tarry[77] blackguard[78], and recreate himself with

---

에 뒤집어쓰고

71 ransack: 샅샅이 뒤지다, 기억을 더듬다

72 take ... to task: ~를 몹시 꾸짖다(비난하다)

73 swollen: 부은

74 ludicrous: 터무니없는, 웃기는, 익살스러운

75 freak: 변덕, 장난

76 valiantly: 용감하게, 뛰어나게

77 tarry: 타르의, 타르를 칠한

a few improper jests, {such as dissolute[79] sailors so abound with}, and a volley[80] of good[81], round, solid[82], satisfactory, and heaven-defying oaths[83]! It was <u>not so much</u> a better principle, as partly his natural good taste, and still more his buckramed[84] habit of clerical decorum[85], {that carried him safely through the latter crisis}.

"What is it {that haunts and tempts me thus}?" cried the minister to himself, at length, <u>pausing</u> in the street, and <u>striking</u> his hand against his forehead. "Am I mad? or am I given over utterly to the fiend? Did I make a contract with him in the forest, and sign it with my blood? And does he now summon me to its[86] fulfilment, by suggesting the performance of every wickedness {which his most foul imagination can conceive}?"

At the moment {when the Reverend Mr. Dimmesdale thus

78　blackguard: 불한당

79　dissolute: 방탕한

80　volley: (공이 땅에 떨어지기 전에) 발 맞받아치기, 공세

81　good: 재미있는, 실컷[맘껏] 하는

82　solid: 순~, 순수한, (색깔이) 다른 색깔이 섞이지 않은, 속이 꽉 찬

83　heaven-defying oaths: 하늘[신]을 모독하는 맹세

84　buckram: 버크램(과거 책 표지 등에 쓰이던, 면이나 마를 뻣뻣하게 만든 천)

85　still more his buckramed habit of clerical decorum: 오히려 목사로서의 범절을 지키려는 굳건한 습성 때문이다

86　its: =the contract's

communed with himself, and struck his forehead with his hand}, old Mistress Hibbins, the reputed[87] witch-lady, is said to have been passing by. She made a very grand appearance; having on a high head-dress[88], a rich[89] gown of velvet, and a ruff done up with the famous yellow starch[90], {of which Anne Turner[91], her especial friend, had taught her the secret, before this last good lady had been hanged for Sir Thomas Overbury's murder}. {Whether the witch had read the minister's thoughts, or no}, she came to a full stop, looked shrewdly[92] into his face, smiled craftily[93], and — {though little given[94] to converse with clergymen} — began a conversation.

"So, reverend Sir, you have made a visit into the forest," observed the witch-lady, nodding her high head-dress at him.

---

87 reputed: (사실 여부와는 별도로) 평판이 난, 알려져 있는

88 head-dress: (특별행사 때) 머리에 쓰는 수건[장식물]

89 rich: 호화로운, 사치스러운

90 a ruff done up with the famous yellow starch: 당시 유행했던 노란 풀을 먹여서 멋을 부린 주름 깃

91 Anne Turner(1576~1615). 토머스 오버베리 경(Sir Thomas Overbury)의 독살에 연루되어 교수형을 당했다. *9장 「의사」(The Leech)에서 청교도사회로 이주하기 이전인 약 30여 년 전에 영국 런던에서 발생한 토머스 오버베리 경 살인사건을 기억하고 있는 나이 든 수공업자에 따르면 칠링워스가— 당시에는 다른 이름이 었는데—그 살인사건에 연루된 포맨(Forman)이라는 의사와 함께 있는 것이 목격되었다고 한다.

92 shrewdly: 빈틈없이, 약삭빠르게

93 craftily: 간사[교활]하게

94 given: ~에 빠져 버린, ~하기를 좋아하는, ~하는 경향이 있는

"The next time, I pray you to allow me only a fair warning[95], and I shall be proud to bear you company. [Without taking overmuch upon myself[96]], my good word will go far[97] towards gaining any strange gentleman a fair reception from yonder potentate[98] {you wot of}!"

"I profess[99], madam," answered the clergyman, with a grave[100] obeisance[101], {such as the lady's rank demanded, and his own good-breeding[102] made imperative[103]}, — "I profess, on my conscience and character, that I am utterly bewildered[104] as touching the purport of your words! I went not into the forest to seek a potentate; neither do I, at any future time, design a visit thither, with a view to gaining the favor of such personage. My one sufficient object was to greet that pious friend of mine, the Apostle Eliot, and rejoice with him over the many precious souls {he hath won from heathendom}[105]!"

---

95 fair warning: 정당한 예고. *행동하기 전에 적절한 시간적인 여유를 두는 것

96 Without ... myself: 과도하게 나를 내세우는 것은 아니지만.
   *take upon[on] oneself: ~의 책임[의무]을 지다, 맡다, 가장하다.

97 go far: 크게 도움이 되다

98 potentate: 유력자

99 profess: 공언, 선언, 고백하다

100 grave: 중대한, 근엄한, 위엄 있는, 의젓한

101 obeisance: 존경, 순종, (존경의 표시로 하는) 절[고개 숙임]

102 good-breeding: 올바른 예의범절

103 imperative: 반드시 해야 하는, 긴요한

104 bewildered: 당혹한, 갈피를 못 잡은

"Ha, ha, ha!" cackled[106] the old witch-lady, still nodding her high head-dress at the minister. "Well, well, we must needs talk thus in the daytime! You carry it off[107] like an old hand[108]! But at midnight, and in the forest, we shall have other talk together!"

She passed on [with her aged stateliness], but [often turning back her head and smiling at him, like one [willing to recognize a secret intimacy of connection]].

"Have I then sold myself," thought the minister, "to the fiend {whom, [if men say true], this yellow-starched and velveted old hag has chosen for her prince and master}!"

The wretched minister! He had made a bargain very like it! [Tempted by a dream of happiness], he had yielded himself with deliberate choice, {as he had never done before}, to {what he knew was deadly sin}. And the infectious[109] poison of that sin had been thus rapidly diffused throughout his moral system. It had stupefied[110] all blessed impulses, and awakened

---

105 heathendom: 이교도
106 cackle: 꼬꼬댁 울다, (불쾌하게) 낄낄 웃다
107 carry it off: 멋지게 해내다, 태연하다, 시치미를 떼고 있다
108 like an old hand: 능숙하게
109 infectious: 전염성의
110 stupefy: 마비시키다

[into vivid life] the whole brotherhood of bad ones. Scorn, bitterness, unprovoked[111] malignity, gratuitous[112] desire of ill, ridicule of {whatever was good and holy}, all awoke, to tempt, {even while they frightened him}. And his encounter with old Mistress Hibbins, {if it were a real incident}, did but show its sympathy and fellowship with wicked mortals and the world of perverted[113] spirits.

He had by this time reached his dwelling, on the edge of the burial-ground, and, [hastening up the stairs], took refuge in his study. The minister was glad to have reached this shelter, [without first betraying himself to the world by any of those strange and wicked eccentricities[114] {to which he had been continually impelled while passing through the streets}]. He entered the accustomed room, and looked around him on its books, its windows, its fireplace, and the tapestried comfort of the walls, with the same perception of strangeness {that had haunted him throughout his walk from the forest-dell into the town, and thitherward}[115]. Here he had studied and written; here, gone through fast and vigil, and come forth half alive;

---

111 unprovoked: 정당한 이유 없는
112 gratuitous: 불필요한, 쓸데없는
113 perverted: 비정상적인, 도착된
114 eccentricity: 괴상한 기분
115 thitherward: 저[그]쪽으로. *여기에서는 '자기 집의 그 방으로'라
    는 의미이다.

here, striven to pray; here, borne a hundred thousand agonies! There was the Bible, in its rich old Hebrew, [with Moses and the Prophets speaking to him, and God's voice through all]! There, on the table, [with the inky pen beside it], was an unfinished sermon, with a sentence [broken in the midst], {where his thoughts had ceased to gush out[116] upon the page two days before}. He knew {that it was himself, the thin and white-cheeked minister, [who had done and suffered these things, and written thus far into the Election Sermon]}! But he seemed to stand apart, and eye this former self [with scornful pitying, but half-envious curiosity]. That self was gone! Another man had returned out of the forest; a wiser one; with a knowledge of hidden mysteries {which the simplicity of the former never could have reached}. A bitter kind of knowledge [that]!

While occupied with these reflections, a knock came at the door of the study, and the minister said, "Come in!" — not wholly devoid of an idea {that he might behold an evil spirit}[117]. And so he did! It was old Roger Chillingworth that entered. The minister stood, white and speechless, with one hand on the Hebrew Scriptures, and the other spread upon his

---

116 gush out: 분출되다

117 not wholly devoid of an idea that he might behold an evil spirit: 혹 악령을 볼 것이라는 생각이 전혀 없었던 것도 아니었다

breast.

"Welcome home, reverend Sir!" said the physician. "And how found you that godly man, the Apostle Eliot? But methinks, dear Sir, you look pale; as if the travel through the wilderness had been too sore[118] for you. Will not my aid be requisite to[119] put you in heart and strength[120] to preach your Election Sermon?"

"Nay, I think not so," rejoined the Reverend Mr. Dimmesdale. "My journey, and the sight of the holy Apostle yonder, and the free air {which I have breathed}, have done me good, [after so long confinement in my study]. I think to need no more of your drugs, my kind physician, {good though they be, and administered by a friendly hand}."

All this time, Roger Chillingworth was looking at the minister [with the grave and intent regard of a physician towards his patient]. But, [in spite of this outward show], the latter was almost convinced of the old man's knowledge, or, at least, his confident suspicion, with respect to his own interview with Hester Prynne. The physician knew, then, {that, [in the minister's regard], he was no longer a trusted friend, but his

---

118 sore: 아픈, 쓰라린, 괴로운
119 be requisite to: ~에 필요하다
120 heart and strength: 마음과 힘, 심력

bitterest enemy}. [So much being known], it would appear natural {that a part of it should be expressed}. It is singular, however, {how long a time often passes [before words embody things]}; and with what security two persons, {who choose to avoid a certain subject}, may approach its very verge, and retire without disturbing it. Thus, the minister felt no apprehension {that Roger Chillingworth would touch, in express[121] words, upon the real position [which they sustained towards one another]}. Yet did the physician, in his dark way, creep frightfully near the secret.

"Were it not better," said he, "that you use my poor skill to-night? Verily, dear Sir, we must take pains [to make you strong and vigorous for this occasion of the Election discourse]. The people look for great things from you; apprehending[122] {that another year may come about, and find their pastor gone}."

"Yea, to another world," replied the minister, with pious resignation[123]. "Heaven grant it be a better one; for, in good sooth, I hardly think to tarry with my flock[124] through the flitting seasons of another year! But, [touching your medicine],

---

121 express: 급행의, 속달의, 분명한, 명시적인
122 apprehend: 우려하다, 염려하다
123 resignation: 체념, 단념
124 I hardly think to tarry with my flock: 나는 신도들과 늑장 부리며 시간을 보낼 것이라고 거의 생각지 않는다

kind Sir, [in my present frame of body] I need it not."

"I joy to hear it," answered the physician. "It may be that my remedies, [so long administered in vain], begin now to take due effect. Happy man were I, and well deserving of New England's gratitude, {could I achieve this cure}!"

"I thank you from my heart, most watchful friend," said the Reverend Mr. Dimmesdale, with a solemn smile. "I thank you, and can but requite your good deeds with my prayers."

"A good man's prayers are golden recompense[125]!" rejoined old Roger Chillingworth, {as he took his leave}. "Yea, they are the current gold coin of the New Jerusalem, with the King's own mint-mark on them[126]!"

[Left alone], the minister summoned a servant of the house, and requested food, {which, being set before him, he ate with ravenous[127] appetite}. Then, [flinging the already written pages of the Election Sermon into the fire], he forthwith began another, {which he wrote with such an impulsive flow of thought and emotion, that he fancied himself inspired;

---

125 recompense: 보상, 보답
126 with the King's own mint-mark on them: 그 위에 왕이신 주님의 조폐국 각인이 찍힌
127 ravenous: 탐욕스러운, 게걸스러운

and only wondered that Heaven should see fit to transmit the grand and solemn music of its oracles [through so foul an organ-pipe as he]. However, [leaving that mystery to solve itself, or go unsolved for ever], he drove his task onward, [with earnest haste and ecstasy]. Thus the night fled away, {as if it were a winged steed, and he careering[128] on it}; morning came, and peeped blushing through the curtains; and [at last] sunrise threw a golden beam into the study, and laid it right across the minister's bedazzled[129] eyes. There he was, with the pen still between his fingers, and a vast, immeasurable[130] tract[131] of written space behind him!

---

128 career: 달리다
129 bedazzle: 눈부시게 하다
130 immeasurable: 헤아릴 수 없는
131 tract: (넓은) 지역[지대], 글, 소책자

The Scarlet Letter 21장

The New England Holiday

Betimes[1] in the morning of the day {on which the new Governor was to receive his office at the hands of the people}, Hester Prynne and little Pearl came into the market-place. It was already thronged with[2] the craftsmen and other plebeian[3] inhabitants of the town, in considerable numbers; among whom, likewise, were many rough figures, {whose attire of deer-skins marked them as belonging to some of the forest settlements, [which surrounded the little metropolis[4] of the colony]}.

On this public holiday, {as on all other occasions, for seven years past}, Hester was clad in a garment of coarse gray cloth. [Not more by its hue than by some indescribable[5] peculiarity in its fashion], it had the effect of making her fade personally out of sight[6] and outline[7]; while, again, the scarlet letter brought her back from this twilight indistinctness[8], and revealed her under the moral aspect of its own illumination.[9]

---

1 betimes(=early): 일찍

2 thronged with: ~로 붐비는

3 plebeian: 평민의, 서민의

4 metropolis(=capital): 수도, 중심도시

5 indescribable: 형언할 수 없는

6 sight: (눈에 보이는) 광경(모습)

7 outline: 윤곽, 외형

8 twilight indistinctness: 흐릿한 희미함

9 Not more ... illumination: 이 대목에서도 A자를 단 헤스터의 모습이 생생하고 인상적으로 묘사된다. 즉, 독특한 패션의 옷차림으로 인해 그녀의 존재가 제 모습과 윤곽을 잃고 희미해지는 동시에 그런

Her face, [so long familiar to the townspeople], showed the marble quietude[10] {which they were accustomed to behold there}. It was like a mask; or rather, like the frozen calmness of a dead woman's features; owing this dreary resemblance to the fact {that Hester was actually dead, [in respect to any claim of sympathy], and had departed out of the world [with which she still seemed to mingle]}.

It might be, on this one day, that there was an expression [unseen before], [nor, indeed, vivid enough to be detected now; unless some preternaturally[11] gifted observer should have first read the heart, and have afterwards sought a corresponding development in the countenance and mien]. Such a spiritual seer[12] might have conceived, that, [after sustaining the gaze of the multitude through seven miserable years as a necessity, a penance, and something {which it was a stern religion to endure}],[13] she now, for one last time more,

---

희미함으로부터 A자가 그녀를 다시 두드러지게 하지만 이때 다시 드러나는 헤스터의 모습은 원래 그녀의 모습이 아니라 A자가 뿜어 내는 빛이 지닌 도덕적인 양상에 따라 재구성된 모습이라는 것이다.

10 quietude: 고요, 평온, 정적

11 preternaturally: 불가사의하게

12 a spiritual seer: 영적인 관찰자[선지자]

13 after sustaining the gaze of the multitude through seven miserable years as a necessity, a penance, and something which it was a stern religion to endure: 비참한 7년의 세월 동안 내내 군중의 시선을 하나의 필연으로, 참회로, 그리고 엄격한 신앙생활에 따라 견뎌야 할 무엇인가로 견뎌 온 후에

encountered it freely and voluntarily[14], in order to convert {what had so long been agony} into a kind of triumph[15]. "Look your last on the scarlet letter and its wearer!" — the people's victim and life-long bond-slave, {as they fancied her}, might say to them. "Yet a little while, and she will be beyond your reach! A few hours longer, and the deep, mysterious ocean will quench[16] and hide for ever the symbol {which ye have caused to burn on her bosom}!" Nor were it an inconsistency[17] [too improbable to be assigned to human nature], {should we suppose a feeling of regret in Hester's mind, at the moment [when she was about to win her freedom from the pain {which had been thus deeply incorporated with her being}]. Might there not be an irresistible[18] desire to quaff[19] a last, long, breathless draught of the cup of wormwood[20] and aloes[21], {with which nearly all her years of womanhood had been perpetually

---

14 she now, for one last time more, encountered it freely and voluntarily: 그녀는 지금, 마지막으로 다시 한 번, 기꺼이, 그리고 자발적으로 그 시선을 대면했다. *it은 the gaze of multitude를 말하다.

15 in order to convert what had so long been agony into a kind of triumph: 오랫동안의 고통을 일종의 승리로 바꾸기 위해서

16 quench: 불을 끄다

17 inconsistency: 불일치, 모순, 일관성이 없음

18 irresistible: 저항할 수 없는, 억누를 수 없는

19 quaff: 꿀꺽꿀꺽 마시다

20 wormwood: 다북쑥속의 식물

21 aloes: 알로에, 노회[남아프리카 원산의 백합과 (약용 · 관상용) 식물], 노회즙

flavored[22]}?[23] The wine of life, [henceforth[24] to be presented to her lips], must be indeed rich, delicious, and exhilarating[25], in its chased[26] and golden beaker; or else leave an inevitable and weary languor[27], after the lees[28] of bitterness {wherewith she had been drugged[29]}, as with a cordial of intensest potency.[30]

Pearl was decked[31] out with airy gayety[32]. It would have been impossible to guess {that this bright and sunny apparition owed its existence to the shape of gloomy gray}; or {that a

★ MP3
21장 (2)
시작

---

22 flavor: 맛을 내다, 풍미를 곁들이다

23 Might there ... flavored?: 이 대목의 묘사도 매우 탁월한 심리 묘사를 보여 준다. 청교도사회에 머물 경우 남은 생애 동안 조금씩 나눠 마셔야 할 고난의 쓴 잔을 떠나기 전에 한꺼번에 들이켜고 싶은 헤스터의 심리를 묘사하고 있다. 이는 바로 다음 대목의 묘사와도 잘 어울린다. 그렇게 쓴맛을 한꺼번에 들이켜고 나면, 쓰디쓴 뒷맛이 강하게 남을 터이므로 그 반작용으로 앞으로 이곳을 벗어나 누릴 삶에서 그녀의 입술에 닿을 포도주는 한결 더 달콤하고 원기를 회복시키는 것일 수밖에 없을 것이다. 하지만 이런 강렬한 쓴맛을 미리 맛보지 않은 채 포도주를 마신다면 (술을 마시면 늘 그렇듯) 술기운만 강할 것이기에 피곤한 나른함만 불러올 의미이라는 것이다.

24 henceforth: 이후로 [죽]

25 exhilarating: 기분을 돋우는, 상쾌한

26 chase: 돋을새김하다

27 languor: 권태, 무기력

28 lee: 앙금, 찌꺼기

29 drug: 약물을 투여[주입]하다

30 as with a cordial of intensest potency: 강렬한 효능이 있는 강장제를 마신 경우에 그런 것처럼

31 deck: 갑판, 입히다, 치장하다

32 gayety: 명랑, 쾌활, (복장) 화려함

fancy, [at once so gorgeous and so delicate as must have been requisite to contrive the child's apparel], was the same [that had achieved a task perhaps more difficult, in imparting so distinct a peculiarity to Hester's simple robe]}. The dress, [so proper was it to little Pearl], seemed an effluence, or inevitable development and outward manifestation of her character, no more to be separated from her {than the many-hued brilliancy from a butterfly's wing, or the painted glory from the leaf of a bright flower}. [As with these], so with the child; her garb was all of one idea with her nature. On this eventful[33] day, moreover, there was a certain singular inquietude and excitement in her mood, resembling nothing so much as the shimmer of a diamond, {that sparkles and flashes with the varied throbbings of the breast [on which it is displayed]}. Children have always a sympathy in the agitations of those [connected with them]; always, especially, a sense of any trouble or impending revolution, of whatever kind, in domestic circumstances; and therefore Pearl, {who was the gem on her mother's unquiet bosom}, betrayed, [by the very dance[34] of her spirits], the emotions {which none could detect in the marble passiveness of Hester's brow}.

This effervescence[35] made her flit with a bird-like move-

---

33 eventful: 다사다난한, 중대한

34 dance: (흥분 따위로) 뛰어 돌아다니다, 껑충껑충 뛰다, 또는 그러함

35 effervescence: 거품이 읾, 비등 작용, 흥분, 활기

ment, {rather than walk by her mother's side}. She broke continually into shouts of a wild, inarticulate, and sometimes piercing music[36]. {When they reached the market-place}, she became still more restless, on perceiving the stir[37] and bustle {that enlivened the spot}; for it was usually more like the broad and lonesome green before a village meeting-house, than the centre of a town's business.

"Why, what is this, mother?" cried she. "Wherefore have all the people left their work to-day? Is it a play-day for the whole world? See, there is the blacksmith! He has washed his sooty face, and put on his Sabbath-day clothes, and looks {as if he would gladly be merry, if any kind body would only teach him how}! And there is Master Brackett[38], the old jailer, nodding and smiling at me. Why does he do so, mother?"

"He remembers thee a little babe, my child," answered Hester.

---

36 music: 소리, 음조, 지저귐

37 stir: 소동, 소란

38 Master Brackett: 이 인물은 4장 「면회」(The Interview)의 앞 대목에 등장한 바 있다. Master는 대개 일정한 지위가 있는 사람에 대한 호칭으로 쓰였고 점잖은 사람 일반으로 확장되어 사용되었다. 19세기 말까지 일상 대화에서 성인남자를 Mister로 대체하여 쓰면서 Master는 아직 사회에 입문하지 않은 사내아이들을 가리키는 말로도 쓰였다. 여기에서는 '~님' 정도의 의미로 쓰였다고 볼 수 있다.

"He should not nod and smile at me, for all that,—the black, grim, ugly-eyed old man!" said Pearl. "He may nod at thee if he will; for thou art clad in gray, and wearest the scarlet letter. But, see, mother, how many faces of strange people, and Indians among them, and sailors! What have they all come to do here in the market-place?"

"They wait to see the procession pass," said Hester. "For the Governor and the magistrates are to go by, and the ministers, and all the great people and good people, with the music, and the soldiers marching before them."

"And will the minister be there?" asked Pearl. "And will he hold out both his hands to me, as when thou ledst me to him from the brook-side?"

"He will be there, child," answered her mother. "But he will not greet thee to-day; nor must thou greet him."

"What a strange, sad man is he!" said the child, as if speaking partly to herself. "In the dark night-time, he calls us to him, and holds thy hand and mine, {as when we stood with him on the scaffold yonder}! And in the deep forest, {where only the old trees can hear, and the strip of sky see it}, he talks with thee, sitting on a heap of moss! And he kisses my forehead, too, {so that the little brook would hardly wash it off}! But, here, in the sunny day, and among all the people, he knows us not; nor must we know him! A strange, sad man is he, with his hand always over his heart!"

"Be quiet, Pearl! Thou understandest not these things," said her mother. "Think not now of the minister, but look about thee, and see how cheery is every body's face to-day. The children have come from their schools, and the grown people from their workshops and their fields, [on purpose to be happy]. For, to-day, a new man is beginning to rule over them; and so — {as has been the custom of mankind ever since a nation was first gathered} — they make merry[39] and rejoice[40]; {as if a good and golden year were at length to pass over the poor old world}!"

It was as Hester said, in regard to the unwonted jollity[41] {that brightened the faces of the people}. Into this festal season of the year — as it already was, and continued to be during the greater part of two centuries — the Puritans compressed[42] {whatever mirth and public joy they deemed allowable to

---

39 make merry: 흥겨워하다, 즐겁게 놀다
40 rejoice: 기뻐하다, 좋아하다
41 jollity: 즐거움, 유쾌함
42 compress: 압축하다, 응축시키다

human infirmity[43]}; thereby so far dispelling[44] the customary cloud, {that, [for the space of a single holiday], they appeared scarcely more grave than most other communities at a period of general affliction}.

But we perhaps exaggerate the gray or sable tinge, {which undoubtedly characterized the mood and manners of the age}. The persons [now in the market-place of Boston] had not been born to an inheritance of Puritanic gloom. They were native Englishmen, {whose fathers had lived in the sunny richness of the Elizabethan epoch}; a time {when the life of England, [viewed as one great mass], would appear to have been as stately, magnificent, and joyous, [as the world has ever witnessed]}. {Had they followed their hereditary taste}, the New England settlers would have illustrated[45] all events of public importance by bonfires, banquets, pageantries[46], and processions. Nor would it have been impracticable[47], [in the observance of majestic ceremonies], to combine mirthful recreation with solemnity, and give, {as it were}, a grotesque and brilliant embroidery to the great robe of state, {which a nation, at such festivals, puts on}. There was some shadow[48]

---

43 infirmity: 허약, 쇠약, 우유부단, (도덕적 · 성격적) 약점, 결함
44 dispel: 떨쳐 버리다, 없애다
45 illustrate: 삽화를 쓰다, 실제로 보여 주다
46 pageantry: 화려한 행사
47 impracticable: 실행할 수 없는

of an attempt of this kind in the mode of celebrating the day
{on which the political year of the colony commenced}. The
dim reflection of a remembered splendor, a colorless and
manifold diluted repetition[49] of {what they had beheld in
proud old London,—we will not say at a royal coronation[50],
but at a Lord Mayor's[51] show},—might be traced in the
customs {which our forefathers instituted[52], with reference
to the annual installation[53] of magistrates}. The fathers and
founders of the commonwealth[54]—the statesman, the priest,
and the soldier—deemed it a duty then [to assume the
outward state and majesty, {which, in accordance with antique
style, was looked upon as the proper garb of public and social
eminence}]. All came forth, [to move in procession before the
people's eye, and thus impart a needed dignity to the simple
framework of a government {so newly constructed}].

---

48 shadow: 기미, 흔적, 희미한 모습
49 colorless and manifold diluted repetition: 개성이 없이 여러 차례
    희석되며 반복됨
50 coronation: 대관식
51 Lord Mayor: (런던 및 영국 일부 대도시의) 시장
52 institute: (제도·정책 등을) 도입하다, 시작하다
53 installation: 설치[설비], 시설, 취임[임명]
54 commonwealth: 공동의 이익을 위해 세워진 정치 공동체를 의미
    한다. 미국의 경우 켄터키(Kentucky), 매사추세츠(Massachusetts),
    펜실베이니아(Pennsylvania), 버지니아(Virginia) 4개 주를 이렇게
    불러 왔다.

Then, too, the people were countenanced[55], if not encouraged, in relaxing[56] the severe and close application[57] to their various modes of rugged industry, {which, [at all other times], seemed of the same piece and material with their religion}. Here, it is true, were none of the appliances[58] {which popular merriment would so readily have found in the England of Elizabeth's time, or that of James};—no rude[59] shows of a theatrical kind; no minstrel[60] with his harp and legendary ballad, nor gleeman[61], [with an ape dancing to his music]; no juggler, [with his tricks of mimic witchcraft]; no Merry Andrew[62], to stir up the multitude [with jests, perhaps hundreds of years old, but still effective, by their appeals to the very broadest sources of mirthful sympathy]. All such professors[63] [of the several branches of jocularity] would have been sternly repressed, not only by the rigid discipline of law, but by the general sentiment {which gives law its vitality}. Not the less, however, the great, honest face of the people smiled,

---

55 countenance: 너그럽게 봐주다

56 relax: 완화하다

57 application: 전념, 근면. *a man of close application: 부지런한 사람

58 appliance: 장치, 설비, 응용

59 rude: (섹스·인체와 관련된) 저속한[남부끄러운, 낯뜨거운]

60 minstrel: 음악가[음유시인]

61 gleeman: 방랑시인, 음유시인

62 Merry Andrew: (옛날의) 거리의 약장수의 앞잡이, 어릿광대

63 professor: ~의 자격을 내세운 자, ~을 직업으로 하는 자

grimly, perhaps, but widely too. Nor were sports wanting, {such as the colonists had witnessed, and shared in, long ago, at the country fairs and on the village-greens of England}; and {which it was thought well to keep alive on this new soil, for the sake of the courage and manliness [that were essential in them]}. Wrestling-matches, in the different fashions of Cornwall and Devonshire[64], were seen here and there about the market-place; in one corner, there was a friendly bout[65] at quarterstaff[66]; and—what attracted most interest of all—on the platform of the pillory, [already so noted in our pages], two masters of defence[67] were commencing an exhibition with the buckler[68] and broadsword. But, much to the disappointment of the crowd, this latter business was broken off by the interposition of the town beadle, {who had no idea of permitting the majesty of the law to be violated by such an abuse of one of its consecrated places}.

It may not be too much to affirm, on the whole, (the people being then in the first stages of joyless deportment[69], and the

---

64 Cornwall and Devonshire: 영국 서부 고장의 레슬링 방식으로 재 킷을 입고 경기를 하며 땅바닥에서는 경기를 진행하지 않는다. Devonshire 방식에서는 발로 차는 것이 허용된다.

65 bout: 한차례, 한바탕, (권투 · 레슬링) 시합

66 quarterstaff: 육척봉(六尺棒, 양끝에 쇠를 댄 막대기)

67 master of defence: 수성의 귀재

68 buckler: 둥근 방패

69 deportment: 몸가짐, 행실

offspring of sires {who had known how to be merry, in their day,}) that they would compare favorably, in point of holiday keeping, with their descendants, even at so long an interval as ourselves. Their immediate posterity, the generation next to the early emigrants, wore the blackest shade of Puritanism, and so darkened the national visage with it, {that all the subsequent years have not sufficed to clear it up}. We have yet to learn again the forgotten art of gayety.

The picture of human life in the market-place, {though its general tint was the sad gray, brown, or black of the English emigrants}, was yet enlivened by some diversity of hue. A party of Indians — [in their savage finery[70] of curiously embroidered deer-skin robes, wampum[71]-belts, red and yellow ochre[72], and feathers, and armed with the bow and arrow and stone-headed spear] — stood apart, with countenances of inflexible gravity, beyond {what even the Puritan aspect could attain}. Nor, {wild as were these painted barbarians}, were they the wildest feature of the scene. This distinction could more justly be claimed by some mariners, — a part of the crew of the vessel from the Spanish Main, — {who had come ashore to see the humors[73] of

---

70 finery: (특히 특별한 경우에 입는) 화려한 옷과 보석
71 wampum: 조가비 구슬(옛날 북미 인디언이 화폐 또는 장식으로 사용)
72 ochre: 오커(페인트 · 그림물감의 원료로 쓰이는 황토)
73 humor: 익살, 기행

Election Day}. They were rough-looking desperadoes[74], [with sun-blackened faces, and an immensity of beard]; their wide, short trousers were confined[75] about the waist by belts, [often clasped[76] with a rough plate of gold, and sustaining always a long knife, and, in some instances, a sword]. [From beneath their broad-brimmed hats of palm-leaf[77]], gleamed eyes {which, even in good nature and merriment, had a kind of animal ferocity}. They transgressed, [without fear or scruple], the rules of behaviour {that were binding on all others}; smoking tobacco under the beadle's[78] very nose, {although each whiff would have cost a townsman a shilling}; and quaffing, at their pleasure, draughts[79] of wine or aqua-vitæ[80] from pocket-flasks, {which they freely tendered[81] to the gaping[82] crowd around them}. It remarkably characterized the incomplete morality of the age, {rigid as we call it}, that a license[83] was allowed the seafaring class, not merely for their freaks[84] on shore, but for far

---

74 desperado: 무법자, 악당
75 confine: 가두다, 졸라매다
76 clasp: (걸쇠를 걸어) 잠그다
77 palm-leaf: 야자나무 잎
78 beadle: 교구 직원
79 draught: 죽 들이마시기, 한 모금, (병이 아니라) 통에서 따라 파는
80 aqua-vitæ: 알코올, 독한 술(brandy, whiskey 등)
81 tender: 제공하다
82 gape: (놀라서) 입을 딱 벌리고 바라보다
83 license(=licence): 자격, 허가. 〈격식〉(흔히 좋지 못한 것을 마음대로 할 수 있는) 자유, 방종
84 freak: 기이한[희한한] 일

more desperate[85] deeds on their proper element[86]. The sailor of that day would go near to be arraigned[87] as a pirate in our own. There could be little doubt, for instance, that this very ship's crew, [though no unfavorable[88] specimens of the nautical[89] brotherhood], had been guilty, {as we should phrase it}, of depredations[90] on the Spanish commerce, {such as would have perilled all their necks in a modern court of justice}.

MP3★
21장 (4)
시작 But the sea, [in those old times], heaved, swelled, and foamed very much at its own will, or subject only to the tempestuous wind, [with hardly any attempts at regulation by human law]. The buccaneer[91] on the wave might relinquish his calling, and become at once, {if he chose}, a man of probity[92] and piety on land; nor, even in the full career of his reckless life, was he regarded as a personage {with whom it was disreputable[93] to traffic, or casually[94] associate}. Thus, the Puritan elders, in their black cloaks, starched bands, and

---

85 desperate: 자포자기의, 무모한, 될 대로 되라는 식의, 극단적인

86 proper element: 본연의 장소[환경]. ＊element: (특히 동물 본래의) 환경

87 arraign: 〈법률〉 기소 인정 여부 절차를 밟다

88 unfavorable: 호의적이 아닌, 알맞지[적합하지] 않은

89 nautical: 선박의, 해상의, 항해의

90 depredation: 약탈

91 buccaneer: 해적

92 probity: 정직성

93 disreputable: 평판이 나쁜, 불명예스러운

94 casually: 격식을 차리지 않고, 태평스럽게, 대충

steeple-crowned hats, smiled not unbenignantly[95] at the clamor and rude deportment of these jolly seafaring men; and it excited neither surprise nor animadversion[96] {when so reputable a citizen as old Roger Chillingworth, the physician, was seen to enter the market-place, in close and familiar talk with the commander of the questionable vessel}.

The latter was by far the most showy and gallant figure, {so far as apparel went}, anywhere to be seen among the multitude. He wore a profusion of ribbons on his garment, and gold lace on his hat, {which was also encircled by a gold chain, and surmounted with a feather}. There was a sword at his side, and a sword-cut on his forehead, {which, by the arrangement of his hair, he seemed anxious rather to display than hide}. A landsman could hardly have worn this garb and shown this face, and worn and shown them both with such a galliard air, [without undergoing stern question before a magistrate, and probably incurring a fine or imprisonment, or perhaps an exhibition in the stocks]. {As regarded the shipmaster}, however, all was looked upon as pertaining to the character, as to a fish his glistening scales.

---

95 unbenignantly: 불친절하게, 악의적으로. *benignant: 인자한, 온화한

96 animadversion: 비평, 비난

[After parting from the physician], the commander of the Bristol ship strolled idly through the market-place; until, happening to approach the spot {where Hester Prynne was standing}, he appeared to recognize, and did not hesitate to address her. {As was usually the case wherever Hester stood}, a small, vacant area—a sort of magic circle—had formed itself about her, {into which, [though the people were elbowing one another at a little distance], none ventured, or felt disposed to intrude}. It was a forcible type of the moral solitude {in which the scarlet letter enveloped its fated wearer; partly by her own reserve, and partly by the instinctive, though no longer so unkindly, withdrawal of her fellow-creatures}. Now, if never before, it answered a good purpose, by enabling Hester and the seaman to speak together without risk of being overheard; and so changed was Hester Prynne's repute before the public, {that the matron in town most eminent for rigid morality could not have held such intercourse with less result of scandal than herself}.

"So, mistress," said the mariner, "I must bid the steward make ready one more berth {than you bargained for}! No fear of scurvy or ship-fever, this voyage! [What with the ship's surgeon and this other doctor], our only danger will be from drug or pill; more by token, as there is a lot of apothecary's stuff aboard, {which I traded for with a Spanish vessel}."

"What mean you?" inquired Hester, startled more than she permitted to appear. "Have you another passenger?"

"Why, know you not," cried the shipmaster, "that this physician here—Chillingworth, he calls himself—is minded to try my cabin-fare with you? Ay, ay, you must have known it; for he tells me {he is of your party, and a close friend to the gentleman [you spoke of],—he [that is in peril from these sour old Puritan rulers]}!"

"They know each other well, indeed," replied Hester, with a mien of calmness, though in the utmost consternation. "They have long dwelt together."

Nothing further passed between the mariner and Hester Prynne. But, at that instant, she beheld old Roger Chillingworth himself, [standing in the remotest corner of the market-place, and smiling on her]; a smile {which—across the wide and bustling square, and through all the talk and laughter, and various thoughts, moods, and interests of the crowd—conveyed secret and fearful meaning}.

The Scarlet Letter 22장

The Procession[1]

{Before Hester Prynne could call together[2] her thoughts, and consider what was practicable[3] to be done in this new and startling aspect of affairs}, the sound of military music was heard approaching along a contiguous[4] street. It[5] denoted[6] the advance of the procession of magistrates and citizens, on its way towards the meeting-house; where, in compliance with[7] a custom [thus early established, and ever since observed], the Reverend Mr. Dimmesdale was to deliver an Election Sermon.

Soon the head of the procession showed itself, with a slow and stately march, turning a corner, and making its way across the market-place. First came the music. It[8] comprised[9] a variety of instruments, [perhaps imperfectly adapted to one another, and played with no great skill, but yet attaining the great object {for which the harmony of drum and clarion[10] addresses itself to[11] the multitude}, — that of imparting a higher and more heroic air to the scene of life {that passes

---

1 procession: 행렬(= parade)
2 call together: 소집하다, 불러 모으다
3 practicable: 실행[실현] 가능한
4 contiguous: 인접한(= adjacent)
5 It: = the sound
6 denote: 표시하다, 알리다
7 in compliance with: ~에 따라, ~에 순응하여
8 It: = the music
9 comprise: 구성되다
10 clarion: 〈악기〉 클라리온
11 address oneself to: ~에게 말을 걸다, 전념하다[힘을 쏟다]

214

before the eye}]. Little Pearl at first clapped her hands, but then lost, for an instant, the restless agitation {that had kept her in a continual effervescence[12] throughout the morning}; she gazed silently, and seemed to be borne upward, like a floating sea-bird, on the long heaves and swells of sound[13]. But she was brought back to her former mood by the shimmer[14] of the sunshine on the weapons and bright armour of the military company, {which followed after the music, and formed the honorary escort[15] of the procession}. This body of soldiery[16] — {which still sustains a corporate[17] existence, and marches down from past ages with an ancient and honorable fame} — was composed of no mercenary materials[18]. Its ranks were filled with gentlemen, {who felt the stirrings of martial impulse[19], and sought to establish a kind of College of Arms[20], [where, as in an association of Knights Templars, they might learn the

---

12 effervescence: 흥분, 활기

13 like a floating sea-bird, on the long heaves and swells of sound: 길게 높이 올라 굽이치는 음악을 타고 날아오른 물새처럼

14 shimmer: 희미한 반짝임

15 honorary escort: 명예를 기리는[명예상의] 호위대

16 soldiery: 군대

17 corporate: 법인조직의, (공동) 단체의, 공동의, 기업의. *어원 =united in one body

18 mercenary materials: 용병. *material은 인재, 인물이라는 뜻이 있음.

19 who felt the stirrings of martial impulse: 군인다운 호기로 자극받은 사람

20 College of Arms(=the College of Heralds): 문장원(紋章院). *college: 단체, 협회, 학회

science, and, {so far as peaceful exercise would teach them},
the practices of war]}. The high estimation [then placed upon
the military character] might be seen in the lofty port of each
individual member of the company. Some of them, indeed,
[by their services in the Low Countries[21] and on other fields of
European warfare], had fairly won their title[22] to assume the
name and pomp of soldiership[23]. The entire array[24], moreover,
[clad in burnished steel, and with plumage nodding over their
bright morions[25]], had a brilliancy of effect {which no modern
display[26] can aspire to[27] equal}.

And yet the men of civil eminence, {who came immediately
behind the military escort}, were better worth a thoughtful
observer's eye. [Even in outward demeanour] they showed
a stamp[28] of majesty {that made the warrior's haughty[29]
stride look vulgar, if not absurd}. It was an age {when [what

---

21 the Low Countries: 북해연안 저지대(벨기에, 네덜란드, 룩셈부르
    크를 지칭함)

22 win their title: 권리를 얻다

23 to assume the name and pomp of soldiership: 군인이라는 명성
    과 화려함을 지닐

24 array: 대열, 구색을 갖춘 것, 치장. *in full array: 한껏 차려 입고;
    in holiday array: 나들이옷을 입고

25 morion: 면갑(面甲)이 없는 모자 같은 투구

26 display: 진열, 전시, 과시

27 aspire to: 갈망하다

28 stamp: 표시, 소인, 검인

29 haughty: 도도한

we call talent] had far less consideration than now, but the massive materials [which produce stability and dignity of character[30]] a great deal more}. The people possessed, [by hereditary right[31]], the quality of reverence[32]; which, [in their descendants], [if it survive at all], exists [in smaller proportion, and with a vastly diminished force] in the selection and estimate of public men.[33] The change may be for good or ill, and is partly, perhaps, for both. In that old day, the English settler on these rude shores,—[having left king, nobles, and all degrees of awful rank behind, while still the faculty and necessity of reverence[34] were strong in him,]—bestowed it[35] on the white hair and venerable brow of age; on long-tried integrity[36]; on solid[37] wisdom and sad-colored experience; on endowments of that grave and weighty[38] order[39], {which gives the idea of permanence[40], and comes under the general

---

30 stability and dignity of character: 성격의 안정성과 위엄성
31 by hereditary right: 세습적으로, 조상으로부터
32 reverence: 공경하기, 존경받기, 위엄
33 The people ... public men: 공경하거나 공경을 받는(reverence) 사람들의 자질이 후손으로 내려오면서 더 줄어들기도 했지만 공직 자를 뽑거나 평가할 때 미치는 영향도 줄어들었다는 의미
34 faculty and necessity of reverence: 존경하는 능력과 필요
35 it: = reverence
36 long-tried integrity: 오래 단련된 고결함
37 solid: 속속들이 알찬
38 weighty: 영향력 있는, 유력한, 중후한
39 order: 종류, 계층, 집단
40 the idea of permanence: 한결같다(영구적이고 내구력이 있다)는

definition of respectability[41]}. These primitive statesmen, therefore, — Bradstreet, Endicott, Dudley, Bellingham, and their compeers[42], — {who were elevated to power by the early choice of the people}, seem to have been not often brilliant, but distinguished by a ponderous sobriety[43], rather than activity of intellect. They had fortitude[44] and self-reliance[45], and, in time of difficulty or peril, stood up for the welfare of the state like a line of cliffs against a tempestuous tide[46]. The traits of character [here indicated] were well represented in the square[47] cast[48] of countenance and large physical development of the new colonial[49] magistrates. {So far as a demeanour of natural authority was concerned}, the mother country need not have been ashamed to see [these foremost men[50] of an actual

---

생각

41 respectability: 존경할 만함

42 compeers: 동료들. *여기의 인물들 사이먼 브래드스트리트(Simon Bradstreet, 1603~1697), 존 엔디콧(John Endicott, 1588~1665), 토머스 더들리(Thomas Dudley, 1576~1653)는 리처드 벨링햄 (Richard Bellingham)과 마찬가지로 뉴잉글랜드의 초기 총독이 었음.

43 but distinguished by a ponderous sobriety: 엄숙한 진중함으로 두각을 나타내었다. *sobriety: (취하지 않아서) 맑은 정신

44 fortitude: 불굴의 정신

45 self-reliance: 자립

46 like a line of cliffs against a tempestuous tide: 거센 조류에 맞서 는 절벽과 같이

47 square: 정사각형, 넓적한, 각진

48 cast: 틀, 외형, 외관

49 colonial: 식민지의, 식민지 시대의

democracy] adopted into the House of Peers[51], or make the Privy Council[52] of the sovereign.

[Next in order to the magistrates] came the young and eminently distinguished divine[53], {from whose lips the religious discourse of the anniversary[54] was expected}. His was the profession, at that era, {in which intellectual ability displayed itself far more than in political life}; for — leaving a higher motive out of the question[55] — it offered inducements[56] powerful enough, [in the almost worshipping respect of the community], to win[57] the most aspiring ambition into its service. Even political power — as in the case of Increase Mather[58] — was within the grasp of a successful priest.

It was the observation of those {who beheld him now}, that never, [since Mr. Dimmesdale first set his foot on the New England shore], had he exhibited such energy [as was seen in the gait and air {with which he kept his pace in the

---

50 foremost men: 선구자들
51 the House of Peers: 귀족원, 상원
52 Privy Council: 추밀원
53 divine: 목사
54 the religious discourse of the anniversary: 경축일 설교
55 out of the question: 논외인
56 inducements: 자극, 동기
57 win: (남을) 끌어당기다, 설득하여 ~하게 하다
58 Increase Mather(1639~1723). 미국의 청교도 목사, 저술가

procession}]. There was no feebleness of step, [as at other times]; his frame was not bent[59]; nor did his hand rest ominously[60] upon his heart. Yet, {if the clergyman were rightly viewed}, his strength seemed not of the body. It might be spiritual, and imparted to him by angelic ministrations[61]. It might be the exhilaration[62] of that potent cordial[63], {which is distilled[64] only in the furnace-glow of earnest and long-continued thought}. Or, perchance, his sensitive temperament was invigorated by the loud and piercing music, {that swelled heavenward[65], and uplifted him on its ascending wave}. Nevertheless, so abstracted[66] was his look, it might be questioned {whether Mr. Dimmesdale even heard the music}. There was his body, [moving onward, and with an unaccustomed force]. But where was his mind? Far and deep in its[67] own region, busying itself, with preternatural activity[68], to marshal[69] a procession of stately thoughts {that were soon to issue thence}; and so he saw nothing, heard nothing, knew

---

59 bent: 굽은, 구부러진

60 ominously: 불길하게

61 ministration: 목사의 직무, 봉사, 원조, 돌보기

62 exhilaration: 들뜸, 유쾌한 기분

63 cordial: 강장제

64 distill: 증류되다

65 heavenward: 하늘을 향하는

66 abstracted: 마음이 쏠리는, 정신이 딴 데 팔린

67 its: =his mind's

68 with preternatural activity: 비상한 활동으로

69 marshal: 모으다, 결집시키다

nothing, [of what was around him]; but the spiritual element took up the feeble frame, and carried it along, [unconscious of the burden, and converting it to spirit like itself]. Men of uncommon intellect, {who have grown morbid}, possess this occasional power of mighty effort, {into which they throw the life of many days, and then are lifeless for as many more}.

Hester Prynne, [gazing steadfastly at the clergyman], felt a dreary influence come over her, but [wherefore or whence] she knew not; {unless that he seemed so remote from her own sphere, and utterly beyond her reach}. One glance of recognition, {she had imagined}, must needs pass between them. She thought of the dim forest, [with its little dell of solitude, and love, and anguish], and the mossy tree-trunk, {where, sitting hand in hand, they had mingled their sad and passionate talk with the melancholy murmur of the brook}. How deeply had they known each other then! And was this the man? She hardly knew him now! He, [moving proudly past, enveloped, as it were, in the rich music, with the procession of majestic and venerable fathers]; he, [so unattainable[70] in his worldly position, and still more so in that far vista of his unsympathizing[71] thoughts, {through which she now beheld him}]! Her spirit sank with the idea {that all must have been

---

70 unattainable: 얻기 어려운, 도달하기 어려운
71 unsympathizing: 인정이 없는, 동정 않는

a delusion}, and {that, [vividly as she had dreamed it], there could be no real bond betwixt the clergyman and herself}. And thus much of woman was there in Hester, {that she could scarcely <u>forgive</u> him, — least of all now, [when the heavy footstep of their approaching Fate might be heard, nearer, nearer, nearer!] — <u>for</u> being able so completely to withdraw himself from their mutual world; {while she groped darkly, and stretched forth her cold hands, and found him not}.

Pearl either saw and responded to her mother's feelings, or herself felt the remoteness and intangibility[72] {that had fallen around the minister}. {While the procession passed}, the child was uneasy, fluttering up and down[73], like a bird on the point of taking flight[74]. {When the whole had gone by}, she looked up into Hester's face.

"Mother," said she, "was that the same minister {that kissed me by the brook}?"

"Hold thy peace, dear little Pearl!" whispered her mother. "We must not always talk in the market-place of {what happens to us in the forest}."

---

72 intangibility: 손으로 만질 수 없음, 불가해함
73 fluttering up and down: 퍼덕거리다
74 on the point of ~ing: 바야흐로 ~하려고 하여, ~의 순간에.
　　＊take flight: 날다, 비행하다

"I could not be sure that it was he; so strange he looked," continued the child. "Else I would have run to him, and bid him kiss me now, before all the people; {even as he did yonder among the dark old trees}. What would the minister have said, mother? Would he have clapped his hand over his heart, and scowled on[75] me, and bid me begone?"

"What should he say, Pearl," answered Hester, "save {that it was no time to kiss}, and {that kisses are not to be given in the market-place}? Well for thee, foolish child, {that thou didst not speak to him}!"

Another shade of the same sentiment, in reference to Mr. Dimmesdale, was expressed by a person {whose eccentricities[76] — [or insanity, as we should term it] — led her to do [what few of the townspeople would have ventured on]; to begin a conversation with the wearer of the scarlet letter, in public}. It was Mistress Hibbins, {who, [arrayed in great magnificence, with a triple ruff, a broidered stomacher[77], a gown of rich velvet, and a gold-headed cane], had come forth to see the procession}. As this ancient lady had the renown (which subsequently cost her no less a price than her life)

---

75 scowl on: ~에게 얼굴을 찌푸리다, 노려보다
76 eccentricity: 괴벽스러움, 별남
77 stomacher: 여자의 가슴옷

of being a principal actor in all the works of necromancy[78] {that were continually going forward}, the crowd gave way before her, and seemed to fear the touch of her garment, {as if it carried the plague among its gorgeous folds[79]}. Seen in conjunction with[80] Hester Prynne,—{kindly as so many now felt towards the latter},—the dread [inspired by Mistress Hibbins] had doubled, and caused a general movement from that part of the market-place {in which the two women stood}.

"Now, what mortal imagination could conceive it!" whispered the old lady confidentially to Hester. "Yonder divine man! That saint on earth, {as the people uphold him to be, and as—I must needs say—he really looks}! Who, now, {that saw him pass in the procession}, would think {how little while it is since he went forth out of his study,—chewing a Hebrew text of Scripture in his mouth, I warrant,—to take an airing in the forest}! Aha! we know {what that means}, Hester Prynne! But, truly, forsooth, I find it hard to believe him the same man. Many a church-member saw I, walking behind the music, {that has danced in the same measure with me, when Somebody[81]

---

78 necromancy: 강령술, 마법
79 among its gorgeous folds: 호화로운 주름 사이에
80 in conjunction with: ~와 함께
81 Somebody: 대문자로 쓴 것으로 미루어 이 '어떤 분'은 악마를 가리키는 것으로 보인다.

was fiddler[82], and, it might be, an Indian powwow[83] or a Lapland[84] wizard changing hands[85] with us}! That is but a trifle, {when a woman knows the world}. But this minister! Couldst thou surely tell, Hester, whether he was the same man {that encountered thee on the forest-path}?"

"Madam, I know not of what you speak," answered Hester Prynne, feeling Mistress Hibbins to be of infirm mind; yet strangely startled and awe-stricken[86] by the confidence {with which she affirmed a personal connection between so many persons (herself among them) and the Evil One}. "It is not for me to talk lightly of a learned and pious minister of the Word[87], like the Reverend Mr. Dimmesdale!"

"Fie[88], woman, fie!" cried the old lady, shaking her finger at Hester. "Dost thou think I have been to the forest so many times, and have yet no skill to judge {who else has been there}? Yea; though no leaf of the wild garlands, {which they wore

---

82 fiddler: 바이올리니스트

83 powwow: 주술사

84 Lapland: 북극권에 속하는 유럽 최북부의 지역을 가리키며, 노르웨이, 스웨덴, 핀란드, 러시아에 걸쳐 있다.

85 change hands: 손을 바꾸다. *여기서는 파트너를 바꾸면서 춤을 추는 것을 묘사한다.

86 startled and awe-stricken: 깜짝 놀라고 두려움에 휩싸였다

87 the Word: 하느님의 말씀, 성경의 가르침

88 fie: 쳇, 에잇

while they danced}, be left in their hair! I know thee, Hester; for I behold the token. We may all see it in the sunshine; and it glows like a red flame in the dark. Thou wearest it openly; so there need be no question about that. But this minister! Let me tell thee in thine ear! {When the Black Man sees one of his own servants, [signed and sealed[89]], so shy of[90] owning to the bond as is the Reverend Mr. Dimmesdale}, he hath a way of ordering matters {so that the mark shall be disclosed in open daylight to the eyes of all the world}! What is that the minister seeks to hide, with his hand always over his heart? Ha, Hester Prynne!"

"What is it, good Mistress Hibbins?" eagerly asked little Pearl. "Hast thou seen it?"

"No matter, darling!" responded Mistress Hibbins, making Pearl a profound reverence[91]. "Thou thyself wilt see it, one time or another. They say, child, thou art of the lineage of the Prince of the Air[92]! Wilt thou ride with me, some fine night, to see thy

---

89 sealed: 초기 노턴(Norton)판에는 'scaled'로 되어 있던 것이 현재 의 노턴판에는 'sealed'로 수정되었다. 오하이오 주립대학 출판부에 서 나온 표준판인 센테너리(Centenary)판에도 'sealed'로 되어 있 다. 'signed and sealed'는 '서명되어 봉랍되었다'는 의미이다.

90 shy of: 꺼리는, 두려워하는

91 making Pearl a profound reverence: 펄에게 공손하게 절하면서

92 the Prince of the Air(=the Prince of the Power of the Air): 공중 의 권세 잡은 자, 사탄, 악마의 우두머리. *'허공', '공기'의 이미지 는 인간과 같은 한정적인 육신의 형태를 띠고 있지 않음을 의미하

father? Then thou shalt know {wherefore the minister keeps his hand over his heart}!"

[Laughing so shrilly that all the market-place could hear her], the weird old gentlewoman took her departure.

By this time the preliminary[93] prayer had been offered in the meeting-house, and the accents of the Reverend Mr. Dimmesdale were heard commencing his discourse. An irresistible[94] feeling kept Hester near the spot. {As the sacred edifice was too much thronged to admit another auditor}, she took up her position close beside the scaffold of the pillory. It was in sufficient proximity to bring the whole sermon to her ears, in the shape of an indistinct, but varied, murmur and flow[95] of the minister's very peculiar voice.

This vocal organ[96] was in itself a rich endowment; insomuch[97] that a listener, [comprehending nothing of the language {in which the preacher spoke}], might still have been swayed to and fro by the mere tone and cadence[98]. Like all

★ MP3
22장 (3)
시작

는 것으로 보인다.

93 preliminary: 예비적인, 준비의
94 irresistible: 저항할 수 없는
95 flow: 계속 이어지는 말, 말의 흐름
96 vocal organ: 발성기관
97 insomuch: ~할 정도까지, ~이므로

other music, it breathed passion and pathos[99], and emotions high or tender, in a tongue [native to[100] the human heart], {wherever educated[101]}. {Muffled as the sound was by its passage through the church-walls}, Hester Prynne listened with such intentness, and sympathized so intimately, that the sermon had throughout[102] a meaning for her, [entirely apart from its indistinguishable words]. These, perhaps, {if more distinctly heard}, might have been only a grosser medium, and have clogged the spiritual sense. Now she caught the low undertone, [as of the wind sinking down to repose itself]; then ascended with it, {as it rose through progressive gradations of sweetness and power, [until its volume seemed to envelop her with an atmosphere of awe and solemn grandeur]}. And yet, {majestic as the voice sometimes became}, there was for ever [in it] an essential character of plaintiveness[103]. A loud or low expression of anguish,—the whisper, or the shriek, {as it might be conceived}, of suffering humanity, {that touched a sensibility in every bosom}! At times this deep strain of pathos was all {that could be heard}, and scarcely heard, sighing [amid a desolate[104] silence]. But {even when the minister's voice grew

---

98 cadence: 운율, 억양
99 pathos: 비애감
100 native to: ~에 고유한
101 wherever educated: 어디에서 교육받았든. *지역에 따른 언어와 는 관계가 없다는 의미
102 throughout: 전부, 죄다, 철두철미
103 plaintiveness: 구슬픔, 애처로움

high and commanding}, — {when it gushed irrepressibly[105] upward}, — {when it assumed its utmost breadth and power, so overfilling[106] the church as to burst its way through the solid walls, and diffuse itself in the open air}, — still, {if the auditor listened intently, and for the purpose}, he could detect the same cry of pain. What was it? The complaint of a human heart, [sorrow-laden, perchance guilty, telling its secret, {whether of guilt or sorrow}, to the great heart of mankind; beseeching its sympathy or forgiveness, — at every moment, — in each accent, — and never in vain]! It was this profound and continual undertone {that gave the clergyman his most appropriate power}.

During all this time Hester stood, statue-like, [at the foot of the scaffold]. {If the minister's voice had not kept her there}, there would nevertheless have been an inevitable[107] magnetism[108] in that spot, {whence she dated the first hour of her life of ignominy}. There was a sense within her, — [too ill-defined[109] to be made a thought, but weighing heavily on her mind], — that her whole orb[110] of life, both before and after,

---

104 desolate: 황량한, 쓸쓸한
105 irrepressibly: 제어할 수 없는
106 overfilling: 지나치게 가득 채워진
107 inevitable: 필연적인
108 magnetism: 자력, 자기 작용
109 ill-defined: (설명, 기술 등이) 불분명한
110 orb: 구, 구체, 궤도

was connected with this spot, as with the one point {that gave it[111] unity}.

Little Pearl, meanwhile, had quitted her mother's side, and was playing at her own will about the market-place. She made [the sombre crowd] cheerful by her erratic[112] and glistening ray; even as a bird of bright plumage illuminates a whole tree of dusky foliage[113] [by darting[114] to and fro, half seen and half concealed, amid the twilight of the clustering leaves]. She had an undulating[115], but, oftentimes, a sharp[116] and irregular movement. It indicated the restless vivacity[117] of her spirit, which to-day was doubly indefatigable[118] in its tip-toe[119] dance, because it was played upon and vibrated with her mother's disquietude[120]. Whenever Pearl saw any thing to excite [her ever active and wandering[121] curiosity], she flew thitherward[122], and, {as we might say}, seized upon that

---

111 it: = her whole orb of life
112 erratic: 불규칙한, 변덕스러운
113 foliage: 잎
114 dart: 쏜살같이[휙] 달리다[움직이다]
115 undulate: 물결치다, 파동치다
116 sharp: (커브 등이) 급격한. *a sharp bend in the road: 도로의 급커브 부분; a sharp turn to the left: 급좌회전
117 vivacity: 생기, 활기
118 indefatigable: 지치지 않는, 끈기 있는
119 tip-toe: 발끝, 까치발
120 disquietude: 불안한 상태, 동요
121 wandering: 헤매는, 종잡을 수 없는

man or thing as her own property, {so far as she desired it}; but without yielding the minutest degree of control over her motions in requital[123]. The Puritans looked on, and, {if they smiled}, were none the less inclined to pronounce the child a demon offspring, from the indescribable charm of beauty and eccentricity {that shone through her little figure, and sparkled with its activity}. She ran and looked the wild Indian in the face; and he grew conscious of a nature [wilder than his own]. Thence, [with native audacity[124]], but still [with a reserve as characteristic], she flew into the midst of a group of mariners, the swarthy-cheeked[125] wild men of the ocean, {as the Indians were of the land}; and they gazed wonderingly and admiringly at Pearl, {as if a flake of the sea-foam had taken the shape of a little maid, and were gifted with a soul of the sea-fire[126], [that flashes beneath the prow[127] in the night-time]}.

One of these seafaring[128] men — the shipmaster, indeed, {who had spoken to Hester Prynne} — was so smitten[129] with Pearl's aspect, that he attempted to lay hands upon her, [with

---

122 thitherward(=thither)：저쪽으로
123 requital：보답, 보상
124 audacity：대담함
125 swarthy-cheeked：거무스레한 낯빛의
126 sea-fire：바다 생물의 발광(發光)
127 prow：이물, 뱃머리
128 seafaring：선원의, 항해의
129 smitten：홀딱 반한

purpose to snatch a kiss]. [Finding it as impossible to touch her as to catch a humming-bird in the air], he took [from his hat] the gold chain {that was twisted about it}, and threw it to the child. Pearl immediately twined it around her neck and waist, [with such happy skill, that, once seen there, it became a part of her, and it was difficult to imagine her without it].

"Thy mother is yonder woman with the scarlet letter," said the seaman. "Wilt thou carry her a message from me?"

"{If the message pleases me} I will," answered Pearl.

"Then tell her," rejoined he, "that I spake again with the black-a-visaged[130], hump-shouldered[131] old doctor, and he engages to bring his friend, the gentleman {she wots[132] of}, aboard with him. So let thy mother take no thought, save for herself and thee. Wilt thou tell her this, thou witch-baby?"

"Mistress Hibbins says my father is the Prince of the Air!" cried Pearl, with her naughty smile. "If thou callest me that ill-name, I shall tell him of thee; and he will chase thy ship with a tempest!"

---

130 black-a-visaged: 검은 얼굴의
131 hump-shouldered: 곱사등의
132 wot: 알다, 알고 있다

[Pursuing a zigzag course across the market-place], the child returned to her mother, and communicated {what the mariner had said}. [Hester's strong, calm steadfastly enduring spirit] almost sank, at last, on beholding this dark and grim countenance of an inevitable doom, {which — [at the moment when a passage seemed to open for the minister and herself out of their labyrinth of misery] — showed itself, with an unrelenting[133] smile, right in the midst of their path}.

With her mind harassed by the terrible perplexity {in which the shipmaster's intelligence involved her}, she was also subjected to another trial. There were many people present, from the country roundabout, {who had often heard of the scarlet letter}, and {to whom it had been made terrific by a hundred false or exaggerated rumors}, but {who had never beheld it with their own bodily eyes[134]}. These, [after exhausting other modes of amusement], now thronged about Hester Prynne [with rude and boorish[135] intrusiveness[136]]. {Unscrupulous[137] as it[138] was}, however, it could not bring

---

133 unrelenting: 엄한, 무자비한
134 own bodily eyes: 직접 자신의 눈으로
135 boorish: 상스러운, 천박한
136 intrusiveness: 침입, 밀고 들어옴
137 unscrupulous: 사악한, 파렴치한, 부도덕한
138 it: 여기에서의 'it'은 바로 앞에 나온 'rude and boorish intrusiveness'(거칠고 상스러운, 무조건 밀고 들어오는 태도)라고 볼 수 있다.

them nearer than a circuit of several yards. [At that distance] they accordingly stood, fixed there by the centrifugal force of the repugnance[139] {which the mystic symbol inspired}. The whole gang of sailors, likewise, [observing the press[140] of spectators, and learning the purport of the scarlet letter], came and thrust their sunburnt and desperado-looking faces[141] into the ring. Even the Indians were affected by a sort of cold shadow of the white man's curiosity, and, [gliding through the crowd], fastened their snake-like black eyes on Hester's bosom; conceiving, perhaps, {that the wearer of this brilliantly embroidered badge must needs be a personage of high dignity among her people}. Lastly, the inhabitants of the town (their own interest in this worn-out subject languidly[142] reviving itself, by sympathy with {what they saw others feel}) lounged idly to the same quarter, and tormented Hester Prynne, perhaps more than all the rest, with their cool, well-acquainted gaze at her familiar shame. Hester saw and recognized the self same faces of that group of matrons, {who had awaited her forthcoming from the prison-door, seven years ago}; all save one, the youngest and only compassionate among them, {whose burial-robe she had since made}. At the final hour, {when she

---

139 centrifugal force of the repugnance: 혐오의 원심력
140 press: 누르기, 압박, 밀려들기, 웅성거리기, 인파. *a great press of people: 대혼잡
141 desperado-looking faces: 무법자처럼 생긴 얼굴
142 languidly: 나른하게

was so soon to fling aside the burning letter}, it had strangely become the centre of more remark and excitement, and was thus made to sear her breast more painfully than at any time [since the first day {she put it on}].

{While Hester stood in that magic circle of ignominy, [where the cunning cruelty of her sentence seemed to have fixed her for ever]}, the admirable preacher was looking down from the sacred pulpit upon an audience, {whose very inmost spirits had yielded to his control}. The sainted minister in the church! The woman of the scarlet letter in the market-place! What imagination would have been irreverent enough to surmise {that the same scorching stigma[143] was on them both}!

---

143 scorching stigma: 맹렬히 타오르는 오명, 치욕

The Scarlet Letter **23장**

The Revelation[1]
of the Scarlet Letter

The eloquent[2] voice, {on which the souls of the listening audience had been borne aloft, as on the swelling waves of the sea[3]}, at length came to a pause. There was a momentary silence, profound as {what should follow the utterance of oracles[4]}. Then ensued a murmur and half-hushed tumult[5]; as if the auditors, [released from the high spell {that had transported them into the region of another's mind}], were returning into themselves, with all their awe and wonder still heavy on them. In a moment more, the crowd began to gush forth from[6] the doors of the church. {Now that there was an end}, they needed other breath, more fit to support the gross and earthly life {into which they relapsed[7]}, than that atmosphere {which the preacher had converted into words of flame, and had burdened with the rich fragrance of his

---

1 revelation: 폭로

2 eloquent: 웅변의, 말 잘하는, 능변인, 감동적인, 청중을 사로잡는, (표현이) 풍부한. *eloquent looks[gestures]: 표정이 풍부한 얼굴 [몸짓]

3 The eloquent voice, on which the souls of the listening audience had been borne aloft, as on the swelling waves of the sea: 바다의 넘실거리는 파도에 실리듯이 청중의 영혼이 실려 높이 오르던 감동 적인 목소리, 바다의 넘실거리는 파도처럼 청중의 영혼을 싣고 높이 오르던 감동적인 목소리

4 the utterance of oracles: 신탁의 발언

5 Then ensued a murmur and half-hushed tumult: 뒤이어 속삭임과 반쯤 소리를 낮춘 소란이 뒤따랐다

6 gush forth from: ~에서 분출하다, 쏟아져 나오다

7 relapse into: 되돌아가다, ~에 다시 빠지다

thought[8]}.

In the open air their rapture broke into speech. The street and the market-place absolutely babbled, from side to side, with applauses of the minister. His hearers could not rest {until they had told one another of [what each knew better than he could tell or hear]}. [According to their united testimony[9]], never had man spoken in so wise, so high, and so holy a spirit, as he {that spake this day}; nor had inspiration ever breathed through mortal lips more evidently {than it did through his}. Its[10] influence could be seen, [as it were], descending upon him, and possessing him, and continually lifting him out of the written discourse {that lay before him}, and filling him with ideas {that must have been as marvellous[11] to himself as to his audience}. His subject, [it appeared], had been the relation between the Deity[12] and the communities of mankind, with a special reference to the New England {which they were here planting in the wilderness}. And, {as he drew towards the close}, a spirit[13] as of prophecy[14] had come upon him,

---

8 the rich fragrance of his thought: 풍성한 사상의 향기

9 testimony: 증언

10 Its: = inspiration's

11 marvellous: 기막히게 좋은, 경탄할 만한

12 Deity: 신

13 spirit: 여기에서의 의미는 holy spirit(성령)를 가리키는 것으로 보인다.

14 prophecy: 예언

constraining[15] him to its purpose <u>as</u> mightily {as the old prophets of Israel were constrained}; only with this difference, {that, [whereas the Jewish seers[16] had denounced[17] judgments and ruin on their country], it was his mission to foretell[18] a high and glorious destiny for the newly gathered people of the Lord}. But, [throughout it all, and through the whole discourse], there had been a certain deep, sad undertone of pathos[19], {which could not be interpreted otherwise than as the natural regret of one [soon to pass away[20]]}. Yes; their minister {whom they so loved}—and {who so loved them all, that he could not depart heavenward without a sigh}—had the foreboding[21] of untimely death upon him, and would soon leave them in their tears! This idea of his transitory[22] stay on earth gave the last emphasis to the effect {which the preacher had produced}; it was as if an angel, [in his passage to the skies], had shaken his bright wings over the people for an instant,—at once a shadow and a splendor,—and had shed down a shower of golden truths upon them.

---

15 constrain: ~하게 만들다, 강요하다

16 seer: 선지자들, 예언자들

17 denounce: 예시하다, 예언하다(＝portend)

18 foretell: 예언하다

19 sad undertone of pathos: 슬픈 비애의 저음

20 pass away: 사망하다, 돌아가시다, 없어지다, 사라지다

21 foreboding: 예언, 예감

22 transitory: 일시적인, 잠시 동안의

Thus, there had come to the Reverend Mr. Dimmesdale —
[as to most men, in their various spheres, though seldom
recognized {until they see it[23] far behind them}] — an epoch
of life [more brilliant and full of triumph than any previous
one, or than any {which could hereafter be}]. He stood, [at this
moment], on the very proudest eminence of superiority, {to
which the gifts of intellect, rich lore, prevailing eloquence, and
a reputation of whitest sanctity[24], could exalt[25] a clergyman in
New England's earliest days, [when the professional character
was of itself a lofty pedestal[26]]}. Such was the position {which
the minister occupied, [as he bowed his head forward on the
cushions of the pulpit, at the close of his Election Sermon]}.
Meanwhile, Hester Prynne was standing beside the scaffold of
the pillory, [with the scarlet letter still burning on her breast]!

Now was heard again the clangor[27] of the music, and the
measured tramp[28] of the military escort, [issuing from the
church-door]. The procession was to be marshalled[29] thence to

---

23 it: 바로 다음에 나오는 'an epoch of life'를 가리킨다.
24 sanctity: 고결함
25 exalt: 격상시키다, 칭송하다
26 when the professional character was of itself a lofty pedestal: (목
    사라는) 직업의 특성만으로도 높은 지위를 누렸던 때(← 직업의 특
    성 그 자체가 높은 기단이었을 때)
27 clangor: 뗑그렁 소리
28 tramp: 쿵쿵거리며 걷기, 무겁게 울리는 발소리
29 marshal: (특정 목적을 위해) 모으다[결집시키다], 통제하다

the town-hall[30], {where a solemn banquet would complete the ceremonies of the day}.

Once more, therefore, the train of venerable and majestic fathers was seen moving through a broad pathway of the people, {who drew back reverently, on either side, as the Governor and magistrates, the old and wise men, the holy ministers, and all [that were eminent and renowned[31]], advanced into the midst of them}. {When they were fairly in the market-place}, their presence was greeted by a shout. This — {though doubtless it might acquire additional force and volume from the child-like loyalty [which the age awarded to its rulers]} — was felt to be an irrepressible outburst[32] of the enthusiasm [kindled[33] in the auditors by that high strain[34] of eloquence {which was yet reverberating in their ears[35]}]. Each felt the impulse [in himself], and, [in the same breath], caught it from his neighbour. Within the church, it had hardly been kept down; beneath the sky, it pealed upward to the zenith. There were human beings enough, and enough [of highly

---

30 town-hall: 시청, 공회당

31 renowned: 유명한, 명성 있는

32 irrepressible outburst: 제어할 수 없는 폭발, 분출

33 enthusiasm kindled: 불붙은 열광

34 strain: 가락[선율]

35 by that high strain of eloquence which was yet reverberating in their ears: 아직도 귓전을 울리는 최고조로 긴장된 능변으로 인해

wrought[36] and symphonious[37] feeling], to produce that more impressive sound [than the organ-tones[38] of the blast[39], or the thunder, or the roar of the sea]; even that mighty swell of many voices, blended[40] into one great voice [by the universal impulse {which makes likewise one vast heart out of the many}]. Never, [from the soil of New England], had gone up such a shout! Never, [on New England soil], had stood the man [so honored by his mortal brethren as the preacher]!

How fared[41] it with him[42] then? Were there not the brilliant particles of a halo[43] in the air about his head? {So etherealized[44] by spirit as he was, and so apotheosized[45] by worshipping admirers}, did his footsteps in the procession really tread upon the dust of earth?

{As the ranks of military men and civil fathers moved

---

36 highly wrought: 정교한, 매우 흥분된
37 symphonious: 조화를 이루는, 화성의
38 organ-tone: 오르간의 음조, 음색. *강한 바람에 의한 소리를 오르간 소리로 비유하고 있다.
39 blast: 강한 바람
40 blend: 섞이다, 혼합하다[혼합되다]
41 fare: 되어 가다, 일어나다. *How fared it with him?: 그는 어떠했는가?
42 him: =preacher
43 halo: 후광
44 etherealize: 영묘하게 되다, 영화롭게 되다
45 apotheosize: 신격화하다

onward}, all eyes were turned towards the point {where the minister was seen to approach among them}. The shout died into a murmur, {as one portion of the crowd after another obtained a glimpse of him}. How feeble and pale he looked amid all his triumph! The energy—or say, rather, the inspiration {which had held him up, [until he should have delivered the sacred message that brought its own strength along with it from heaven]}—was withdrawn, {now that it had so faithfully performed its office}. The glow, {which they had just before beheld burning on his cheek}, was extinguished[46], like a flame {that sinks down hopelessly among the late-decaying embers[47]}. It seemed hardly the face of a man alive, [with such a deathlike hue]; it was hardly a man [with life in him], {that tottered[48] on his path so nervelessly, yet tottered, and did not fall}!

MP3 ★
23장 (2)
시작 One of his clerical brethren,—{it was the venerable John Wilson},—[observing the state {in which Mr. Dimmesdale was left by the retiring wave of intellect and sensibility}], stepped forward hastily to offer his support. The minister tremulously, but decidedly, repelled[49] the old man's arm. He still walked onward, {if that movement could be so described,

---

46 extinguish: 끄다
47 the late-decaying embers: 이제는 약화되어 가는 타다 남은 부분
48 totter: 비틀거리다
49 repel: 물리치다, 거절하다

[which rather resembled the wavering effort of an infant, with its mother's arms in view, outstretched to tempt him forward]}. And now, {almost imperceptible as were the latter steps of his progress}, he had come opposite the well-remembered and weather-darkened scaffold, {where, [long since, with all that dreary lapse of time between], Hester Prynne had encountered the world's ignominious stare[50]}. There stood Hester, [holding little Pearl by the hand]! And there was the scarlet letter on her breast! The minister here made a pause; {although the music still played the stately and rejoicing march [to which the procession moved]}. It summoned him onward,—onward to the festival!—but here he made a pause.

Bellingham, [for the last few moments], had kept an anxious eye upon him. He now left his own place in the procession, and advanced to give assistance; judging [from Mr. Dimmesdale's aspect] {that he must otherwise inevitably fall}. But there was something [in the latter's expression] {that warned back the magistrate, [although a man[51] not readily obeying the vague intimations {that pass from one spirit to another}]}. The crowd, meanwhile, looked on with awe and wonder. This earthly faintness was, in their view, only another phase of the minister's celestial strength; nor would it have seemed a

---

50 ignominious stare: 치욕의 응시
51 although a man: =although he was a man

miracle [too high to be wrought for one so holy]⁵², {had⁵³ he ascended before their eyes, waxing⁵⁴ dimmer and brighter, and fading at last into the light of heaven}!

He turned towards the scaffold, and stretched forth his arms.

"Hester," said he, "come hither! Come, my little Pearl!"

It was a ghastly⁵⁵ look {with which he regarded them}; but there was something [at once tender and strangely triumphant] in it. The child, [with the bird-like motion {which was one of her characteristics}], flew to him, and clasped her arms about his knees. Hester Prynne—[slowly, as if impelled by inevitable fate⁵⁶, and against her strongest will]—likewise drew near, but paused {before she reached him}. [At this instant] old Roger Chillingworth thrust himself through the crowd,—or, perhaps, {so dark, disturbed, and evil was his look}, he rose up out of some nether region,—to snatch back his victim {from

---

52 nor would it have seemed a miracle [too high to be wrought for one so holy]: 그렇게 성스러운 사람에게는 그 일[if 절의 일]이 너무 숭고하여 일어날 수 없을 기적으로 보이지는 않았을 것이다

53 had: if[even if] ... had

54 wax: 커지다, 증대하다, 점점 ~이 되다

55 ghastly: 무시무시한, 섬뜩한, 송장 같은, 몹시 창백한

56 as if impelled by inevitable fate: 마치 어쩔 수 없는 운명에 이끌린 듯

what he sought to do}! {Be that as it might[57]}, the old man rushed forward and caught the minister by the arm.

"Madman, hold! What is your purpose?" whispered he. "Wave back that woman! Cast off this child! All shall be well! Do not [blacken your fame[58], and perish in dishonor[59]!] I can yet save you! Would you bring infamy on your sacred profession[60]?"

"Ha, tempter[61]! Methinks thou art too late!" answered the minister, encountering his eye, fearfully, but firmly. "Thy power is not {what it was}! [With God's help], I shall escape thee now!"

He again extended his hand to the woman of the scarlet letter.

"Hester Prynne," cried he, with a piercing earnestness[62], "in the name of Him, [so terrible and so merciful], {who gives me grace, at this last moment, to do what—for my own heavy sin

---

57 Be that as it might: 어쨌든
58 blacken your fame: 명예를 더럽히다
59 perish in dishonor: 불명예스럽게 죽다
60 sacred profession: 성직
61 tempter: 유혹자, 악마
62 with a piercing earnestness: 열의를 다해 귀청이 찢어질 듯하게

and miserable agony[63]—I withheld myself from doing seven years ago}, come hither now, and twine thy strength about me! Thy strength, Hester; but let it be guided by the will {which God hath granted me}! [This wretched and wronged old man] is opposing it with all his might!—with all his own might and the fiend's! Come, Hester, come! Support me up yonder scaffold!"

The crowd was in a tumult. The men of rank and dignity, {who stood more immediately around the clergyman}, were so taken by surprise, and so perplexed as to the purport of {what they saw},—[unable to receive the explanation {which most readily presented itself}, or to imagine any other],—that they remained silent and inactive spectators of the judgment {which Providence seemed about to work}. They beheld the minister, [leaning on Hester's shoulder and supported by her arm around him], approach the scaffold, and ascend its steps; {while still the little hand of the sin-born child was clasped

---

63 for my own heavy sin and miserable agony: 여기의 'for'는 두 가지로 해석이 가능하다. 우선, '~에 대해'로 해석할 수 있다. 딤즈데일이 직접 'gives me grace, at this last moment, to do what—for my own heavy sin and miserable agony'라고 말하는 어순을 살펴 번역하면, '이 마지막 순간에 내 자신의 무거운 죄와 비참한 고뇌를 위해 무엇을 하도록 내게 은총을 베풀다'라는 의미가 된다. 한편, 뒷부분에 연결지어 해석할 경우 '~에도 불구하고'의 의미가 자연스럽다. 즉, 'what ... ago' 부분은 '내 자신의 무거운 죄와 비참한 고뇌에도 불구하고 7년 전에는 하지 못했던 것'이라는 의미가 된다.

in his}. Old Roger Chillingworth followed, as one [intimately connected with the drama of guilt and sorrow {in which they had all been actors}, and well entitled, therefore, to be present at its closing scene].

"{Hadst thou sought the whole earth over}[64]," said he, looking darkly at the clergyman, "there was no one place [so secret], — [no high place nor lowly place, {where thou couldst have escaped me}], — save on this very scaffold!"

"Thanks be to Him {who hath led me hither}!" answered the minister.

Yet he trembled, and turned to Hester with an expression of doubt and anxiety in his eyes, not the less evidently betrayed, that there was a feeble smile upon his lips.[65]

"Is not this better," murmured he, "than {what we dreamed of in the forest}?"

---

64 Hadst thou sought the whole earth over: 그대가 전 세계를 낱낱이 뒤졌다고 해도

65 Yet he ... his lips: 이 문장은 눈에는 의심과 근심의 표정을 담고 있으면서도 입술에는 미소를 띠고 있다는 내용을 전달하고 있다. 이 문장의 뒤쪽 'not the less evidently betrayed, that there was a feeble smile upon his lips' 부분의 문장구조는 다소 혼란스럽다. 'but his lips not the less evidently betrayed a feeble smile' 정도의 의미라고 볼 수 있다.

"I know not! I know not!" she hurriedly replied. "Better? Yea; so we may both die, and little Pearl die with us!"

"For thee and Pearl, be it as God shall order," said the minister; "and God is merciful! Let me now do the will {which he hath made plain before my sight}. For, Hester, I am a dying man. So let me make haste to take my shame upon me."

Partly supported by Hester Prynne, and holding one hand of little Pearl's, the Reverend Mr. Dimmesdale turned to the dignified and venerable rulers; to the holy ministers, {who were his brethren}; to the people, {whose great heart was thoroughly appalled, yet overflowing with tearful sympathy, as knowing [that some deep life-matter—which, if full of sin, was full of anguish and repentance[66] likewise—was now to be laid open to them]}. The sun, [but little past its meridian[67]], shone down upon the clergyman, and gave a distinctness to his figure, {as he stood out from all the earth to put in[68] his plea of guilty[69] at the bar of Eternal Justice}.

MP3 ★
23장 (3)
시작 "People of New England!" cried he, with a voice {that rose over them}, high, solemn, and majestic,—yet had always a

---

66 repentance: 참회
67 meridian: 자오선
68 put in: 제기[제출]하다
69 a plea of guilty: 유죄인정. *a plea of not guilty: 무죄의 항변

tremor[70] through it, and sometimes a shriek, [struggling up out of a fathomless depth of remorse and woe[71]], — "ye, {that have loved me}! — ye, {that have deemed me holy}! — behold me here, the one sinner of the world! At last! — at last! — I stand upon the spot {where, seven years since, I should have stood}; here, with this woman, {whose arm, [more than the little strength wherewith I have crept hitherward], sustains me, at this dreadful moment, from grovelling[72] down upon my face}! Lo, the scarlet letter {which Hester wears}! Ye have all shuddered at it! {Wherever her walk hath been}, — {wherever, so miserably burdened, she may have hoped to find repose}, — it hath cast a lurid gleam of awe and horrible repugnance[73] round about her. But there stood one in the midst of you, {at whose brand of sin and infamy ye have not shuddered}!"

It seemed, at this point, {as if the minister must leave the remainder of his secret undisclosed[74]}. But he fought back the bodily weakness, — and, still more, the faintness of heart, — {that was striving for the mastery with him}. He threw off all assistance, and stepped passionately forward a pace [before the

---

70 tremor: 떨림, 전율

71 woe: 비통, 비애

72 grovel: 굽실거리다, 기어 다니다

73 cast a lurid gleam of awe and horrible repugnance: 경외와 끔찍한 혐오의 충격적인 빛을 던지다

74 undisclosed: 폭로되지 않은, 비밀에 부쳐진

woman and the child].

"It[75] was on him!" he continued, with a kind of fierceness; so determined was he to speak out the whole. "God's eye beheld it! The angels were for ever pointing at it! The Devil knew it well, and fretted[76] it continually with the touch of his burning finger! But he[77] hid it cunningly from men, and walked among you with the mien[78] of a spirit, mournful, {because so pure in a sinful world}!—and sad, {because he missed his heavenly kindred}! Now, at the death-hour, he stands up before you! He bids you look again at Hester's scarlet letter! He tells you, {that, [with all its mysterious horror[79]], it is but the shadow of [what he bears on his own breast]}, and {that even this, his own red stigma, is no more than the type of [what has seared his inmost heart]}![80] Stand any here {that question God's judgment on a sinner}? Behold! Behold a dreadful witness of it[81]!"

[With a convulsive[82] motion] he tore away the ministerial

---

75 It: =the brand of sin and infamy

76 fret: ~을 애태우다, 괴롭히다

77 he: 딤즈데일 자신

78 mien: 풍채, 모습, 태도

79 with all its mysterious horror: 온갖 기이한 공포심을 불러일으킴에도 불구하고

80 He tells you ... his inmost heart!: 이 대목을 보면, 딤즈데일은 헤스터가 달고 있던 낙인이 자신의 가슴속 낙인의 그림자에 불과할 뿐이라고 함으로써 헤스터의 고통이 자신의 것에 비해 부차적인 것이라고 여기고 있음을 알 수 있다.

81 a dreadful witness of it: 그것[신의 심판]의 끔찍한 증거

band from before his breast. It was revealed! But it were irreverent [to describe that revelation]. [For an instant] the gaze of the horror-stricken[83] multitude was concentrated on the ghastly miracle[84]; {while the minister stood with a flush of triumph[85] in his face, as one [who, in the crisis of acutest pain[86], had won a victory]}. Then, down he sank upon the scaffold! Hester partly raised him, and supported his head against her bosom. Old Roger Chillingworth knelt down beside him, with a blank, dull countenance[87], {out of which the life seemed to have departed}.

"Thou hast escaped me!" he repeated more than once. "Thou hast escaped me!"

"May God forgive thee!" said the minister. "Thou, too, hast deeply sinned!"

He withdrew his dying eyes from the old man, and fixed them on the woman and the child.

---

82 convulsive: 경련성의, 발작적인

83 horror-stricken: 공포에 질린

84 ghastly miracle: 무시무시한[섬뜩한] 기적

85 a flush of triumph: 승리의 홍조

86 in the crisis of acutest pain: 극심한 고통의 절정 속에서

87 a blank, dull countenance: 공허하고 멍한 표정

"My little Pearl," said he feebly,—and there was a sweet and gentle smile over his face, as of a spirit sinking into deep repose[88]; nay, {now that the burden was removed}, it seemed almost {as if he would be sportive with the child},—"dear little Pearl, wilt thou kiss me now? Thou wouldst not yonder, in the forest! But now thou wilt?"

Pearl kissed his lips. A spell was broken. The great scene of grief, {in which the wild infant bore a part}, had developed all her sympathies; and {as her tears fell upon her father's cheek}, they were the pledge {that she would grow up amid human joy and sorrow, nor for ever do battle with the world, but be a woman in it}. Towards her mother, too, [Pearl's errand as a messenger of anguish] was all fulfilled.

"Hester," said the clergyman, "farewell!"

"Shall we not meet again?" whispered she, bending her face down close to his. "Shall we not spend our immortal life together? Surely, surely, we have ransomed[89] one another, with

---

88 repose: 휴식
89 ransom: 몸값을 치르다. *이 대목에서 헤스터는 지난 시기 동안 극단적인 고통의 값을 치르고 연인을 되찾은 비유를 사용하고 있다. 그러므로 이제부터는 영원히 서로 헤어지지 않고 함께 영생을 누릴 것이라는 기대를 품고 있다. 반면, 딤즈데일은 다음의 말에서 보이듯, 헤스터의 그런 기대와 희망을 불경스러운 것으로 보고 있다.

all this woe! Thou lookest far into eternity, with those bright dying eyes! Then tell me {what thou seest}?"

"Hush, Hester, hush!" said he, with tremulous solemnity[90]. "The law {we broke}! — the sin here [so awfully revealed]! — let these alone be in thy thoughts! I fear! I fear! It may be, {that, [when we forgot our God], — [when we violated our reverence each for the other's soul], — it was thenceforth vain to hope {that we could meet hereafter, in an everlasting[91] and pure reunion}. God knows; and He is merciful! He hath proved his mercy, most of all, in my afflictions. By giving me this burning torture to bear upon my breast! By sending yonder dark and terrible old man, to keep the torture always at red-heat! By bringing me hither, to die this death of triumphant ignominy before the people! {Had either of these agonies been wanting}, I had been lost for ever! Praised be his name! His will be done! Farewell!"

That final word came forth with the minister's expiring breath. The multitude, [silent till then], broke out [in a strange, deep voice of awe and wonder], {which could not as yet find utterance, save in this murmur {that rolled so heavily after the departed spirit}.

---

90 solemnity: 장엄함, 엄숙함
91 everlasting: 영원히 계속되는, 영원한

The Scarlet Letter **24장**

Conclusion

After many days, {when time sufficed for the people to arrange their thoughts in reference to the foregoing scene}, there was more than one account of {what had been witnessed on the scaffold}.

Most of the spectators testified to having seen, [on the breast of the unhappy minister], a SCARLET LETTER—the very semblance of that [worn by Hester Prynne]—imprinted in the flesh. [As regarded its origin], there were various explanations, {all of which must necessarily have been conjectural[1]}. Some affirmed {that the Reverend Mr. Dimmesdale, [on the very day when Hester Prynne first wore her ignominious badge], had begun a course of penance[2],—which he afterwards, [in so many futile methods], followed out[3],—by inflicting a hideous torture on himself}. Others contended[4] that the stigma had not been produced [until a long time subsequent, {when old Roger Chillingworth, [being a potent necromancer[5]], had caused it to appear, through the agency of magic and poisonous drugs}. Others, again,—and those [best able to appreciate the minister's peculiar sensibility, and the wonderful operation of his spirit upon the body],—whispered their belief, {that

---

1 conjectural: 추측의, 억측하기 좋아하는
2 penance: 속죄, 참회
3 follow out: 끝까지 해내다, 실행하다
4 contend: 주장하다
5 necromancer: 마술사

the awful symbol was the effect of the ever active tooth of remorse, [gnawing from the inmost heart outwardly, and at last manifesting Heaven's dreadful judgment by the visible presence of the letter]}. The reader may choose among these theories. We have thrown all the light {we could acquire upon the portent[6]}, and would gladly, {now that it has done its office}, erase its deep print [out of our own brain; {where long meditation[7] has fixed it in very undesirable distinctness}.

It is singular, nevertheless, {that certain persons, [who were spectators of the whole scene, and professed never once to have removed their eyes from the Reverend Mr. Dimmesdale], denied [that there was any mark whatever on his breast, more than on a new-born infant's]}. Neither, by their report, had [his dying words] acknowledged, nor even remotely implied, [any, the slightest connection, on his part, with the guilt {for which Hester Prynne had so long worn the scarlet letter}]. [According to these highly respectable witnesses], the minister, [conscious {that he was dying}, — conscious, also, {that the reverence of the multitude placed him already among saints and angels}], — had desired, [by yielding up his breath in the arms of that fallen woman], to express to the world {how utterly nugatory[8] is the choicest[9] of man's own righteousness[10]}.

---

6 portent: 조짐, 전조
7 meditation: 명상

[After exhausting life in his efforts for mankind's spiritual good], he had made [the manner of his death] a parable, [in order to impress on his admirers the mighty and mournful lesson, {that, in the view of Infinite Purity, we are sinners all alike}]. It was to teach them, {that the holiest among us has but attained so far above his fellows as to discern more clearly the Mercy [which looks down], and repudiate[11] more utterly the phantom[12] of human merit, [which would look aspiringly upward]}. [Without disputing a truth so momentous], we must be allowed to consider this version of Mr. Dimmesdale's story as only an instance of that stubborn fidelity[13] {with which a man's friends — and especially a clergyman's — will sometimes uphold[14] his character; [when proofs, clear as the mid-day sunshine on the scarlet letter, establish him a false and sin-stained creature of the dust]}.

The authority {which we have chiefly followed} — a manuscript of old date, drawn up from the verbal testimony of

---

8 nugatory: 하찮은, 쓸모없는

9 the choicest: 가장 훌륭한 것

10 righteousness: 정의, 정직, 공정

11 repudiate: 거절하다, 부인하다

12 phantom: 실체가 없는 것, 이름[겉모양]뿐인 것. *a phantom of a leader: 이름뿐인 지도자; a phantom of human merit: 이름뿐인 인간적 미덕

13 fidelity: 충성

14 uphold: 유지시키다, 옹호하다

individuals, {some of whom had known Hester Prynne, while others had heard the tale from contemporary witnesses} — fully confirms the view [taken in the foregoing pages]. Among many morals {which press upon us from the poor minister's miserable experience}, we put only this into a sentence: — "Be true! Be true! Be true! Show freely [to the world], if not your worst, yet some trait {whereby the worst may be inferred}!"

Nothing was more remarkable than the change {which took place, [almost immediately after Mr. Dimmesdale's death], [in the appearance and demeanour of the old man known as Roger Chillingworth]}. All his strength and energy — all his vital and intellectual force — seemed at once to desert him; {insomuch that he positively[15] withered[16] up, shrivelled away[17], and almost vanished from mortal sight, like an uprooted weed [that lies wilting[18] in the sun]}. This unhappy man had made [the very principle of his life] to consist in[19] the pursuit and systematic exercise of revenge; and {when, by its[20] completest triumph and consummation[21], that evil principle was left with no further material to support it}, — {when, in short, there

---

15 positively: 전적으로
16 wither: 신선함을 잃고 시들다, 마르다
17 shrivel away: 시들다, 쪼글쪼글해지다
18 wilt: 시들다
19 consist in: ~에 존재하다
20 its: 사악한 원칙의
21 consummation: 완성, 완료, 죽음

was no more devil's work on earth for him to do}, it only remained for the unhumanized mortal to betake himself[22] {whither his Master would find him tasks enough, and pay him his wages duly}. But, to all these shadowy beings, so long our near acquaintances[23], — as well Roger Chillingworth as his companions, — we would fain[24] be merciful. It is a curious subject of observation and inquiry, {whether hatred and love be not the same thing at bottom}. Each, [in its utmost development], supposes a high degree of intimacy and heart-knowledge; each renders [one individual] dependent [for the food of his affections and spiritual life] upon another; each leaves the passionate lover, or the no less passionate hater, forlorn and desolate [by the withdrawal of his object]. [Philosophically considered], therefore, the two passions seem essentially the same, {except that one happens to be seen in a celestial radiance, and the other in a dusky and lurid glow}. [In the spiritual world], the old physician and the minister — {mutual victims as they have been} — may, unawares, have found [their earthly stock[25] of hatred and antipathy[26]] transmuted into golden love.

---

22 betake oneself: 가다

23 to all these shadowy beings, so long our near acquaintances: 오랫동안 우리의 가까운 지인들이었던 이 모든 그림자 같은 존재들에게

24 fain: 기꺼이, 흔쾌히

25 stock: 재고, 축적, 저장

26 antipathy: 반감, 혐오

[Leaving this discussion apart], we have a matter of business to communicate to the reader. [At old Roger Chillingworth's decease[27] (which took place within the year), and by his last will and testament[28], {of which Governor Bellingham and the Reverend Mr. Wilson were executors[29]}], he bequeathed[30] a very considerable amount of property, both here and in England, to little Pearl, the daughter of Hester Prynne.

So Pearl—the elf-child,—the demon offspring, as some people, up to that epoch, persisted in considering her— became the richest heiress[31] of her day, in the New World. Not improbably, this circumstance wrought a very material change in the public estimation; and, {had the mother and child remained here}, little Pearl, [at a marriageable[32] period of life], might have mingled her wild blood with the lineage of the devoutest Puritan among them all. But, [in no long

★ MP3
24장 [2]
시작

---

27 decease: 죽음

28 last will and testament: 유언을 가리키는 말로 will과 testament 는 같은 의미를 지닌 법률적 이중어(legal doublet)이다. 중세에 기 원을 둔 이중어 사용관습은 대다수의 영국민이 고대영어를 사용한 반면 법률가 등 교육층은 고대프랑스어나 라틴어를 사용한 상황을 감안하여 두 용어를 병기한 데서 유래하였는데 원래의 동기가 소 멸한 뒤에도 두 언어로 같은 개념을 표현하는 관습이 여전히 남아 있다(http://en.wikipedia.org/wiki/Legal_doublet 참조).

29 executor: 유언 집행자

30 bequeath: 유언으로 증여하다

31 heiress: 여자 상속인. *heir: 상속인, 계승자

32 marriageable: 혼인하기에 알맞은

time after the physician's death], the wearer of the scarlet letter disappeared, and Pearl along with her. For many years, {though a vague report would now and then find its way across the sea,—like a shapeless piece of driftwood[33] [tost ashore], with the initials of a name upon it},—yet no tidings of them [unquestionably authentic] were received. The story of the scarlet letter grew into a legend. Its spell, however, was still potent[34], and kept the scaffold [awful[35]] {where the poor minister had died}, and likewise the cottage by the sea-shore, {where Hester Prynne had dwelt}. Near this latter spot, one afternoon, some children were at play, {when they beheld a tall woman, in a gray robe, approach the cottage-door}. [In all those years] it had never once been opened; but either she unlocked it, or the decaying wood and iron yielded to her hand, or she glided[36] shadow-like through these impediments[37],—and, at all events, went in.

[On the threshold] she paused,—turned partly round,—{for, perchance, [the idea of entering, all alone, and all so changed, the home of so intense a former life], was more

---

33 driftwood: 떠돌아다니는 나무
34 potent: 강력한
35 awful: 경외심을 불러일으키는, 무시무시한. *awful은 kept의 2개
   의 목적어인 the scaffold와 the cottage의 목적보어로 쓰였다.
36 glide: 미끄러지다
37 impediment: 장애물

dreary[38] and desolate[39] than even she could bear}. But her hesitation was only for an instant, {though long enough to display a scarlet letter on her breast}.

And Hester Prynne had returned, and taken up her long-forsaken shame. But where was little Pearl? {If still alive}, she must now have been in the flush[40] and bloom[41] of early womanhood. None knew — nor ever learned, with the fulness of perfect certainty — {whether the elf-child had gone thus untimely[42] to a maiden grave}; or {whether her wild, rich nature had been softened and subdued[43], and made capable of a woman's gentle happiness}. But, [through the remainder of Hester's life], there were indications {that the recluse of the scarlet letter was the object of love and interest with some inhabitant of another land}. Letters came, [with armorial[44] seals[45] upon them, though of bearings[46] unknown to English

---

38 dreary: 음울한, 따분한. *a dreary winter day: 어느 음울한 겨울날

39 desolate: 황량한, 적막한, 너무나 외로운

40 flush: 홍조, 싹틈, 발랄함, 왕성함, 한창

41 bloom: 꽃, (건강한) 혈색. *the bloom in her cheeks: 그녀 뺨의 건강한 혈색

42 untimely: 〈형용사〉 때 아닌, 너무 이른. 〈부사〉 너무 일찍

43 subdue: 진압하다, (감정을) 가라앉히다, 진정시키다

44 armorial: 문장(紋章)의

45 seal: 인장(印章), 도장, 인감, 문장(紋章)

46 bearing: 관계, 관련, 의미, 취지. *bearings: 방패에 그려진 문장 (紋章, 상징적으로 도안된 그림이나 문자)

heraldry[47]]. [In the cottage] there were articles of comfort[48] and luxury, {such as Hester never cared to use}, but {which only wealth could have purchased, and affection have imagined for her}. There were trifles, too, little ornaments, beautiful tokens of a continual remembrance, {that must have been wrought by delicate fingers, at the impulse of a fond[49] heart}. And, once, Hester was seen embroidering a baby-garment, [with such a lavish richness of golden fancy {as would have raised a public tumult[50], [had any infant, thus apparelled, been shown to our sombre-hued[51] community]}].

In fine[52], the gossips of that day believed, —and Mr. Surveyor Pue, {who made investigations a century later}, believed, —and one of his recent successors[53] in office, moreover, faithfully believes, —{that Pearl was not only alive, but married, and happy, and mindful of her mother}; and {that

---

47 heraldry: 문장, 문장학

48 comfort: 위안, 편의, 생활을 편하게 해 주는 물건

49 fond: 다정한, 애정 어린

50 as would have raised a public tumult: 사회적 물의를 일으켰을

51 sombre-hued: 칙칙한[침울한] 색깔의. *표준판인 오하이오 주립대학 센테너리(Centenary)판을 따라 'sombre-hued'로 하였다. 1850년의 초판과 재판에는 'sobre-hued'로, 이후 3판에서 7판까지는 'sober-hued'[침착(냉정)한 색깔의]로 되어 있고, 2005년의 노턴(Norton) 판에도 'sober-hued'로 되어 있다. 여기의 맥락에서는 두 경우의 의미가 상통한다.

52 in fine: 결국, 요는

53 successor: 후임자

she would most joyfully have entertained[54] that sad and lonely mother at her fireside}.

But there was a more real life for Hester Prynne, here, in New England, than in that unknown region {where Pearl had found a home}. Here had been her sin; here, her sorrow; and here was yet to be her penitence. She had returned, therefore, and resumed, — of her own free will, {for not the sternest magistrate of that iron period would have imposed it}, — resumed the symbol {of which we have related[55] so dark a tale}. Never afterwards did it quit her bosom. But, [in the lapse[56] of the toilsome[57], thoughtful, and self-devoted years {that made up Hester's life}], the scarlet letter ceased to be a stigma {which attracted the world's scorn and bitterness}, and became a type of something [to be sorrowed over, and looked upon with awe, yet with reverence too]. And, {as Hester Prynne had no selfish ends, nor lived in any measure for her own profit and enjoyment}, people brought all their sorrows and perplexities[58], and besought[59] her counsel, [as one {who had herself gone through a mighty trouble}]. Women, more especially, — in the

---

54 entertain: 접대하다, 즐겁게 해 주다
55 relate: ~에 대하여 이야기하다[들려주다]
56 lapse: (부주의로 인한) 실수, 과실, (시간적) 경과. *in the lapse of: ~ 지나는 동안
57 toilsome: 고생스러운, 고된
58 perplexity: 당혹스러운[이해하기 힘든] 것
59 beseech: 간청하다, 애원하다

continually recurring[60] trials of wounded, wasted[61], wronged[62], misplaced[63], or erring[64] and sinful passion, — or with the dreary burden of a heart [unyielded, because unvalued[65] and unsought[66]], — came to Hester's cottage, demanding {why they were so wretched}, and {what the remedy}! Hester comforted and counselled them, {as best she might}. She assured them, too, of her firm belief, {that, [at some brighter period, when the world should have grown ripe for it, in Heaven's own time], a new truth would be revealed, in order to establish the whole relation between man and woman on a surer ground of mutual happiness}. [Earlier in life], Hester had vainly imagined {that she herself might be the destined prophetess}, but had long since recognized the impossibility {that any mission of divine and mysterious truth should be confided to a woman [stained with sin, bowed down with shame, or even burdened with a life-long sorrow]}. The angel and apostle[67] of the coming revelation must be a woman, indeed, but [lofty, pure, and

---

60 recurring: 되풀이하여 발생하는, 순환하는
61 wasted: 헛된, 쇠약한
62 wronged: 부당한 취급을 받은, 학대받는
63 misplaced: (상황에) 부적절한, 잘못된 대상을 향한
64 erring: 잘못되어 있는, 부정한
65 unvalued: 소중히 여겨지지 않는, 변변찮은, 아직 평가되지 않은
66 unsought: 찾지 않는, 구하지 않는, 원치 않는. *a heart [unyielded, because unvalued and unsought]: [소중히 여겨지지 않고 남들이 찾지 않기 때문에 건네주지 못한] 마음
67 apostle: 사도

268

beautiful]; and wise, moreover, [not through dusky grief, but the ethereal[68] medium of joy]; and showing {how sacred love should make us happy}, by the truest test of a life successful to such an end!

So said Hester Prynne, and glanced her sad eyes downward at the scarlet letter. And, [after many, many years], a new grave was delved, near an old and sunken one, in that burial-ground {beside which King's Chapel[69] has since been built}. It was near that old and sunken grave, yet with a space between, {as if the dust of the two sleepers had no right to mingle}. Yet one tombstone served for both. All around, there were monuments [carved with armorial bearings]; and [on this simple slab of slate[70]] — {as the curious investigator may still discern, and perplex himself with the purport} — there appeared the semblance of an engraved escutcheon[71]. It bore a device[72], {a herald's wording[73] of which might serve for a motto and brief description of our now concluded legend}; so sombre is it, and

---

68 ethereal: 천상의
69 King's Chapel: 제임스 2세 치하의 뉴잉글랜드에 세워진 첫 번째 앵글리칸 교회로 1686년에 총독 에드먼드 앤드로스 경(Sir Edmund Andros)에 의해 세워졌다.
70 slab of slate: 석판
71 escutcheon: 가문의 문장이 찍힌 방패
72 device: 궁리, 장치, 고안물, (장식적) 도안, 문장(紋章).
   *a safety device: 안전장치
73 wording: (신중히 골라 쓴) 자구[표현]

relieved only by one ever-glowing point of light [gloomier than the shadow]: —

"ON A FIELD, SABLE, THE LETTER A, GULES."[74]

THE END

---

74 ON A FIELD, SABLE, THE LETTER A, GULES: =On a black background, the letter A in red. *sable: 흑담비, 검은색의; gules: 붉은색(의)